Aftermath

OFF THE SUBJECT
BOOK ONE

DENISE GROVER SWANK

Copyright 2013 by Denise Grover Swank

Cover Design: Momir

ISBN: 978-1-940562-78-0

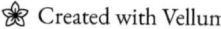 Created with Vellum

To my daughters:
May you find your own Tuckers

Chapter One

I'm late.

I stand outside the doorway of my Western civ class, caught in a dilemma. Either go in and have thirty pairs of eyes stare at me or leave, which means missing my test. The decision is already made. I only need to open the door and walk in.

I suck oxygen into my lungs, past my tightened airway, as I try to calm down and turn the doorknob.

My professor is standing at the white board, writing *Ancient Greece* in a big scrawl with a blue marker that is running out of ink. He barely pauses as he lifts his eyes at the sound of the door hinges before returning to his task, yet my heart still pounds in my chest. My breath still catches.

I can't do this.

In spite of the surety that I will flunk the test and ruin my 4.0 GPA, I choose to leave. I spin around and slam into something hard. When I stumble backward, strong hands grab my arms and right me.

"I know I make girls swoon, but this is a first," a deep voice drawls.

I instantly know whom this voice belongs to. Tucker Price.

Southern University's soccer team superstar and resident man-whore. He sits in the end row, second seat.

I jerk out of his hold and confusion flickers in his eyes before he grins. "You're not the first girl to fall for me."

It has to be one of the worst lines ever, but it doesn't stop half the class from laughing.

I'm about to combust from embarrassment.

Dr. Eggleston looks up this time and puts a hand on his hip. One bushy gray eyebrow hitches as he stares. "Are you two going to stand there for the rest of the class or take a seat?"

My face is on fire. I force my eyes to focus in the empty seat in the middle aisle, middle row—my usual seat—and I take purposeful steps toward it. If I sit down without attracting any more attention, this moment will pass, and I will be alone with my mortification.

With shaky fingers, I dig my Scantron sheet and pencil from my bag as Dr. Eggleston begins to pass out booklets. "When you have completed the test, turn it in at my desk, and you are free to leave."

The guy in the seat in front of me hands me a test, and I set it down on the desk, smoothing the sheet with my hand as I try to get a grip on my emotions. *Arriving late to class is no big deal.* Sure, it's slightly embarrassing, but people like Tucker Price thrive on the attention. People like me want to curl up and die.

Lightheaded from my humiliation, I try to read the questions swimming on the page in front of me. I know this information backward and forward. It doesn't hurt that I've found Ancient Greece fascinating since I first studied the Greek gods in fourth grade. Nevertheless, my heart still beats furiously and blood whooshes in my ears, making it difficult to focus. I might know everything under the sun about the Spartans and Athenians, but it doesn't do me any good if I don't answer the questions.

I hear the rustle of paper and look up. People are already moving onto the second page of the test, and I haven't even read the first question. A quick glance up at the clock tells me I've wasted ten minutes.

Sucking in a deep breath, I close my eyes, holding oxygen in my lungs until I'm sure they will burst. When I release the breath, I imagine pushing all my anxiety out with it. After a couple of rounds, I settle enough to start. Fourteen months of free campus counseling boiled down into a simple breathing exercise.

Forty minutes later, I rise from my chair, my completed test and essay in my hand. Most of the class has finished, but two girls still huddle over their essays, their hands flying as they hurry to finish. In the second row, Tucker stares out the window, his pencil hovering over his composition book. For someone who is about to run out of time, he looks remarkably relaxed.

I should be more like Tucker Price. The thought burns itself in my head, and I want a gallon of bleach to purge the errant idea from my brain. Never in a million years would I want to be like Tucker Price.

Unfocused. Irresponsible. Dangerous.

Tucker Price's reputation is well earned, and if the university rumor factory is correct, Tucker is well on his way to losing his soccer scholarship after his latest DUI.

I turn in my test and grab a quick lunch in the student union before I report for my shift in the math lab. My friend Tina sits next to me, plopping her tray on the table as her backpack slips down her arm. Tina is a sophomore I met last semester. There are few female math majors at Southern, and we tend to hang out together. On Tuesdays and Thursdays, we both have forty-five minutes between our last class and our shift in the lab so we usually meet for lunch.

"My friend Kyle is having a party on Friday night," Tina says before she takes a bite of her sandwich. Her eyes lift to me to gauge my reaction.

Tina is not the typical math student. She straddles both the demanding academic world and a social life. Parties included. For some reason she seems intent on dragging me from my comfortable hovel.

"Tina, we've discussed this before—"

"You don't date. You don't go to parties. Yeah, I know, I know," she grumbles.

I frown. "You don't ask anyone else from the math department to go. Why me?"

"Don't you see that you have so much more potential than spending all of your time studying?"

"But I—"

Her face lowers close to mine. "Look, Scarlett. Everyone knows you're a brilliant mathematics student. But it doesn't mean you can't have some fun. Just once." Her eyes plead with mine. "You don't have to say yes or no. Just think about it. Okay?" She gives me an exaggerated pouty face.

I laugh, shaking my head, my ponytail brushing my back. "You're incorrigible."

"And that's why you love me."

I laugh again and see Tucker at a table twenty feet away. He's sitting with several soccer players and their groupies. Two of the girls openly flirt and Tucker flashes them his cocky grin.

I've paid little attention to him before, other than casually observing his self-destructive behavior. Rumor has it he's on academic, as well as behavioral, probation. Tucker might be Southern University's soccer superstar, but he's close to burning out at the pace he's keeping. Watching him now, I know that people like him bring this upon themselves. Tucker Price has been given a gift I'd kill for—a full-ride scholarship—but he chooses to throw it away so he can party and screw.

He catches me watching him, and I freeze, waiting for the look of derision that's sure to come. I know that my own look of disgust isn't what he's used to seeing. Instead, his face loses all expression before his arrogant grin is plastered back on his face, like he's just taken a stage break and he's jumping back into a performance.

Tina stands to leave, noticing that something has caught my attention. She grins when she sees who it is. "There may be hope for you yet."

"What? No. Way."

"I heard he almost got arrested last weekend for disturbing the peace, but the policeman turned out to be a huge soccer fan and let him off with a warning."

I throw my trash away, but Tucker's face haunts me while I head to the math lab for our afternoon shift, dodging the raindrops that fall as I walk across campus.

As I take my regular seat, the rain continues, heavy drops pounding the window next to me. The January afternoon perfectly reflects my mood when a few hours later, Tucker stands in the doorway of the lab, looking around. His gaze stops, and he moves toward me.

What is Tucker Price doing here?

The room isn't that large, enough room for four tables where tutors can work with a student. The math lab's director's office is off to the side, although we don't see Dr. Carlisle much. Old office chairs, the fabric on the seats torn and faded, line the walls. There's no one waiting so Tucker slides into the chair on the opposite side of my table and lifts an eyebrow with an amused grin. "You're in my Western civ class."

My face burns at the reminder, and I wait for him to call me out for staring at him at lunch. Although why he'd care what I think is beyond me.

He watches me in confusion. "So you teach math?"

"Tutor." The word catches in my throat. "I tutor in math."

I want to scream. I want to hide in a corner. Working in the math lab is perfect for my social anxiety. While my reaction to awkward social situations has eased quite a bit since I've moved away from my dysfunctional family, it's still present, even in its milder form. The math lab is one-on-one and a more controlled situation, but my run-in—literally—with Tucker earlier is pushing all my trigger buttons.

He leans forward, resting his hand on the table, and looking around before his eyes land on mine. "I need help with algebra."

"Then you've come to the right place." I search the room to see who's available. Mark is with a pretty freshman and from the way he's attempting to flirt, I can see they will be a while. But Tina is not only free but practically salivating at the sight of Tucker. I point toward her. "Tina will help you. Right over there."

His forehead wrinkles. "Why can't you do it?"

My mouth parts and a whoosh of air escapes. "I usually work with students in more advanced courses," I say, flustered. Why would he care if I tutored him or not?

All expression leaves his face. "Are you calling me stupid, Scarlett?"

"I...no...that's not..." How does he know my name?

A slow smile lifts his mouth. "I was teasing, but seriously." He leans even closer. "If you teach advanced math, I'd rather have you. I'm in serious trouble if I don't pass this class. I'm going to lose my scholarship."

I want to tell him that's not the only thing putting his scholarship at risk, but I figure he's already well aware of that fact, despite the continuation of his behavior.

He continues to watch me, waiting for my answer.

I've never been this close to him before, and I can't help studying him. I can see why girls fall at his feet. He's gorgeous. Light hair with lots of natural streaks of blond from all that time in the sun. Tanned skin, with a hint of stubble, like he'd forgotten to shave this morning. But those eyes, a pale blue with just a touch of gray. I'm sure they are what seal the deal for him with the women he collects.

Only there's no smile in his eyes. Only sadness and fear.

I should say no. I'm out of my element around him, and it will affect my ability to tutor him, but something in those eyes touches a place deep in my heart that I keep hidden from everyone. I can't help but wonder if there's more to Tucker Price than he shows the world.

I nod. "Okay."

His eyes close, and his body slumps with relief. After a moment, his eyes open, and he's the cocky guy that bumped into me hours earlier. "So let's set up a time."

"It doesn't work that way. The math lab is drop-in. You work with who's available when you come in. We can get started now."

He frowns and his top teeth bite his lower lip.

"Why don't you get out your problems and show me what you need help with?"

He pulls his textbook and a notebook out of his backpack. "You should know right off that math isn't my thing."

I can't help but smile, in spite of my nervousness around him. "I suspect it's more your *thing* than you give yourself credit. It's simply a matter of understanding the rules."

His cocky grin is back. "I'm not a fan of rules."

"And look where that's gotten you." The words are out of my mouth before I realize I'm saying them. My eyes widen in horror. "I'm sorry. That was uncalled for."

He shakes his head, his expression changing again. Tucker's face is a chameleon of emotions. "No." His gaze narrows. "I need that."

"What? Snarky remarks?"

"No. The truth."

I wait for a sarcastic comment to follow but it doesn't come.

We spend the next half an hour starting with the basics of mathematic operations. He's focusing on what I'm telling him, but the concepts are slow to sink in, and he's frustrated.

"Don't worry. You'll get it. The problem is that everyone's brain is wired differently. Some gravitate to words and concepts. Others are hardwired for facts and logical order. The human brain is capable of both. We just need to figure out how to activate your brain."

"So I'm a cyborg?" he teases, but it's not cocky or arrogant. He's sweet. And so unlike his public persona.

"If you were, you wouldn't need me." I grin. "We're the ones who tell our brains we are incapable. Maybe you need to tell yourself that you *are* capable."

He watches me for a moment, his palm resting on his closed book. "When are you in here again?"

"Why?"

"I want you to tutor me. No one's taken the time to work with me the way you have." I wonder if he's flirting, but he seems serious.

"Uh...I work tomorrow from three to six."

He scowls. "Do you do private lessons?"

I shake my head, now worried where this is going. I thought *this* Tucker, the one I've spent the last half hour with, was too good to be true. "No. I only work here in the lab." I force a smile. "But there's always someone here who is more than capable of helping you."

"You like that word. Capable. You've said it multiple times."

I'm caught off guard and a blush rises to my cheeks. My gaze falls to my folded hands on the table. "Maybe it's because I think we tell ourselves that we can't when we should be telling ourselves that we can."

I refuse to face him, instead pretending that my hangnail is fascinating. Several seconds pass before I make myself look up.

Tucker's blue eyes flicker with confusion and surprise. He gives me a soft smile before he scoops up his books, grabs his backpack, and walks out of the lab.

He must think I'm weird, the brainy math geek, and part of me is glad. I've always steered clear of guys like him, and I have no intention of changing. Guys like him were who Momma and my sister ended up with. Smooth talkers who took your money, screwed you until the next piece of ass came along, and then left you pregnant and living in a trailer park for the rest of your life. I'm running away from my past, creating my own future. There is no room for men like him, or for self-destructive relationships. With my schedule and drive to succeed, I don't really consider dating much at all, not that I have men begging me to go out. The male math majors have either tried or considered me untouchable. They leave me alone, and I like it that way. Only classes, work, and mathematics. The logic of math will never let me down.

I stay several more hours, helping other students before my shift ends. I pack up my stuff and head for the exit. "See you tomorrow."

"Scarlett, wait." Dr. Carlisle calls out of his office. He gets out of his chair and stands in the doorway. "I saw you helping Tucker Price earlier. How did it go?"

I shrug. "He doesn't understand some of the basic rules. But despite the impression he likes to give, he's capable of learning the material. I think he just needs repetition."

"And how comfortable were you with him?"

I know what he's asking. Dr. Carlisle is well aware of my anxiety disorder. Although we don't discuss personal relationships, my preference for not dating is well known in the math department. And the entire school knows Tucker's penchant for trying to get every girl in school out of their panties.

"It actually went really well. He surprised me."

He smiles and leans against the doorframe, looking relieved. "Good to know, because I received a phone call from the chancellor. He wants you to personally tutor Tucker Price. Outside the math lab."

My mouth drops. "*What*?"

"The chancellor himself called, Scarlett. You know the department is up for funding for the new computer program. This could..."

Bile burns my throat. The university needs Tucker to keep his eligibility. The math department needs funding. If I can help the university with the former, they'll help with the latter.

Damn it.

I nod with a jerk. "Okay."

"You can tutor him during your scheduled lab hours if you like." He sighs and his brow wrinkles with worry. "Scarlett, if you don't feel comfortable—"

"No, I'm fine. It will be fine. I can do it." But it won't be fine. And I'm sure I can help him as long as I'm dealing with the Tucker from this afternoon. But if I'm dealing with the Tucker I saw in the lunch room, then I'm screwed.

But then again, part of me knows I'm screwed either way.

Chapter Two

My roommate Caroline is at our apartment when I get home. She's curled up on the sofa with an afghan and a bowl of mac and cheese, watching *Gossip Girl* on Netflix. Other than my family, Caroline has known me longer than anyone. Before college, the trailer park in which we grew up was the one commonality that linked us. But while we were friends in grade school, in our high school years we were more acquaintances. Caroline hovered on the periphery of the popular crowd, not quite breaking in because of her address. By high school, I had retreated from everyone and everything, focusing on my goal of graduating with honors and getting a scholarship to college. When we realized we were both going to the same college, we ended up rooming together, then became best friends. We left Shelbyville behind, and we're all that we have left of our past. Now we're more like sisters than friends. We're our own little family.

"Bad day?" I ask.

She twists her mouth to one side but doesn't answer.

Caroline says her goal in life is to be Blair Waldorf, headbands included. Not surprising since she's a fashion major. But in the two and a half years we've lived together—freshman and sophomore years in the dorm and our junior year in our apartment—I've learned that her *Gossip Girl* marathons are her clue that something's wrong.

"Is the sidewalk at the bottom of the stairs still flooded?" she asks, licking her spoon.

The rain has come down in sheets off and on all day. Still, the question seems random. "Yeah."

She scowls. "Damn. I wanted to wear my new suede boots tomorrow."

I shake my head as I scoop up a bowl of the mac and cheese. "It's January in Tennessee, Caroline. It's wet and cold. What's tomorrow?"

She shrugs, but one side is higher than the other. She has a reason but doesn't want to tell me. "How was geek lab?"

I shove her feet off the sofa to sit next to her, but she puts them in my lap, and I pull the corner of her throw over the both of us. "*Math lab* was fine, although I tutored an interesting student."

Laughing, Caroline leans over and scoops some macaroni from my bowl. "Interesting student. In the math lab." She eats my noodles and shrugs. "I give up. I got nuthin'."

"Tucker Price."

Her eyes narrow, and her mouth puckers around her spoon. "Yeah, right."

"Ever heard of *academic probation*?"

"You're kidding?"

"Nope." I give her a smug smile. "And guess who will start privately tutoring him?"

She bolts upright. "Shut. Up."

Ever since I've agreed to do this, I've been trying to see this in a positive light. The mathematics department needs the new program that maps arbitrary complex functions, and experience with this program will look fantastic on my résumé. I already have the disadvantage of Southern University being a relatively small school with a slightly above-average mathematics department. Besides, I tutor students one-on-one all the time. Why is tutoring Tucker any different? To my surprise, Tucker wasn't the cocky asshole I'm used to hearing about. As long as he checks his attitude at the door, I can live with tutoring him.

I shrug. "He wasn't anything like I expected. He was... polite."

Sinking back into the cushions, an ornery grin lights up her face and she scoops several noodles. "Oh, he's *polite* all right."

"Not like that. Kind of quiet. Other than a few slips into character, he was...normal."

"Are we talking about the same Tucker Price? Blond with incredible blue eyes? About six foot? Stunning legs when he wears those soccer shorts? Guy who flaunts his good looks and his *sportsmanship*?"

"Good Lord. Is everything a sexual innuendo to you tonight?"

"Pretty much."

"Well, it was the same guy. Different personality."

"Shh!" She grabs the remote and increases the volume. "Chuck's about to trade Blair for a hotel."

My jaw drops. "You're kidding, right?" I've never been able to get into *Gossip Girl*, despite Caroline's multiple and relentless attempts to sway me to the dark side. As a poor girl from the other side of the tracks, I just can't relate to spoiled rich kids. Or maybe it's the spoiled, rich bad boys I'm trying to avoid. Why anyone would willingly subject themselves to that type of person is beyond me.

"Want to talk about anything?" I ask.

Tears fill her eyes, but she shakes her head.

"I'm here if you need me, okay?"

She gives me a tearful smile, and I wrap an arm around her shoulders, leaning my head into hers. I suspect her despondency is related to her breakup from her boyfriend, Justin. He broke up with her several months before, but she's still not over it. She'll talk when she's ready, probably in another hour or two.

I force myself off the sofa, not an easy task since it's so cozy under the afghan with Caroline. "I've got some equations to work on."

Caroline fakes a snore.

I put a hand on my hip and look down my nose at her. "Don't the nerdy-math jokes ever get old?"

She twists her mouth to the side as though she's giving it thought. "Nope. Never do."

"I could tease you mercilessly about your fashion design degree. Tons of fodder there."

"Go for it." She grins with exaggerated glee, the tears still in her eyes. My heart breaks for her, yet I don't know what to do to help her get over this awful pain. For the moment, we ignore the elephant in the room.

"Turns out I'm a nicer person than you," I call out to her as I walk down the hall to my bedroom.

"You just keep telling yourself that."

I turn my desk light on then lie down on my bed and listen to the ping of the rain on my window, taking a deep breath. I try to do my relaxation exercises every night to help my overall anxiety, and the soothing sound of the rain helps.

One of many godsends about college was my access to free counseling. After struggling to control my anxiety since the sixth grade, I was grateful to find ways to not only cope with it, but improve my life. I can thank Caroline for making me go only a few weeks into our freshman year after she found me lying on my bed struggling to breathe during a panic attack.

My therapist taught me to use guided imagery to help reduce anxiety before a potential situation that makes me nervous, but I also like to do it after situations that upset me. I relive what happened and reimagine how I wanted it to go. I focus on the incident in Western civ and how I should have appropriately responded to being late—walking in without feeling embarrassed. When people turn their attention to me, I smile and walk to my seat. But when I think about how I should have reacted to running into Tucker, my anxiety rises. I know the situation would have been humorous to anyone else. Why do I have to make such a big deal of it? But whenever I try to relive how I should have handled it, I see Tucker's face in the student union.

The disinterest. The sadness in his eyes. I hardly even know him so I'm not sure why I care.

Perhaps it's because I see the same expression every morning when I look in the mirror.

With a sigh, I sit upright and take my long, dark hair out of its ponytail, then run my fingers through the strands. I'm imagining things. That's the thing about people: you never really know where they stand. You have to rely on gestures and social cues, and still, you really don't know.

I move to the desk and get out my homework. Anxious prickles have poked the back of my neck since I began thinking about Tucker. I pull out my book and study the equation for my linear algebra class. As I write the numbers onto the paper, my shoulders begin to unfurl, my tension fading away. Some people knit or read to relax. I do math problems. My mother and little sister never let me live it down when I was younger, making fun of my love of arithmetic. With math, as long as you have all the necessary factors, you can find the answer. Life, on the other hand, is so much messier.

I stay up another two hours working on my equations before I quit for the night. When I go into the kitchen to make a cup of tea, Caroline's exactly where I left her hours ago. She doesn't comment when I pass her on my way to the kitchen.

I grab a pint of Ben & Jerry's from the freezer along with two spoons and sit next to her on the sofa, throwing the afghan over my legs. I toss the lid onto the coffee table and hand Caroline a spoon.

She digs in, eating several bites before she finally talks. "I saw him today. With someone else. It's been three months, Scarlett. Why is it so hard to see him?"

I've never been in a relationship that I wanted to stay in, but I know the pain she went through when they broke up. The pain she still goes through. "Three years is a long time to be with someone, Caroline. I'm sure it takes time to get over it."

"I don't like feeling this way. It hurts too much."

"Maybe you should start dating again." I'm not really sure it's an appropriate response, but I can't stand to see her this miserable. This moping person isn't the vivacious girl that took the campus by storm her freshman year. The girl I knew when we grew up together. Hiding out in our apartment for the last several months has made her more like me, a terrifying thought. "If nothing else, you need to get out and at least go to parties again."

She sits up and points her spoon at me. "You know, Scarlett. I think you're on to something. It just so happens I've been invited to a party at a guy named Kyle's house Friday night."

"Well, there you go. Tina was invited to the same party."

Her eyes light up. "Oh really? Then the fates have aligned. I'm going to the party, and you're coming with me."

My breath caught. "What? Oh, no. No way."

"Yes! Come on! You never go to parties. You need to loosen up and have some fun."

"I *do* have fun." Caroline went out all the time when she was with Justin. Our freshman year, she invited me to parties, but she soon gave up after my many refusals. Plus, Justin began to suck up more and more of her time, and my lack of a social life was simply accepted.

She scrunches her nose. "With math problems. Don't you want any boy problems?"

"Look how well that's worked out for you." I immediately regret my words, but they are at the root of my hesitancy to date. I can't afford to get close to someone, to let him get close to me, only to have him break my heart. I've made too much progress over the last two years to throw it away over the risk of potential heartbreak. But Caroline thrives on human contact and connections. Staying holed up in our apartment is making her worse.

Tilting her head to the side, her lips pucker. "True. That's because I stuck with one guy for so long." Her eyes widen with excitement. "Let's make it the semester of boys. We'll go out with a different boy every week."

"Are you drunk? When was the last time *I* went on a date?"

"My point exactly! When was the last time *either* one of us went on a date?" She puts the back of her hand against her forehead and arches her back. "Two beautiful young women, home alone night after night. It's a tragedy."

"You should have been a theater major," I say dryly. "I like my life the way it is. Neat and orderly."

"But life is meant to be messy, Scarlett. You need to live a little."

"You can't live a little or a lot, Caroline. You simply live."

"Says the girl who's never lived at all." There's no malice or sarcasm, only a hint of pity.

I'd prefer the sarcasm. I take the empty ice cream container and toss it in the trash. "I'm not going to a party, Caroline."

She gives me a wicked smile. "Oh, we'll see about that."

Oh, yes we will.

The next morning when I wake up, there's an e-mail in my inbox time stamped ten minutes earlier.

I would have texted, but the school refused to give me your number. We need to set up a tutoring time.

Tucker. I'm almost surprised he got in contact with me so soon. Not to mention he's awake before eight-thirty. Maybe he's taking this seriously after all.

I email him my free times then get in the shower, worrying about the Friday night party. Individually, Tina and Caroline are manageable, but I made the fatal mistake of introducing them last November. Now they've made it their combined effort to force me into some kind of social life. I seriously don't understand why they can't leave me alone. I'm happy with the way things are. Don't they get that?

But when I rub my towel across the mirror to wipe off the steam, the expression on my face says differently. Funny how I never considered whether I was happy or unhappy until the last twenty-four hours. After I saw Tucker's face in the cafeteria.

I shake off my melancholy and dry my hair, mulling over the question of happiness. Isn't happiness getting what you want? If so, I'm the epitome of happy. My academic track has me well on my way to helping me get my dream job: working for the CIA or DOD, analyzing data. I have a great roommate and a handful of friends. I have student loans, but nothing monstrous to pay off after I graduate.

By my definition, I'm happy. So why does it feel like something is missing?

I get dressed and check my e-mail, surprised to see Tucker has responded already.

3:00 at the coffee shop on campus.

The hair on my neck prickles. I breathe in, filling my lungs and blowing out the air as I imagine blowing my anxiety away, and try to reason through my fear. I didn't have problems with tutoring Tucker in the lab, so why does meeting him at the coffee shop make me nervous? It's an easy answer. I'm comfortable in the lab. It's a familiar environment. The coffee shop is an unknown variable.

Also, Tucker is a wild card. He was behaved in my environment, but I know that isn't his usual behavior. I'm having major second thoughts about this endeavor, but I shake my head and force myself to calm down. This situation is manageable as long as I don't flake out.

I pack my messenger bag for the day and pour a cup of coffee in my travel mug before I poke my head into Caroline's room. Her clothes are scattered everywhere, and her sheets and blanket are a tangled mess. She's lying sideways on the bed, her feet hanging off the side.

"Caroline."

She buries her face into her pillow. "What?" she mumbles.

"You're going to miss your textiles class. Get up." She's not usually like this, but this isn't uncommon after late-night *Gossip Girl* and ice cream binges.

She pulls the covers over her head.

I step into the room, and grab a handful of the sheet and jerk it down to her waist. "Come on. This is your last warning. I'm leaving now or I'll be late for class."

"You're so mean, Scarlett."

"I can't even imagine how you'll survive in the real world," I mumble and walk out of the room.

"I heard that!" she yells after me.

I meant her to, knowing it would get her out of bed. The more I study people in my attempt to fit into life, the more I realize that people are often driven by their fear. With my mother and her drinking and her many men, it was her fear of being alone. But with Caroline, whose family insisted she was wasting her time with college, her fear was that she'd never escape her trailer park roots. My own fears are too numerous to list.

I grab my coffee and a banana, and head for the front door, pausing until I hear her padding around in her room.

The rain has stopped, but heavy gray clouds hang in the sky. My first class is at ten, but I want to get there early. Set and logic is the class that separates the wheat from the chaff in mathematics majors, and I want to make sure I'm doing everything possible to ensure I do well. This includes getting to class early enough so I don't have a repeat of what happened in Western civ yesterday. I can't afford to spend ten minutes recovering from the embarrassment of being late. I can't afford to miss even thirty seconds in this class.

Some days the lessons are more difficult, but I'm thankful when today's concepts slip easily into place. When I struggle, all my fears that I can't do this—that I'm destined to fail—swamp my head. And I need all the confidence I can muster to face this afternoon.

After my Arabic III class, I head to the coffee shop with a knot in my stomach. I arrive ten minutes early and order my drink and sit at a table by the window, pulling my Arabic homework out to work on while the subject matter is still fresh in my head. I lose myself in verb conjugation, and I'm surprised when I see that it's already twenty after three. Tucker hasn't shown. I pull out my phone and double-check his e-mail to verify the time. He said three o'clock, and this is the only coffee shop on campus.

Tucker enters the shop with two friends as I'm packing up. They are loud and boisterous, drawing the attention of everyone in the room. My anger flares at his lackadaisical attitude as well as his disrespect. But mostly I find myself disappointed with him, although for the life of me, I can't figure out why. Tucker Price is Tucker Price. The guy I saw yesterday was a figment of my imagination.

Tucker sees me and wanders over, a lazy smile on his face. "Where are you going?"

This part I dread. The attention Tucker has drawn follows over to me. My face flames, and I keep my head down as my shaky hand stuffs my books into my bag. It would be so much easier to stay and avoid the eyes of everyone in the room, but the truth is that all these eyes would be on me anyway. Tucker is the center of chaos everywhere he goes. I refuse to be sucked into it. Computer program or not.

He puts his hand on my bag. "Scarlett, where are you going?"

I look up into his face. Confusion wrinkles his brow. He really doesn't get it.

I dig deep down and find the strength to do this. "You said three o'clock, Tucker. It's now three twenty-two. You're late, and my time is valuable."

His eyebrows rise in surprise.

I jerk my bag from his hand and loop the strap over my shoulder.

He holds his hands out from his sides, his cocky attitude bleeding through his stance. "I'm here now."

"Good for you. I'm not." I head for the door.

Tucker follows behind, cutting in front of me and blocking the exit. "Scarlett." My name rolls off his tongue, smooth as silk. I'm sure many a girl has given him much more than their attention when he's used that voice. Fortunately for me, I'm not one of them. "Let's just sit back down, and we'll work during the time I have left."

"Tucker, if you don't get out of my way, I'll call campus security."

All eyes in the shop are on us. He shakes his head in disbelief. I'm quite certain he's used to getting what he wants whenever he wants it. He's not sure how to handle me.

My throat tightens and my lungs burn for oxygen. My body wants to gasp for air, but I fight the sensation, focusing every speck of my attention on the puzzled blue eyes less than a foot in front of my face.

We have a standoff, in the doorway of The Higher Ground coffee shop. People are outside the door waiting to get in, but Tucker's hand is on the handle, preventing their entrance as well as my escape.

I lift my chin and grit my teeth to keep them from chattering. "Get out of my way. Now."

He stares for another three seconds before he curses under his breath. His hand drops, and he takes a step back.

Someone outside pulls the door open, and I push through the group, my eyes stinging from my unshed tears and the cold. I walk at a brisk pace until I get to the mathematics building, then find a back stairwell and sink to a step. Closing my eyes, I bury my face in my hands and give into a full-blown attack as the realization of my fate sinks in my head.

I may have stood up for my principles, but I've just committed career suicide.

Chapter Three

After fifteen minutes of sitting on the stairs fighting to breathe, I feel like I'm ready to move. Thankfully, only a few people have passed me on the seldom-used staircase, and I've struggled to look relatively normal as they pass. As normal as someone sitting on the stairs crying can look.

My scheduled time in the tutoring center is three to six on Wednesdays. If I'm not going to tutor Tucker, I may as well head back to the lab and face my fate. I doubt I'll lose my job in the tutoring center, but Dr. Carlisle is bound to be disappointed in me despite the fact he said I wasn't required to tutor Tucker. Still, I can't help but wonder what it means for the department's funding. As well as my résumé.

After I make my decision to go upstairs, it still takes me another ten minutes to calm down enough to move off the step I'm perched on. I may be able to breathe again, but my nerves are raw and jittery.

Dr. Carlisle isn't in the room when I arrive. The other tutors are all busy with students who are waiting for assistance. I dive right in, helping with calculus and statistics problems. I keep glancing to the door, my anxiety rising as I wait for Dr. Carlisle to show up so I can share my bad news.

When my shift is over, I stay half an hour later and help the last of the students. If nothing else, it will make up for the time I should have spent with Tucker. Dr. Carlisle still hasn't returned, but I can fill him in on the details tomorrow. If the chancellor hasn't beat me to it.

I sigh and grab my bag, heading out the door. My study group meets off campus every Wednesday night at Panera, and I should be only a few minutes late. The sun has already set and the lights in the hall are dim, casting dark shadows. My gaze is lowered as I replay the incident with Tucker in my head. I don't notice the person leaning against the wall.

"Scarlett."

Tucker.

My feet stick to the floor, but I stumble as my body continues its forward momentum. My chest constricts when I see it's him. Anger fueled my backbone earlier. Now I'm dealing with worry, and I know it's not enough to face Tucker *and* stand my ground.

"I'm sorry about this afternoon," he says softly.

My mouth opens to answer him, but nothing comes out. I can't say *it's okay*, because it's not. Instead, I wait.

He takes a step toward me out of the shadows, and I notice right away his cocky swagger is missing. His shoulders are slumped in defeat. "Look, Scarlett, I screwed up. I was disrespectful of your time and rude to you when I finally got there. I know that I don't have any right to ask this, but I'd really like for you to give me another chance."

I stare at him in shock, still unable to answer. Who is this person in front of me? Because it's definitely not the Tucker Price I saw hours earlier. He sounds so formal, like he's rehearsed his appeal. I shake my head to clear it. "I'm not the only person who can tutor you." I pause to assemble my thoughts. "We're just not a good fit, and that's okay. It happens. But don't worry. I know at least two or three people who would jump at the chance." Tina included.

He takes another step closer, his eyes pleading. "I don't want anyone else. I want you."

I blink. "Why? I don't understand. You don't even know me."

"I know you're not going to take my shit. Today was proof of that."

Anger blooms in my chest, catching me by surprise. "So today was a *test*? To see if I'd put up with *your shit*?"

He grabs both sides of his head and shakes it. "No! That's not it at all! I fucked up, okay?" His hands lower, and pain and fear fill his eyes. "I fucked up, just like I fuck up everything."

I swallow, unsure how to answer. His response is unlike anything I ever expected to hear from him.

He takes my silence as encouragement. "Please, Scarlett. I swear to God I'll be on time the next time."

"I still don't understand. Why me?"

His lips press together, and he runs his hand through his wavy blond hair. He sighs and gives me a sad smile. "You treat me like I'm everyone else. You're not star-struck by Tucker Price, the soccer star."

My heart is softening.

He cocks his head to the side. "Please. One more chance."

Something in his eyes melts the guard I have up. There's something so familiar there. It's as though I'm staring into a bottomless pit of regret and sadness. I groan, frustrated with myself for falling for this. "Okay." The word flows out so softly even I have trouble hearing it.

But he doesn't miss it. His mouth lifts into a soft smile, and I realize he has a dimple in his right cheek. "Thank you."

I shift the strap of my messenger bag on my shoulder, hooking my thumb underneath to relieve some of the weight. "What do you have in mind? How much tutoring do you need?"

"What do you suggest?"

I know deep in my heart that I will regret this decision, yet I can't stop the words from tumbling out. "You're still struggling with the basic concepts of algebra. Let's work on it two days a week, right after your algebra class while what you just learned is still fresh in your mind. If you need more, we'll add another session."

He nods. "Yeah, that's good."

"Why don't you e-mail me your schedule, and I'll tell you what will work. And we won't meet at The Higher Ground. We can meet at the library since you have an aversion to the math lab."

The happiness fades from his eyes, and his breath shallows. "Not the library. Please. How about somewhere off campus then? Like Starbucks?"

His reaction is odd. While I know people study better in different environments, I can't help but wonder if this is a ploy to goof off in public again. "Fine. How about Panera?" I reason that while it's still public, there are tables tucked to the side, whereas Starbucks is completely in the open.

Relief floods his face. "Thanks, Scarlett."

I lift my chin and thrust my shoulders back, trying to show a strength I'm not currently feeling. "I will give you only one more chance, Tucker Price. And that's one more chance than I give most people."

The emotion that flickers in his eyes is unreadable yet intense. He swallows and nods but doesn't say a word.

I head toward the stairwell, and he falls in step behind me. When we reach the exit, he pushes the door open, and I look up at him with wariness. What's he up to?

He grins, a mixture of the Tucker upstairs just now and the Tucker from this afternoon. "I'm not some kind of stalker, I promise. I just happen to be going this way, too."

"Oh." *I'm an idiot.* I walk through the door and head for the parking lot as he heads for the fitness center.

The look in his eyes haunts me during the short drive to Panera. Why does he affect me so? Strangely enough, it's not the way every other girl on campus reacts.

The study group has already taken our usual table in the corner. Stephen looks up from our group of eight as I head to the counter to order a bowl of soup. In high school, it would have been every girl's daydream to be in a study group with seven guys and two girls. But this is not your average study group. We're all in set and logic and determined to pass this gauntlet to continue our degree path, which means we are hyper-focused on the work and not the company.

Everyone but Tim, who has asked me out three times in the last year and a half. Each time I say no. Each time he says I'll eventually see the logic and change my mind. He never says it with malice, merely with the surety of someone who has definite plans in life that for some bizarre reason include me.

When I take my seat, everyone looks up from their notebooks.

"Where have you been? You're never late to anything." Stephen pins me with a questioning gaze.

I shrug. "There were people still waiting when my shift was over at six."

"We were just discussing Monday's lecture."

We spend the next ten minutes going over our notes, but everyone's eyes keep darting to me. I can feel my face reddening.

When we move onto today's lecture, I find it harder and harder to concentrate. My study group is usually a safe place, but tonight it feels like anything but. I lock eyes with Tim for a brief second then shift my gaze to the table next to us. "Why is everyone acting so weird?"

"We heard about this afternoon."

When I turn back, all eyes are on me. Waiting for my response. The blood in my veins rises ten degrees. I set the pen in my hand on the table with a careful movement. As though the correct placement will affect the direction this conversation is headed. "What did you hear?"

"That you blew off Tucker Price in The Higher Ground."

I stare at the pen, noticing the logo is partially hidden the way it is laying. I resist the urge to turn it. "He was late."

Tony, a quiet Asian boy, clears his throat. "We need that program, Scarlett."

My mouth parts in astonishment. Tony is the most non-confrontational person I know, even more so than I am. But seeing how we have the same career plans, he of all people knows how essential this program is to our résumés.

Against my better judgment, I look up at their faces and realize the truth. They all *know* about the arrangement. Am I the mathematics concubine, offered to the soccer god as a payment?

Without a word, I slide out of my seat, grab my books and pick up my bag.

"Scarlett." Miranda's eyes are wide. "Where are you going?"

"I have a headache." I throw my trash away and walk out the door to my car.

How have I gotten here? How has my life taken this detour? I know I've overreacted. They are huddled over their sandwiches and equations, worrying that meek Scarlett Goodwin has sabotaged their academic careers. I should have stayed and told them Tucker and I have worked out a new arrangement. That their lives are safe for now, but another part of me rebels.

Screw them.

I drive home and walk into an empty apartment. Caroline has an evening class on Wednesdays so I pull out my homework, searching for solace in numbers. Math is the one constant in my life, the one thing I can count on to always be the same. I brush the stray strands of hair from my face, ignoring how sad my life is if that statement is true.

Tucker has algebra on Tuesdays and Thursdays so I schedule a session with him the next afternoon at three o'clock, at Panera.

He's sitting in a booth staring out the window when I pull up, his face void of expression. He doesn't notice me as I walk in and order a bagel and a coffee. I stop several feet away and study him, trying to prepare myself for our session. He's wearing jeans and a gray long-sleeve thermal shirt. His jacket is folded and in the seat next to him, his bag on top of it. His hair is tousled, as though the gusty wind blew the strands around, and he hadn't thought to right it. It's easy to understand why girls follow him around like lost puppies.

I've stood here for several seconds, long enough to make it awkward if I'm caught. I sit across from him and offer him a small smile. He looks so sad, it pulls a thread on my heart.

When he sees me, he instantly changes, a smile spreads across his face, and he holds his hands out from his sides. "On time. Early even."

I can't help grinning. "I noticed." And I also can't help noticing his dimple.

He opens his book. "Ready."

We spend fifteen minutes going over the orders of operation again and then move onto the lesson from today. His professor has covered linear equations using one variable, and he doesn't understand how to use the multiplication and division properties of equality.

"Tucker, what's your major?"

His face lifts, confusion crinkling his eyes. "History."

"Why history?"

His mouth opens to say something then he unconsciously licks his lower lip. I'm sure most girls would drool over it, but I see a guy who's suddenly lost his shield of confidence. Still, I can't ignore the slight stir in my emotions from the movement. Finally, he shrugs. "I like history."

His answer is a lie, but I don't see what good will come from pointing it out. "So what exactly do you like about history? It's full of dates, which are numbers."

He shakes his head. "Not the numbers. They get scrambled in my head. That's the hardest part." He pauses. "I like the stories. People who did extraordinary things and people remember them. They're not forgotten and lost forever."

I watch him as he speaks, the pain that flickers in his eyes.

"Do you like soccer?"

My question catches him by surprise. He blinks and sits up slightly. "Yeah. I'm good at it."

"I know you're good at it. I asked you if you liked it."

His gaze turns out the window, and his mouth turns to a slight frown. "Do you know you're the first person to ever ask me that question?"

I realize he hasn't answered, and although I'm curious, I refuse to invade Tucker's personal life any more than necessary. "I'm trying to figure out how you learn. Some people are auditory learners, while others are kinesthetic. Most guys are visual."

He shoots me a wicked glance, and to my surprise, I'm happy to see his cockiness return. Sad Tucker makes me feel too personally involved.

I lean forward, my forearms on the table. "I think there's more to learning than just the senses. If we can tie learning to something we love, we can remember it, and it sticks in our heads longer. So then when we retrieve the information later, it's easier to find. Does that make sense?"

"Yeah."

"So what do you love? What excites Tucker Price?" As soon as the words leave my mouth, I realize I've set myself up for a raunchy response.

He ignores it. His jaw works, and he leans back against the seat, stretching his hands across the table. I notice the multiple scars on his knuckles and the back of his hand. "No one's ever asked me that before either." His gaze returns to the gray sky.

While I wait for an answer that never comes, it occurs to me that he doesn't know. As he shuffles through his thoughts, I search my own and ask myself the same question that no one has ever asked me either.

I press my head into the seat, stretching my hands out on the table top, and close my eyes. I'm surrounded by people every day, yet I always feel alone, no matter how hard I try to connect. It's as though a veil has been thrown over my heart, and no one has ever been able to tear it down. Until this boy. This unattainable, untouchable, unreliable boy.

My eyelids flutter open, and I see the despair I've stirred in him.

My fingers flex, millimeters from his hand, his palms splayed on the table.

For the first time, I feel genuinely connected to another human being and just my luck, it turns out to be Tucker Price.

And that's the saddest fact of all.

Chapter Four

"**S**carlett, you look *gorgeous*!" Caroline squeals.

I smile in the mirror, surprised I actually look pretty. My long dark hair is loosely curled, and I'm wearing makeup. Caroline has lent me a silky shirt and pair of boots to wear with my jeans. I have to admit that I don't look anything like the real me. I feel like I'm dressed for a masquerade.

Tina stands in the doorway. "Let's hope Tim doesn't see you tonight or he might become more aggressive in his pursuit."

I laugh. "It's far more likely an asteroid will crash into the earth and send us into another ice age than I'll see Tim Wilson at this party tonight."

"Thank God," Caroline mutters. She stuffs her makeup brushes into a small bag. "Okay, let's go."

Huge winged creatures battle in my stomach as I go into the living room.

"Calm down, Scarlett." Caroline laughs, handing me my coat. "They usually reserve the waterboarding torture for later in the night. I'm sure you'll be safely tucked in bed before then."

"And hopefully with some good-looking guy," Tina adds.

I ignore Tina's ridiculous statement. I suspect Caroline would go batshit crazy if I slept with some guy tonight. Her goal for me tonight is to actually go to the party and hopefully meet a guy. She's been coaching me on what to do and not do all evening, knowing how awkward I can be in unfamiliar situations. The benefit and the curse of our friendship is that she knows me better than anyone. I force a smile at Tina. "Is it that obvious I'm nervous?"

"Worse." Tina leans around me. "What do you have to drink around here? I think Scarlett needs a head start."

Caroline shakes her head. "Nothing. I drank the rest of the wine during my *Gossip Girl* marathon."

No wonder she had so much trouble getting out of bed yesterday.

"No worries. We'll get a drink in her hand within thirty seconds of hitting the door. Although, if we give it sixty seconds, two guys will be fighting over who's going to get her a drink first."

Caroline slips on her coat and pulls her hair out and over her collar. "She'll never be able to handle that without a buzz. Our first mission is to get her a drink as quickly as possible before she scares all the guys away."

Tina nods her agreement with the plan.

I'm nervous enough, but all this talk about guys is making me want to vomit. "I think I changed my mind. Besides we're late. It's almost nine-thirty, and it started at eight."

Caroline lowers her face to mine. She's four inches taller than me in her stiletto boots. "Scarlett, that's what people do when they go to parties. They're supposed to show up late. It's expected." She enunciates her words slowly as though she's explaining this to a small child.

"That makes absolutely no sense." My dread increases.

"Oh, no you don't! No changing your mind." Tina loops her arm around mine and drags me to the door. "Quick, let's get her outside and lock the door before she goes and hides in her closet."

Caroline pushes me outside onto the landing and turns around to lock up. "You know her so well already."

"I used to be her."

Caroline and I turn to her, our mouths gaping. "You're kidding?" Caroline asks. "You mean there's hope for her yet?"

"Yep, but we don't have a moment to spare. Drinking, dancing, and boy shenaniganery are the prescription. Stat."

They both take one of my arms, and we walk the two blocks from our apartment complex to the house that's hosting the party. I ask myself for the hundredth time why I agreed to go. I attribute it to Tina and Caroline wearing me down with their badgering, but if I'm honest with myself, part of it is because of Tucker. Whether he knows it or not, he's made me aware of things about myself, things I don't necessarily like. I'm smart enough to know that if I'm going to change things, I need to alter my behavior, but suddenly this party seems like too much, too soon.

"No cold feet, Scarlett." Caroline tugs on my arm.

We're standing at the curb in front of the house. The house is brightly lit, and we can hear the heavy bass all the way out here on the street.

"Just give me a moment." I gulp deep breaths of air. The air is nippy, and my breath comes out in wispy white clouds.

Caroline leans into my ear. "Scar, it'll be fine. I promise. Just give it a chance."

I'm suddenly reminded of a party I went to during my senior year of high school. It turned out to be a disaster. The boy who took me did so as a joke. There was a bet to see if he could nail the geeky math girl that night.

My heart pounds out of control.

Caroline squeezes my arm. She knows about my history, even that. "Do you think I'd bring you here if I thought you'd get hurt? Just try to relax and have fun. If it gets too much, we'll go home. Okay?"

I nod. She's right, and I know she won't let me get into a situation where I feel completely out of control.

The house is packed, and I'm bombarded by noise and chaos. Tina is on one side of me and Caroline is on the other. They're both shrugging off their coats as we walk. True to her word, Tina leads me to a table, and a guy hands her a bottle. She thrusts it into my hand. "Here. Drink."

I'm smart enough to know that alcohol isn't the answer to my problems, but I'm wise enough to accept it as a crutch. I take a sip and nearly choke. "God, this is awful." The last time I had beer was in high school, and I'd been hoping that I remembered the taste incorrectly.

"You'll get used to it. Drink." Tina pushes the bottle to my mouth and tilts it up. I take several swigs before I push it away.

"Slow down," Caroline says. "She rarely drinks. We want her buzzed, not drunk."

"True."

I take several more sips as Tina gets a bottle and Caroline scans the room.

The guy handing us drinks smiles. "You can put your coats in the spare room, the first door on the left." He eyes me up and down. "I don't think I've met you before."

Tina steps between us. "Kyle, this is Scarlett. Scarlett, Kyle. It's her first time to one of your parties."

He grins. "Then, welcome. I'm really glad you came. It's usually BYOB, but Tina knows she's always welcome to whatever I have. You two are included."

I unbutton my coat and slide it down my arms. Anything to avoid having to talk to Kyle. I'm so awkward in these situations, and my awkwardness makes me even more uncomfortable. Talk about a vicious cycle.

He reaches toward me. "Here. I'll take that for you as long as you let me get you a drink later."

I nod and reluctantly accept. "Okay."

After he takes our coats, Tina turns to me and squeals. "I told you you'd be here less than a minute before a guy hits on you."

"He wasn't hitting on me." Yet I know he was. I just can't admit it to Tina, let alone myself. The all-too-familiar wariness I live with pokes me with its spiky barbs. I take another sip of the beer. Tina was right, you do get used to the taste.

We push our way into the crowd. Some couples are dancing, others are making out. Other people line the walls and bend their heads together in conversation. I stand next to the wall with Caroline, feeling the alcohol loosen the knot in my shoulders.

"Can I get you another drink?"

My head jerks up, and I'm staring into the face of a guy who's smiling. Not a leering smile, a friendly smile. I wave my bottle at him. "I already have one."

His smile turns to a teasing grin. His eyes dart down then back up to my face. "Do you?"

When I look down, I see the bottle is empty. "I guess I don't."

His eyebrow lifts slightly, and a mischievous challenge flickers in his eyes. "So can I get you that drink?"

Normally, I'd be wary, but he seems nice, and the beer has lowered my defenses. "Yeah."

He holds up his hand and pats the air as his other takes my empty bottle from my hand. "Wait here. Don't go anywhere."

I laugh. "Okay." I look away, my nerves pinging because I talked to a guy. And even more so because he's coming back.

Caroline waggles her eyebrows at me.

"What do I do *now*?" My stomach tightens. What have I gotten myself into?

"Scarlett, *relax*. Talk to him. Dance with him. Have fun."

I nod. *Talk. Dance. Have fun.*

Her mouth puckers, and she rolls her eyes. "Stop taking notes."

She knows me too well.

He returns less than a minute later, two beer bottles in his hand. I study him as he makes his way through the crowd. I'd guess him to be less than six feet tall, average build. His hair is dark brown, and he has chocolate brown eyes. I stop when I realize I'm categorizing him like I would the results of an experiment in chemistry class. The thought makes me giggle.

Caroline's eyes widen then scrunch in bewilderment. *Stop that*, she mouths.

When he reaches me, he hands me a bottle. "I'm Daniel, by the way."

"Scarlett."

His gaze studies me, and I can feel the heat rising to my cheeks. The beer has tempered my usual reaction, but not killed it entirely. I turn and watch the people in the room.

Caroline is now talking with a guy I recognize from my Arabic class, but I notice she's hanging close to me, listening in on our conversation.

Daniel leans down toward my ear. "Scarlett, do you go to Southern?"

The front door opens, and a gust of cold air floods the room, bringing with it a rowdy group of boys. None of them wear coats, and two of the guys are carrying cases of beer. They spill into the house, literally. A blond guy almost falls on his face before one of his friends grabs his arm. He jumps up and shouts, "That's what fast feet will do for ya!"

Tucker.

The room laughs, and he feeds off the attention, becoming more animated. "I need a fucking beer!" Then he disappears into the kitchen.

I'm not sure why, but his behavior disappoints me. I have no right to own this feeling, yet it's there anyway, chewing at the lining of my stomach.

Daniel is looking down at me, waiting for my answer.

"Um, yeah. I go to Southern." I cast another glance to the kitchen, then back to Daniel.

Daniel's gaze follows where mine went. "Do you know him?"

"I tutor him."

"Lucky you." His tone is dry.

Tutoring Tucker has been a challenge, but not how I foresaw it. He's been receptive during our two sessions and dedicated to learning the material. But nonetheless, my life feels like it's been upended. I've never questioned my life and my choices more than since I've started working with him. Unintentionally, Tucker's the main reason I'm here tonight. He's made me wonder if my life can have more, even if the definition of *more* remains elusive.

I don't want to discuss Tucker with Daniel or anyone else. "Do you go to Southern?"

His smile returns, and it occurs to me that he thought I might be interested in Tucker. "Guilty as charged. I'm a business major. And you?"

I square my shoulders, waiting for the shock and surprise. "Math."

His eyebrows rise, but his smile remains. "Education?"

"No, advanced mathematics."

The derision I'm used to seeing is absent. He whistles and shakes his head in an appreciative manner. "I bow to your greatness. I have to say I'm impressed."

I give him a smile. "Thank you."

"What are your career plans with that? NASA?" I'm used to people who jokingly ask me if I want to be a rocket scientist, but Daniel's question is genuine.

"Actually, no. The CIA." I sip my beer and wait for his response.

"And here I thought my goal of ending up with the most successful small business in Western Tennessee was high." He clicks his bottle to mine. "Here's to lofty career goals and may we both find what we are looking for." He takes a drink while watching me with a smile.

My chest warms and for the first time in ages, it's not from stress or embarrassment. I genuinely like this guy.

Tucker stumbles out of the kitchen with a beer in his hand, then disappears into a back room. Several girls trail after him.

Daniel waves his bottle toward the hall. "So how'd you get stuck with him?"

Two days ago, my answer would have been riddled with irritation over the situation. Tonight, my irritation stems from some irrational desire to defend him. The question is, why? Tucker's behavior isn't helping his flailing reputation.

I sigh. "It's a long story involving a mathematics computer program."

Daniel smirks. "Ah, funding."

I love that he gets it.

We talk for the next hour while Caroline works the crowd. Tina is dancing with Kyle. The house is getting crowded, and it's harder to talk at a normal level.

Daniel sees me watching Tina. "Would you like to dance?"

I don't want to dance with him, but it's not because I don't like him. It's because I'm uncomfortable getting up and dancing in front of people. I consider telling him no but stop and smile. I'm here tonight because I'm trying to change. What's the worst that could happen? I stumble or I look like a fool? But everyone is caught up in their own conversations, and I can't look much worse than the guy across the room who's shaking around like he's having a seizure. No one's even looking at him, let alone making fun of him. So I smile and nod, unable to say the word *yes*. A nod will have to suffice.

He doesn't question the nod, pulling the empty bottle from my hand and setting it on a table with his own. His hand reaches out to me and he's smiling, but his eyes have turned more serious.

Swallowing, I slowly reach my hand to his. My heart warms when his fingers close around mine as he stands, pulling me up with him. He leads me to the middle of the room and wraps his arms around my back. My hands, now hanging awkwardly at my side, search the front of his shirt for a comfortable place to rest.

He smiles down at me as we begin to sway to a slow song.

I glance around the room to see if anyone is watching me. I find myself counting out the beats of the music under my breath.

His eyebrow hitches. "Let me guess. You played piano."

"How'd you know?"

"Easy guess. First, music is math. And second"—a grin spreads across his face—"you're tapping the rhythm on my chest with your fingers as though you're playing piano."

I close my eyes and cringe. "Sorry." For the first time tonight, I feel embarrassed and uncomfortable, which fills me with disappointment. I've enjoyed spending time with him.

His finger gently lifts my chin so that I'm looking into his brown eyes. "Don't be sorry. I think it's cute. Do you still play?"

The reminder of the piano floods me with sadness. My elementary school music teacher saw an untapped talent in me in the second grade and not only gave me free piano lessons when she realized my mother would never pay for them, but also let me stay after school every day to practice on the music room instrument. Once I moved onto middle school, I no longer had access to a piano. I give him a sad smile. "No."

His mouth lowers, his breath fanning my face as he hesitates, his lips hovering over mine.

I tilt my head slightly up, and he accepts my invitation and presses a soft kiss against my lower lip.

Part of me worries that I'm rushing things. I've only just met him, yet I'm kissing him in a room full of people I don't know. But another part of me welcomes it. I like him. His lips are soft and warm, coaxing mine to kiss him back.

His head raises, and he looks down at me and smiles, then pulls my cheek to his chest and we continue to dance.

I close my eyes and think about what just happened. Obviously, I've been drinking, which explains how I got to this place—kissing a boy in front of a roomful of strangers. The kiss itself was nice, and I have to say Daniel's technique is superior to the last guy who kissed me over a year ago. Nevertheless, I squelch the disappointment building in my stomach. I've always heard of fireworks and butterflies, but never felt them. Not once in the handful of men I've dated. I thought my nerves were supposed to tingle and parts of me were supposed to burn with desire. This guy holding his arms around me is very attractive and treats me with respect. What more could a girl want?

So why do I feel nothing?

What the hell is wrong with me?

I bite my lip and force the tears that burn my eyes to dry. I refuse to cry over something so stupid. Fireworks and butterflies are hormones. Long-term relationships are built on hard work and dedication. It doesn't take a genius to see which lasts longer.

Sucking in a deep breath, I force myself to accept the truth: Butterflies are for lust-driven teens. Real relationships are based on mutual respect. Which would I rather base a relationship on? I know the answer deep in my heart, but it doesn't stop the wish that I could have both.

Wishing for more always leads to heartache. There is no happily ever after. There's only here and now.

So why do I still want it?

Chapter Five

Daniel and I continue to dance through several songs until one of his friends taps his shoulder.

"Dude, we're out of here. It's time to go."

Daniel's arm is still draped across my lower back, but he takes a step backward, conflict skirting across his face.

His friend heads to the door. "Bailey! Let's go!"

I smile up at Daniel. "It's okay. Thanks for the dance. And everything." My face burns at the thought of our kiss.

He looks around then back to me. "We just met, and I don't want to leave you."

"I'm about to leave with my friends." I point to Tina, who is making out with Kyle. And Caroline, who is talking to two guys in the corner, obviously drunk by the amount of laughter floating from her group.

His eyes darken. "I want to see you again, Scarlett."

I feel a twinge of nerves flutter in my stomach. This has to be a good sign. "I'd like that, Daniel Bailey."

"See? You already know my last name, and I don't know yours. Give me your phone so I can put in my number."

I hold my hands out apologetically. Since Tina and Caroline and I are all together, none of us saw a reason to bring our phones. "Sorry. I don't have my phone."

His friend pokes his head around the corner. "*Bailey!*"

Daniel takes a step backward, snatching my hand in his. "At least give me your last name."

"Goodwin. Scarlett Goodwin."

He tugs me to him and kisses me with a sweetness that steals my breath. "Thanks for...tonight." He grins before he steps backward, dropping my hand. "Bye."

Daniel darts out the door but leans around the edge of the door once more, a grin on his face.

Still smiling after he disappears, I'm flushed, but it's not from nerves or embarrassment. This feeling is from the anticipation of seeing him again. Even though I didn't give him my number or any way to find me, I have no doubt that he will. Daniel seems resourceful.

This a good sign, right? This feeling of excitement? This quivering inside? Maybe, just maybe, I *am* capable of feeling something. Maybe I'm *not* dead inside.

Without Daniel, the room suddenly seems too loud and too warm. I head toward the kitchen to get a glass of water. A group of rowdy guys crowds around the table playing beer pong. They don't notice me as I pick up an empty red cup and move to the sink, letting the water run before I fill it. My gaze drifts out the window to the house next door, which is currently under renovation, based on the Dumpster parked in the driveway. I'm about to turn away when someone catches my eyes, his hand slamming into the metal sides.

Tucker.

The only light on the outside of the house is the fixture at the side door. He's in the shadows, but from what little I see, he's upset. And he's alone.

My breath catches in my chest as I consider doing something so unlike me it's alarming. I attribute it to the alcohol in my blood even though I haven't had a drink in almost an hour.

One of the guys behind me bumps into my back and groans as he stumbles. "Sorry." He laughs and returns to his game. The ball bounces on the table, and they break into a loud cheer, but I've moved to the side door, my hand on the doorknob.

Outside, the cold air seeps through the silk shirt I'm wearing. I wrap my arms around my chest and walk toward Tucker, who is on the far side of the Dumpster. His hand is up to his face.

"Marcel. Man, don't do it. *Please.*" Tucker's words are heavy with emotion. He hunches forward over his knees, his other hand grabbing a handful of hair.

Tucker must not like what Marcel says because he jams his phone into his pocket and pummels the bin with both fists. He releases a loud cry as his body wracks with sobs.

I take several steps closer, about six feet away, feeling like an interloper as I witness his breakdown, yet I can't make myself walk away. "Tucker."

He doesn't hear me, taking his frustration and pain out on the metal box. His hands darken with blood.

"Tucker," I say louder and with more force.

His fists still beat the metal, but their speed and force weaken. He turns to me, tears streaming down his face. "I couldn't stop him."

The ice covering my heart cracks and sorrow, hot and heavy, flows through my veins. "I know. I heard."

"I tried, Scarlett. This is all my fault."

I move closer, a foot away. He reeks of alcohol. "It's okay, Tucker."

He shakes his head in an exaggerated movement and stumbles sideways. I grab his arm, and he reaches for me with bloody hands.

"It's not. It's all my fault." A fresh batch of tears floods his face, and I wonder how much he's had to drink.

"Tucker, you need to go home."

His head lifts higher, as though he's listening for something, then his shoulders droop again. "Yeah." He reaches into his pocket and winces as he digs for his keys.

"You can't drive. Where are your friends?"

His face tightens with anger. "Those fuckers aren't my friends."

"But they came with you. They can help you get home." Yet I wonder if that's true. They seemed as wasted as Tucker when they came in.

"I'm not going anywhere with those fuckheads." His words slur and he stumbles again.

"You have to go somewhere."

He scowls and removes his keys. "I told you I'm going home." Dangling his keys in the air, he heads to the street.

"Tucker, wait!" I run next to him and grab his arm, tugging him back. I don't know why I'm getting involved. Maybe I'm worried Tucker will kill himself as well as innocent people on the road if he drives in this condition. Or maybe it's because I'm surprised that Tucker Price could break down like this. Or maybe it's a combination of the two. Whatever the reason, I can't stop myself. "Let me take you."

He turns to me and raises his palm to my cheek. "Sweet Scarlett."

My stomach tightens when his hand touches my face. "Will you let me drive you?"

He continues to watch me, remaining silent.

I slowly take his keys, worried I'll spook him if I move too quickly. "I have to tell my friends I'm leaving. Wait here." I lead him toward a plastic chair and push him down. I start to ask him about his coat, then remember when I saw him come in, he wasn't wearing one.

I have no idea how I'll explain this to Caroline, although I'm sure Tina will be thrilled.

Caroline is still sitting with the two guys she was with when I went outside. Her legs are crossed and she's leaning forward and laughing. She looks happy. When I approach, her happiness fades away. She must see something on my face that worries her. "Is everything okay?"

I force a smile, and fist my shaking hands. "Of course." I pause. There's no way Caroline will approve of me taking Tucker home. I'm not sure *I* approve, yet I still feel obligated, for whatever reason. But I know who will. "I'm looking for Tina."

Caroline nudges her head toward the hall. "Last time I saw her she was headed for the bathroom."

"Thanks."

I grab my coat and find Tina coming from a back bedroom, brushing her hair from her face as Kyle sneaks around the back of her, adjusting his shirt. I'm not even going to think about what she's been doing. "Hey, Tina. Tucker Price has to be at least a point-one-two on the blood alcohol meter, so I'm going to take him home."

Her eyes narrow as the corners of her mouth lift into a wicked smile. "I knew you had it in you."

"No," I protest. "That's not it at all."

"You're a big girl, Scarlett. Have fun."

I could argue with her more, but I'm worried Tucker will wander off. "Tell Caroline, okay?"

"Be safe."

I had no intention of putting myself in a position where safety was an issue. But I nod and head out the side door. Tucker is where I left him, mumbling to himself.

"Tucker, let's go." I grab his arm and pull.

He struggles to get up, and I wonder how drunk he actually is.

"Where's your car?"

His unfocused eyes look up and down the street lined with vehicles. Then he laughs. "It's at home."

I blink. "*What*?"

"I didn't drive."

What the hell have I gotten into? I consider leaving him here, but his hands are covered in blood, and I don't trust him or anyone else in the house to take care of cleaning him up. "Come on, we're walking." If nothing else, the cold air and exercise will clear his head a bit if he doesn't freeze to death without a coat. I wonder how long the thermal shirt he's wearing under his t-shirt will keep him warm. I loop my arm over his.

44

"Where are we going?"

"My place."

He shoots me a wicked grin. "I didn't think you were that kind of girl, Scarlett."

My brow furrows with irritation. This was a stupid idea, but it's too late to turn back now. "I'm not. I'm taking you there to clean up your hands since you were stupid enough to use a giant metal garbage can as a punching bag. Then I'm calling one of your friends to take you home."

"I don't have any friends." His words are slurred and sound hollow.

"What are you talking about? You have tons of friends."

"They're not really my friends."

So Tucker is a melancholy drunk. I suppose I shouldn't be surprised. The person I see every time I tutor him isn't the person I see in class or on campus. There are two sides to this mercurial boy, and I fluctuate between being intrigued and wanting to run. I cast a glance to the person trying to walk a straight line for the two blocks to my apartment, and I want to take off in a sprint.

Sometimes being responsible sucks.

We walk an entire block in silence. The only sounds are the click of my boot heels and Tucker's awkward breathing which comes out in gasps and huffs. He releases a groan, then leans over and vomits on the street.

I scrunch my eyes closed and breathe through my mouth, trying to settle my now-queasy stomach.

After several seconds, he wipes the back of his hand across his mouth and resumes walking again.

"Do you do this often?" I ask.

He laughs. "Yeah."

I think about the nastiness he left on the road behind us. "Why?"

"Why not?"

"Maybe because barfing in the street doesn't sound like my kind of fun."

His eyebrows rise and fall in a playful manner. "What *is* your kind of fun, Scarlett?"

I don't answer, knowing he'd think me even stranger than he already does.

"Well?"

I had hoped he'd be too drunk to press the issue, but the walk seems to be sobering him up. "You wouldn't understand."

"Try me."

I inhale through my nose and imagine my nervousness leaving my body with my exhale. "Math. I like doing math problems."

We walk several steps in silence before I sneak a glance at him. He's watching me with a strange look in his eyes, devoid of amusement or malice. Curiosity. "Why?" he finally says.

"They calm me." Why I answer truthfully is beyond me. I find myself incapable of telling Tucker Price falsehoods, which seems irrational. Tucker Price seems like the kind of person who is used to hearing and speaking mostly lies all day long.

Maybe that's why I feel compelled to tell him the truth.

"Your major is math. You tutor several days a week. I can't even imagine how many problems you must do. What makes you so anxious that you need that much calming?"

I've been truthful up to this point. Why lie now? "Life."

He doesn't respond.

I wait for the familiar rush of panic and adrenaline when I've embarrassed myself, but it doesn't come. Why? My eyes shift to him, and the look on his face isn't just sympathetic. It's as though he really understands.

Chapter Six

Several minutes later we climb the staircase to my apartment. I worry that Tucker will fall down the stairs in his stupor, but he only trips once. When we reach my apartment, he leans his shoulder into the brick wall as he watches me fumble with the lock. I push the door open and wait for him to enter. The soft lamp light from the living room welcomes us in from the cold.

He waves to the opening. "Ladies first."

More surprises. I go inside, and he follows, shutting the door behind us.

I go into the kitchen, my stomach churning. I'm suddenly unsure this was a good idea. "Sit down at the table, and I'll clean up your hands."

He obeys, sliding a chair across the floor closer to the wall and landing in the seat with an *oomph*.

I take off my coat and lay it across the back of another chair. "I need to get some towels." When I come back from the bathroom with several hand towels, I wet one with warm water and lay the rest on the counter. I reach for his right hand and begin to tenderly pat the now-drying blood.

"Why are you doing this?" he asks.

I'd love to know the answer to that question myself. "You can't do your homework if you can't hold a pencil."

He slides down in his seat, leaning his head back and shutting his eyes. "Strictly professional reasons."

"Of course."

We both know it's a lie, but he doesn't call me on it.

When I get most of the blood wiped away on his right hand, I sigh. His knuckles are swollen and purple. "I think you should go to the ER and get x-rays. You might have broken your hand."

The back of his head is propped against the kitchen wall, and his eyes are closed. "Good thing I don't need my hands in soccer."

"Tucker, I'm serious."

One side of his mouth lifts into a smirk. "So am I."

Shaking my head, I open the freezer and look for a bag of something frozen to put on his hand. The freezer is unsurprisingly bare. Caroline and I exist on mac and cheese, spaghetti, and ramen noodles. I have to settle for a partially used bag of pizza rolls. I set Tucker's hand on the table, cover it with a washrag, then top it with the bag.

He sits up in alarm, as though I just woke him. "What the fuck?"

"I'm trying to help you, but I won't if you're going to cuss at me."

He closes his eyes again. "You're cute."

Incoherent Tucker is back.

I clean up his left hand, relieved to find the swelling and bruising aren't as bad. When I finish, I put his hands together on the table, scoot the washrag to cover both hands, then adjust the bag on top.

"You should be a doctor, Scarlett."

I move to the sink and wash out the towels. "Nah. I'm just exceptionally practiced at cleaning up injuries."

"Your old boyfriends get in a lot of fights?"

"No. My mother." There goes my filter again.

One eye cocks open. "Your mother was big into fights?"

My chest tightens. I don't like talking about this. Why am I so truthful with this guy? "Let's just say she was on the receiving end."

His other eye opens, and he focuses his full attention on me.

48

Something flashes in his eyes, as though he's seeing me for the first time. I'm not sure I like it.

I turn around and get a glass and fill it with the water pitcher from the refrigerator. "You need to drink this. And we need to call one of your friends."

He groans and leans his forehead into the edge of the table. "I told you I don't have any friends."

I don't want to argue this point with him again. "What about your roommate?"

He doesn't answer.

"Fine, then I'll call a cab."

His head rotates from side to side, still leaning against the table. "No."

"Tucker. You *have* to go somewhere."

His head rises. "Can I just stay here for a little bit with you?"

I press my back into the counter while I study his face. "I don't think that's a good idea."

Confusion scrunches his forehead. "Why?"

I gesture toward him. "You're Tucker Price. You're..." I shake my head. "I'm not like that, Tucker. I'm not that kind of person."

The emotion on his face shifts to a look that resembles contentment. "I know."

Something in his eyes tugs on my heart, unraveling the seam that separates us a bit more. I don't feel threatened by him. I don't even get a feeling that he's looking for sex. It's something deeper than that.

"Can I stay for just a little bit?" he whispers. "Please."

This is the worst idea in the history of ideas, yet I can't stop myself from nodding. He looks so lost. "Okay."

He tries to get up and almost falls on his face.

"How much did you have to drink tonight?" I grab his arm and help him stand.

"Not enough. Not nearly enough."

My plan is to take him into the living room, but it's obvious he needs to lie down. I stop in front of the hallway and close my eyes. I should call a cab *right now.*

"Scarlett." He sighs, resting his cheek on top of my head.

"Come on." I lead him to my room and turn on the lamp on my nightstand. "Don't get any ideas."

I push him so that he's sitting on my bed, and he lays down, grabbing my hand and tugging.

"I told you not to get any ideas."

"Just sit with me."

I sit on the edge of the bed, his hand still wrapped around mine. His eyes are closed as he buries his cheek into my pillow.

"Tucker?"

"Hmm?"

"Who's Marcel?" I expect him to get angry or tell me to mind my own business.

"My brother," he mumbles.

"What was he going to do?"

We sit in silence. His breath is less ragged than it was outside, but still has the shallow rasp of a drunk person.

"Ruin his life. And it's all my fault."

A soft snore comes from his mouth, and his grip relaxes on my wrist. I sit for a few moments then start to pull my hand away, but his fingers tighten. "Don't go," he slurs.

"I have to go to the bathroom."

His grip tightens. "Promise you'll come back."

I pause. "Okay. I will."

His fingers relax, and I pull free, easing off the bed and wandering to the bathroom. I pee and wash my hands, looking up to see my face in the mirror. The girl in the reflection looks just like me, but she can't be me.

The Scarlett Goodwin I know would not have Tucker Price in her bed.

But then again, I don't. He's lying on top of the covers, and I have no intention of having sex with him.

I hear the front door open, and Caroline comes in. "Scarlett! Where are you?"

"What are you doing home so early? You were having fun."

"I was worried about you. Tina told me you took Southern's man-slut home."

I watch her as she takes off her coat, unsure how to answer.

She lifts her gaze to me as she tosses her coat onto the sofa. "Did you really take him home?"

"Define *home*."

My meaning sinks in, and her eyes enlarge to twice their size. "No, Scarlett. Please tell me you didn't."

"It's not what you think."

Her face hardens. "Then what is it?"

I sigh, uncertain what *it* is myself. "I'm not sleeping with him, if that's what you think."

Relief washes away her fear, but wariness remains. "Then why is he here?"

"I found him beating up a Dumpster, and he was so drunk he could hardly stand. His hands were a mess, and I don't know...I felt sorry for him."

Her mouth drops, and then her eyes narrow. "You felt sorry for Tucker Price?"

"There's something more to him, Caroline. Something no one else sees."

"How drunk are you?"

I sigh. "I'm not drunk and it's not just tonight. I've seen it before when I tutor him. He seems so sad. And lonely."

She rolls her eyes. "Is that what he's doing to try to get you to sleep with him? Playing Mr. Sensitive?"

"I seriously doubt he has to play anything to get girls to sleep with him. So why would he waste the effort?"

I head into the kitchen and clean up the mess I left.

Caroline follows me in. "Why is there blood on those washrags?"

Turning my back to her, I wash out the rags in the sink again. "I told you that he beat up a Dumpster."

"And you cleaned him up?"

"Yeah." Why does it sound so wrong the way she asks it?

"If you need something to take care of, we can get a cat."

I turn to face her and burst into laughter. "A cat?"

She shrugs. "I hate cats, but I'd rather see you get attached to a cat than Tucker Price." She looks over her shoulder. "Where is he anyway? Is he gone?"

I take a deep breath and turn back to the sink. "He's passed out on my bed."

"*What*?" She stomps down the hall to my room and throws open the door.

I run after her and put my hand across the doorway. "Caroline! What are you doing?"

She watches him with a scowl. "Well, look at that. Tucker drools."

I swivel my gaze and sure enough, he's drooling on my pillow.

She leans her shoulder into the door jamb. "I have to admit he's kind of cute, passed out in your bed."

"Sure, if you like the drunk look."

Her face softens, and she turns to face me. "You don't, do you, Scarlett?" Her question comes out as a plea.

The corners of my mouth lift into a hint of a smile. "No. You know me better than that." I close the door, and we go back into the kitchen.

"Tell me about the guy I saw you dancing with." Caroline grabs a Chinese container from earlier tonight out of the fridge and eats her leftover lo mein cold.

I put mine in the microwave and watch the glass base spin around and around. "His name is Daniel, and he's a business major at Southern."

Caroline squeals and claps her hands together. "A business major? Two boring people! It's a match made in heaven."

I tilt my head back as I look over my shoulder. "He is not boring. He's sweet. I like him."

"And?"

"And what?" The microwave dings and I take my food to the table. I know what she wants to know, but I'm going to make her dig for it.

"You're so mean!"

I laugh and take a bite of my cashew chicken. "He wants to see me again. I didn't have my phone to put his number into, but he said he'll find me."

Her smile falls. "Oh."

I remember his face and his smile. "He'll find me."

She tips her head to the side, her fork in the air. "Well, listen to you. A man in your bed and a man waiting in the wings. I always knew you were an overachiever."

I purse my lips together. "It's not like that." I look into her eyes. "Sometimes you just know when you connect with someone, you know?"

She grins and nods. "I do. And I'm happy for you."

Sighing, I look down at my food. So why am I thinking about the man in my bed and not the man who kissed me?

Chapter Seven

Caroline and I finish eating, and she gets ready for bed while I clean up the kitchen. I'm still wearing her shirt, and I need to get something to sleep in.

I crack the door to my bedroom. Tucker is still asleep, snoring even louder. Part of me wants to wake him up, have him call someone, and send him on his way. But another part of me wants to let him stay, and that's the part I don't understand. There's no logical explanation. I just do. That fact alone is troubling. I never *just do* anything. Everything is carefully thought out.

Even tonight when I danced with Daniel and let him kiss me, I gave it some thought before it happened. I danced with him because he was nice. I let him kiss me because I liked him and hoped I'd feel something. Split-second decisions, but decisions nonetheless.

But not Tucker. No matter how deeply I search, there is no answer to be found.

Tucker Price is getting under my skin.

I creep in the room and open a drawer. It creaks, and I stop for a second, then continue pulling. Between my mother and her friends, I've been around enough passed-out drunks in my life to know when they're out. Tucker is definitely out.

I grab a t-shirt and a pair of shorts and notice that I no longer hear snoring. When I turn around, Tucker's eyes are open and focused on me.

Turns out Tucker isn't like most drunks.

"You promised to come back."

"And here I am." I press against the dresser. Why do I feel this push-pull? The need to dig deeper into his secrets and the desperation to run away? "Why don't I get you a glass of water?"

He closes his eyes. "Yeah, that's probably a good idea."

I go into the bathroom and change before I get Tucker's water. When I return, he's snoring again. I set the water on the nightstand then turn toward the door.

"Why are you always running away from me?"

I look over my shoulder and his eyes are closed, but the back of his forearm covers his forehead. "You were asleep. I didn't want to bother you."

"Where are you going? This is your bed."

"It's okay. I'm going to sleep on the sofa."

He pushes himself into a sitting position. "No, Scarlett. It's your bed. You should sleep here."

"It's okay, really. You need to sleep it off."

"Please. Stay." He reaches for me, hopelessness washing off of him in thick waves.

Hypnotized by the despair in his eyes, I sink to the edge of the mattress.

He smiles, but it's sad. He slips his hand into mine. "See? That wasn't so hard."

"Tucker...I can't... I'm not..."

"I know, Scarlett. I would never ask you to. I'm still drunk, and you deserve better than that."

The sincerity in his words freezes the air in my lungs.

He pulls me down next to him, and I find myself unable to resist.

We're both on our sides, facing each other. He releases my hand and reaches for the side of my face, brushing the hair off my cheek.

His fingertips barely touch my skin, yet send shivers down my back. My stomach clenches.

"Sweet, sweet Scarlett." His palm presses against my cheek as his fingers dig into my hair.

I close my eyes, my stomach tightening even more.

"I've never felt this with anyone. Ever," he murmurs, his words fading.

Neither have I remains unsaid but buried in my heart.

My panic builds like a storm in the back of my head. How can I be lying next to Tucker Price? How can I let him affect me so? But part of me is tired of basing every single decision in my life on reasoned and thought-out choices. Part of me wants to *live*.

I can't help thinking about my conversation with Caroline days ago, when I told her that one didn't live a little or a lot, they simply lived.

I finally get it.

Nevertheless, I can't give any part of myself to this man. There may be a hidden window to his soul, but it is not my job to plumb its depths. I'm neither experienced nor jaded enough to survive the attempt.

But maybe I can steal this moment. Just for tonight.

Our breathing fills the silence in a synchronized rhythm that soothes my distress. My shoulders begin to unknot. My hands unfist. My jaw unclenches. The only part of us touching is his hand on my face, tangled in my hair. Yet a peace washes over me, loosening my anxiety and peeling it away.

His hand slides down my neck, and brushes the bare skin of my arm, then curves around the small of my back and slowly, ever so slowly, pulls me closer to him. My head tucks under his chin and he continues to pull until my chest is pressed against his. I can feel the thud of his heart, the rise and fall of his ribcage as he breathes. Such simple, involuntary acts, yet they permeate my consciousness, draw me in with a hypnotizing lull.

Several minutes later, I know he's asleep again, and I tell myself to move, to get up and sleep on the sofa, but I can't make myself do it. In twenty years, I've never felt this close to anyone.

That's what makes this all the more dangerous, to let myself feel this with *him*, but I'm like the proverbial moth drawn to the flame.

Why do I think the end result will be any different for me?

I drift off to sleep and wake to sunlight peering through the crack of my curtains. Tucker is still asleep, and thankfully so is Caroline. I duck into the bathroom and spend much longer than necessary in the shower, washing the scent of alcohol and smoke from my body and my hair. When I go back into my room, Tucker is gone and nowhere to be found in the apartment.

Part of me is glad. He stirs too many uncomfortable emotions in me. But part of me misses him. A ridiculous thought. I've obviously lost touch with reality.

On Monday, I leave my set and logic class and see Daniel in the hallway, leaning against the wall and looking down the opposite way.

He turns his head toward me and smiles. "I told you I'd find you."

My mouth turns up into the barest of grins even though I'm beaming inside. I remember telling him I took this class. "I'm glad you did."

"Do you have somewhere you need to be?"

I usually study after this lecture, going over what we learned, but I'd rather spend the time with Daniel. Anything to purge the lingering memory of Tucker. "I have some time before Arabic."

He leans back and studies me with a teasing glint. "*Arabic*?"

"Did I forget to mention I'm minoring in Arabic?"

He winks. "Did I mention I'm minoring in making ramen noodles?"

I laugh, but my guard is still up.

"I have class in about thirty minutes, but I'd love to spend time with you at The Higher Ground."

"I'd like that."

We walk across the small campus to the coffee shop, discussing what we did over the weekend. I leave out any mention of Tucker. In fact, I've tried my best to block him out of my memory as much as possible.

Daniel tells me that he spent most of the weekend helping a friend put a deck on his house.

"You built a deck in January? Isn't it too cold?"

"It's better than the middle of July. I hate the heat."

"Then what are you doing in Tennessee?" I tease as he opens the door to the coffee shop for me.

"I ask myself that every day," he says woefully, then chuckles.

We order our drinks and wait at the counter. I study the bakery case, finding it difficult to look him in the eye.

"Where did you learn construction?"

"My dad owns a construction company, so I've been swinging a hammer since before I could walk."

"I hope you don't have any siblings."

He laughs. "Thankfully for my little brother, I learned some self-control before he was born."

The barista hands us our drinks, and we sit at a table by the window.

Daniel leans his forearms on the table. "We've discussed enough of my exciting weekend. What did you do?"

"My weekend was so much more exciting that yours. My room-mate forced me to watch *Gossip Girl*, but mostly I was studying." Caroline had fallen back into her depressive state on Saturday and spent the weekend re-watching the first season. She wanted to watch people falling in love since she declared it was never going to happen to her again. I made two Ben & Jerry runs until I finally cut her off.

"You really know how to have a good time."

"This semester is the make-it-or-break-it semester of my entire academic career. Set and logic is *the class* that decides my fate. I can't blow it."

"What do you do for fun, Scarlett?"

His change in topic makes me pause. Tucker asked me the same question a few nights ago, but I can't bring myself to give Daniel the same answer. I give him the one I keep on file when I'm asked such questions. "I like to watch movies."

He holds his hands out and a grin covers his face. "What a coincidence? So do I."

I chuckle and look down at my coffee. "What *are* the odds?"

"Since we both like movies, how about we see one together?"

I slowly twist my coffee cup. While he's nice and attractive enough, part of me is reluctant to take this next step. I take a moment to analyze why and come up with no reasonable explanation. I *need* to do this. Maybe this is what is missing in my life and will give me the elusive happiness I've begun to seek. But I want to take it slower. Ease my way into it. "Would you mind if we just stick to coffee for now?" I ask, keeping my gaze on the table.

"Is this you brushing me off or is this really 'let's start with coffee'?"

I look into his anxious face. I realize it seems kind of backward after we've already kissed. Twice. "I like you. I just need to take it slow. If you don't want to, I understand."

"As long as I really have a shot, then I'm fine with coffee. Now that I know where to stalk you on Monday, I'm guessing I can find you at the same place and time on Wednesday." He closes his eyes and groans. "Wow. That sounded wrong when I'm trying to convince you that I'm not a serial killer."

I laugh. "Don't worry. I'm not scared off yet."

"Good." He stands and picks up his bag. "I'm going to be late to class."

"Thanks for the coffee. I'm really glad you tracked me down."

"Me, too. I'll see you Wednesday."

Daniel walks out the door. When he reaches the sidewalk, he turns and waves.

I break into a grin and wave back. I'm actually looking forward to Wednesday. Until I realize I have to get through Tuesday. I still have to face Tucker.

Chapter Eight

Tucker is already at Panera when I arrive on Tuesday afternoon, and I'm ten minutes early. I wasn't sure he'd be here at all since he didn't show up for Western civilization earlier today. *I* didn't want to come here at all, but I had an obligation, awkwardness aside. It's moments like now that I wish I'd agreed to go on some type of anxiety medication, even if I can't afford it.

He's standing inside, next to the door waiting for me, looking a little rough. His eyes are bloodshot, and his skin has a sallow appearance. His shirt is wrinkled, as though he pulled it out of the laundry hamper. He looks hung over, which explains why he wasn't in Western civ. I can't help wondering how effective our tutoring session will be.

When I pause outside, trying to calm my nerves, he watches me for a second with his sad eyes. As though he's aware of my inner struggle, he steps outside, the blustery wind tossing his hair around. He stops in front of me, close enough for me to catch a whiff of his shampoo. He may look disheveled, but at least he's showered.

"Scarlett, before we go in, I want to apologize for Friday night. I'd like to say that doesn't happen very often, but it does." He runs a hand through his hair and looks across the parking lot. "But I'm sorry it happened with *you*." His gaze returns to me. "I want you to know that I don't think of you"—he pauses and looks away again—"like that. What I did was wrong." His chest rises and worry etches lines around his eyes as they shift and search mine. "I understand if you want me to find a new tutor."

Most of me wants him to find another tutor. The rational, logical part, and the reason has less to do with him and more to do with me. Being with him dredges up insecurities from my past. The hopelessness, the fear. I need to keep these feelings locked up and buried.

But one small part of me likes that he makes me feel *something*, even if it's bad.

"No. It's okay." I finally say.

He exhales, and his shoulders sink with relief. "Then let's get started." He opens the door and waits for me to enter. When I order at the counter, he requests a coffee and pays for both.

"You don't have to do that, Tucker."

He gives me a sheepish grin. "I know, but I wanted to."

I'm suddenly aware that I've had two men buy me coffee in two days. Look how things have changed.

We find a table in the corner and Tucker pulls out his book. "I'm getting linear equations now, but I'm having trouble with linear inequality."

I study his work and show him where he went wrong, applying the wrong distributive property. To my surprise, within minutes, he's plowing through several problems. He looks up. "You don't have to sit there and wait for me. Do you have something you need to work on?"

I'm being paid to work with Tucker, not do my own homework.

He sees my hesitation and his eyebrow rises. "You do."

I cast a glance to my bag. "I shouldn't."

"You're creeping me out just sitting there." He grins, and I know he's teasing. "Do your own thing, and I'll tell you if I need you."

"Okay." I feel guilty pulling my own work out, but I have an upcoming test in set and logic a week from Friday, and there aren't enough hours left to make me feel prepared.

He winks. "See? I knew you could do it."

When I open the textbook and my own notebook, Tucker leans over and spins the pages around to face him. "You've got to be kidding." He looks up, his mouth parted. "You actually *like* this?"

"Yeah." I say with confidence even though I feel self-conscious.

His amusement fades to concern. "I didn't mean it to sound negative, Scarlett. If anything, I'm in awe."

I'm shocked he could read me. I'm used to masking my reactions, as long as my flushed skin doesn't make an appearance and give me away. But he's not looking at my cheeks—which are amazingly blotch-free—and is staring instead into my eyes. I notice his aren't as red as before and that some of the color has returned to his complexion. I realize he's not hung over, but he doesn't look sick either. It's as though he was upset before and is getting over it.

"So *why* do you like it?" His gaze holds mine, challenging me to not look away.

"I'm good at it."

"Obviously, but I'm good at soccer. It doesn't mean I like it. I'm asking if you *like* math."

I remember him saying that no one ever asked if he liked soccer. The fact that he asks me whether I really like math warms the inside of my chest. As though my liking it or not matters. I give him a soft smile. "Yeah, I really like it."

"So why do you like it?" He asks again. I hear no challenge in his voice, only genuine curiosity.

"Because as long as you know the rules, you know what's expected of you, and as long as you have the necessary information, you can always find the answer."

He watches me, analyzing my face and what I've said. "You like being in control." There's no malice or derision, only pure observation.

I wait for the heat to rise to my cheeks, but it doesn't come. I suppose I never looked at it that way, but now that he's said it, I realize it's true. "Yes."

"And you do math problems for fun?"

He remembers our discussion on the street.

Memories of Friday night rush into my head, and I start to look down, but his hand reaches for my chin, tilting my face up. "Don't do that. Don't be embarrassed. You didn't do anything wrong. I was the ass, you were only stuck dealing with it. Okay?"

I bite my top lip and slowly nod.

His hand lowers but his eyes hold mine.

"You don't like soccer?" I ask.

Pain flickers in his eyes, but he still holds my gaze. "That's a complicated question."

The last time we met, I wouldn't have pressed the issue. But I feel like what we experienced Friday night gives me the right to ask. "I think I can handle a complicated answer."

He smirks, and a hint of his smart-assness flickers in his eyes. "Let's just say that on rare occasions, the answer is yes, I love to play. But mostly, especially lately, the answer is no."

"Then why do you play?"

"Why do any of us do what we don't want to do?"

I don't respond, unsure what answer he's looking for.

He smiles, but it's sad. "Because we're afraid of what will happen if we don't."

I always considered fear to be a motivator or a reason not to do something, but I never considered it a reason to continue an ongoing behavior. This opens a vault full of questions about my own life. I've always assumed I'm afraid to engage in activities because I'm afraid of what might happen. But maybe I'm looking at it all wrong. Maybe I should be asking myself if I'm really afraid of leaving what makes me comfortable.

Tucker watches me with careful, perceptive eyes. He knows he's stirred something in my head, and he patiently waits for me to respond.

If Caroline saw this Tucker, would she believe he's the same guy that showed up at the party Friday night? I've experienced this doppelganger Tucker multiple times now, and I still struggle to believe it.

A question bubbles in my chest, begging for release. "Why are you so different with me than what I see in class or with your friends?"

He looks surprised, but I'm more surprised than he is. I'm usually a steel trap with my thoughts and emotions. Tucker seems to draw them out against my will.

He hesitates, but his blue eyes hold mine. "Because I trust you."

I want to ask why, but he looks down at his paper. "So you're telling me that I can't multiply x by twenty-three?"

He's changing the subject, and I let him, uncomfortable that I've shared so much. "No." I point to the problem. "See? You need to perform this function first."

We pass the next hour in silence except for Tucker's few questions. It takes him a little longer to understand the concepts, but once he has them, he knows them well. At four, we get up to leave, and Tucker walks me to my car. His mouth twists to one side, showing his dimple, and I realize how much I love when he smiles and lets me see it. How odd that Tucker spends most of his time grinning and cavorting his way through life, but with me, his dimple-producing smiles are rare.

Suddenly, he looks shy. "I've been thinking I might know of another way for you to de-stress, doing something besides math."

My face burns. Is it that obvious that I'm a mess?

"Scarlett, don't." He leans down to look into my eyes and his voice softens. "Don't be embarrassed. I was thinking about it because I'm freaking out over my algebra test on Thursday. I thought how ironic it was that the thing that calms you down stresses me out."

I take a deep breath, but my skin feels like it's crawling with ants. "I can see the irony."

"Anyway, I was thinking maybe I could teach you a different way to relieve your stress. A physical way."

My face is on fire now. I'm sure I know the physical way Tucker relieves his stress.

He smirks. "I'm pretty sure we're thinking of two different things right now."

Mortified, I spin around to open my car door.

"Scarlett, wait." His left hand presses the door, and his right hand rests on my shoulder. "I'm sorry. I forget how sensitive you are. It's just that I think that deep down inside you want to learn how to relax."

If he's trying to make me feel better, it's not working. My hand jerks on the door handle.

His body tenses behind me. "*Damnit*. That didn't come out right."

I don't say anything, frustrated with myself for reacting this way. He's making an effort to try to help me, *Tucker Price*, and I'm acting like a nun in a convent. I take a deep breath. "It's okay. I tend to overreact."

"Look." His mouth is next to my ear. "You've helped me so much, I just thought maybe I could teach you something I know and maybe help you."

I turn around to face him.

He smiles, and it's lopsided. His excitement makes him look like a teenager instead of a jaded college junior. "When you play soccer, your run your ass off on the field, so it's important to keep in shape all year long, even when you're not playing. Most guys hate it, but I like it. I like pushing myself. I like the rush I get during a hard run and meeting my goal. Anyway." He takes a deep breath. "For some reason, I think you'd like it too. It's about control and testing your limits."

"You think I should start running?"

"Yeah, and I want you to work out with me."

My lips part. "You want me to run with *you*?"

"Yeah." He grins, but it's hesitant, like he's worried I'll say no. Which is crazy. Why would he care?

I shake my head. "I haven't run since high school gym class. I'll hold you back."

"It's my offseason and training is boring. You'll help liven it up a bit. Make it more interesting."

"Me?"

"Yeah, I'll get to tutor you for a change."

I laugh, but it's a nervous laugh. Even though I'm not that physical, exercise is supposed to be good for my anxiety. But I'm worried working out with Tucker will make me more anxious. Nevertheless, I'm intrigued by this side of Tucker and the idea of finding something to help my nerves. "What would I have to do?"

"Just show up in workout clothes and running shoes, and I'll take care of the rest."

"And when did you want to start this?"

His grin spreads across his face. "I have to work out tonight. You usually work in the math lab on Tuesdays, and it closes at seven. Right?"

I nod, momentarily caught off guard that he knows this, until I remember we've shared schedules to set up his tutoring sessions.

"What if you come to the fitness center around eight?" He studies my face with a hopeful look. "So you'll do it?"

Say no. Say no. Hanging out with Tucker Price is a terrible idea and will come to no good. But he's giving me a cheesy smile and looks genuinely excited about this venture. I can't help myself. "Yes."

"Okay. Tonight at eight. At the fitness center." He takes off to his car, and I wonder why I can't go to a movie with a nice guy like Daniel, but I'll agree to work out with Tucker.

Chapter Nine

I text Caroline while I'm walking across campus to the tutoring center, asking if I can borrow her running shoes. We wear the same size, and she bought a brand new pair after Justin broke up with her last fall. Her plan was to run away from her problems by taking up jogging. It lasted two sessions.

She quickly responds: *Yes, why?*

I thought I might try running.

No response. She's probably trying to figure out why I've suddenly decided to do something physical. She knows about Daniel and our coffee dates. Maybe she thinks I want to get in shape for him.

The next few hours fly by, but my stomach has begun to tighten like a noose. Why did I agree to this? Sure, I've hung out with Tucker at Panera, but that was for studying.

If the Tucker I knew before our tutoring sessions had suggested we run together, I would have been sure it was a practical joke. But oddly enough, I know this Tucker. We've only been together a handful of times, yet I know he wouldn't hurt me. He said he shows a different side of himself to me because he trusts me. I guess I trust him, too. The revelation is shocking. Other than Caroline, I can't remember the last time I've trusted anyone.

When my session is over, I hurry home. Caroline has left a note that her shoes are in my room. I make a peanut butter sandwich and eat it while I search my dresser drawers for workout clothes. I tried yoga a year ago as a form of relaxation and while it worked, I had trouble finding time when I was alone in the apartment to do it. I was too self-conscious to do it around Caroline.

So what makes me think I can run with Tucker? In front of people? My hands are shaking as I tie Caroline's shoes, and I sit on the side of the bed, sucking in air.

I can't do this, which is stupid and makes me more upset, which increases my anxiety. I consider canceling, but I realize I don't have Tucker's phone number, and the responsible part of me would never leave him there wondering where I am. I lie down on the bed and try to relax, using guided imagery to settle down. When I try to envision running on the track with Tucker, my mind can't go there. For one thing, I'm too anal to imagine a place I've never been. And for another, I simply can't picture Tucker working out with me.

I finally get myself under control and drive to campus. The grounds are dark when I pull into the parking lot, but I've never felt unsafe here, one of several reasons I picked Southern. Still, I'm careful as I walk toward the brightly lit fitness center. I've been in college for two and a half years and never entered that building, but I know it's divided into two sections. One for the student athletes, and the other for the general student population. It never occurred to me to ask Tucker which side. One more thing to worry about.

It's a needless concern. Tucker is standing in the lobby, waiting, with a duffel bag over his shoulder. He smiles when he sees me. "I was worried you'd chicken out."

"I almost did." Why am I always compelled to tell him the truth?

"I'm glad you didn't." The weird thing is he really looks happy.

He opens the door to the general student body side and waits for me to enter. I'm relieved. I'll make enough of a fool of myself without doing it in front of trained athletes.

Tucker sets his bag down on the side of the indoor running track.

Leaning over, he pulls out two water bottles and hands me one. "It's important to stay hydrated."

I nod and take a drink.

"I'm not sure how much physical exercise you've gotten lately, so I decided to start as though you're a beginner."

My eyebrows lift. "Is it that obvious?"

He cocks his head to the side with an ornery look. "Is that a trick question where there is no right answer?"

I laugh. "Probably."

"Then I plead the fifth."

"Smart man."

"Interesting choice of words." He teases. "You may be smarter with algebraic equations, but I know about running. You're in my territory now."

Something about his wording sets off a buzz in my stomach, but it quickly ebbs away. This is a totally friendly venture. I'm amazed how relaxed I am. I expected to be a nervous wreck, and while my nerves are on edge, it's only a twinge. Why? I'm in an unfamiliar situation that sets off all my trigger points, but I'm comfortable. Is it because of the activity or who I'm with? Before I can puzzle it out, Tucker takes the bottle from my hand and sets both on the ground.

"Let's get started."

"Do we need to stretch?"

"You don't want to stretch cold muscles. We'll stretch when we're done."

"Oh." This is no big deal, but I hate not knowing things. My stomach tightens.

"Scarlett." Tucker's voice is soothing, and I look up into his face. "Breathe. For once, you don't have to know everything. Let me be in charge, and you just do what I say."

Does he know what he's asking from me? I inhale a gulp of air and stare into his eyes. Strangely enough, I think he does.

"The goal here is for you use your body to relax you, not just your mind. Okay?"

I nod.

"Good. Now I know how driven you are, but it's important to not push yourself. Not your first time or two. Otherwise you'll overdo it, and this will be counterproductive."

I take another breath and nod.

"I'm going to be watching you closely, but I know you hate people to watch you, so I wanted to warn you."

How much of me does he actually see?

He senses my unease and looks into my eyes. "You have to trust me. Okay?"

Trust. There's that word again. I do trust him, but this is still hard. I nod. "But won't other people watch me?"

"Everyone else is busy with their own workout. They're not going to pay attention to you." He grins. "Not unless you start running like Forrest Gump."

His answer makes me laugh, and I find myself relaxing a bit.

"We're going to start out walking first, then work our way up to a run. The walk will warm up your muscles." He starts walking, and I stay beside him, trying to match my strides to his. Someone approaches from behind us, jogging at a brisk pace, and we move to the side, walking a quarter of the track in silence. I'm concentrating on my breathing and my strides, trying to find equilibrium for the two.

He turns toward me. "Do you have any brothers or sisters?"

My stomach clenches. "A younger sister."

"Why are you tensing up?"

"What?" My head jerks toward him.

"Was it the question or what you're doing?"

I look away. "The question."

"You don't like to talk about your family in general or just your sister?"

He's much too perceptive. "My family."

"Okay, No talking about family. I get that. I'm not a fan of talking about my family, either."

Now I wonder even more about his brother Marcel. "That's okay. We don't have to talk."

"Actually, we do. Your being able to carry a conversation is a good indicator of how much you're pushing yourself."

"Oh."

He winks. "The challenge is to find a safe topic that doesn't make you anxious. Any hints?"

That's a good question. My life is math, school, tutoring, and hanging out with Caroline. "I'm pretty boring, Tucker."

"I highly doubt that." There's a strange tone in his voice that sets off a flutter in my stomach. "Let's start with the basics. I'd ask you where you're from, but I suspect it falls under the *not comfortable topics.*"

I nod.

He smiles. "The past sucks. The future is what's important."

I laugh. "Says the history major."

"Well..." A sheepish grin spreads across his face, and he rubs his hand through his hair. "What do you plan to do with your math major?"

"You really want to know?"

His voice turns serious. "Yes, Scarlett. I only want the truth from you."

I turn to look at him.

"That's what I love about you. You speak the truth, as painful or as uncomfortable it is for you to say and me to hear. People bullshit me all the time. I need the truth."

I always worry people think I'm weird or will make fun of my career plans, but looking into Tucker's face, I know he won't think it's odd. "I want to be an analyst for the CIA."

He pauses. "That's not something you just come up with. How did you find out about that kind of thing?"

"It was in math club in high school. One of our meetings was about careers with math."

"Why did it excite you?"

My head swings to face him. "Why do you think it excites me?"

"Your eyes widened just a bit and got a sparkle that wasn't there before."

"That's kind of scary, Tucker." But I'm not frightened for my physical safety, more for my emotional. I wonder what else he sees in me that no one else does.

He shakes his head then shrugs. "I just pay attention. I read people."

I do this in my own way, study people so I know where I stand and how to react. Tucker and I are more alike than I realize.

"You didn't answer my question," he says. "Why does it excite you?"

"I don't know." It's my turn to shrug. "I guess because I can use something I love to help people and it seems like a challenge. Maybe because it seems so unlike me."

He gives me a soft smile. "I happen to like you the way you are."

"You don't even know me."

Seriousness creeps into his eyes. "I think I know you better than you think."

We walk in silence for several steps, and I know that Tucker's confession should scare me and on some level it does, but mostly it fills me with wonder. For twenty years, I've kept myself, the real me, hidden from everyone. Even Caroline who knows me better than anyone doesn't see it all. Could someone really see past the walls I put up and see *me*?

"And how does someone become an analyst for the CIA?"

"A minimum of a bachelor's degree, although a master's degree would help. I'm going to apply my senior year and see if they accept me without one. I'm not sure I can afford the tuition for a master's. I've got a 4.0. I'm preparing for the GRE. My English and writing skills are strong, and I'm semi-fluent in Arabic. I'm a strong candidate on paper."

"Why do I sense a but in there?"

I take a deep breath. "Oral communication is important."

"Oh." He pauses. "You can do it, Scarlett. You'll be fine."

I wish I were so sure.

We've already circled the track once, and Tucker is still walking at a brisk pace. "One more time around," he says.

"And what about you? What do you plan to do with a history major?"

His mouth twists to the side. "Honestly? I have no idea."

"Then why major in it?"

He laughs. "First of all, unlike you, not everyone in college is hyper-focused on their career plans. But you might find it hard to believe I'm not one of those students." He winks. "I'm majoring in history because the major I want wasn't an option."

"And what do you want to major in?"

His face is devoid of emotion as he studies me. I can see he's trying to decide whether he can trust me. "Physical education."

I shake my head. "I don't understand. It seems like the perfect fit."

"My parents have very definite ideas about my career path, and my major has nothing to do with that."

"You mean soccer?"

He takes a deep breath and nods. "I'm good, and I have a shot at the pros."

"But you don't want that?"

"I don't know what I want."

"I don't believe that."

He shoots me an odd look but doesn't answer.

"Why can't you major in physical education?"

"If I go pro, and I'm successful, I can't go back and teach kids P.E."

"Why not?"

"Can you imagine David Beckham teaching high school students?"

"Did you seriously just equate yourself to David Beckham?"

Tucker bursts out laughing. "Where the hell have you been hiding?"

"Living in Shelbyville, Tennessee."

His eyes widen in surprise at my revelation. I figure if I insulted him, the least I can do is give him something from my past.

"It seems to me that you're pinning a lot on a dream that isn't even yours."

He shrugs.

We walk in silence, but it's not uncomfortable, despite how our conversation ended. When we're about to reach our starting point, Tucker points to it. "We're about to start jogging. We'll go halfway around, then walk, then jog halfway, then walk. Then we'll see how you're doing."

"Okay."

"I'm going to be watching you and checking your form so you can correct any bad habits before they start."

We start to jog and Tucker keeps his attention on me. "Eyes ahead, Scarlett. Don't look down. Your shoulders are too tense. Let them relax."

"That's a lot to think about while I'm running."

"I thought you like to think."

"Not while I'm running." I puff out.

He laughs. "We're just getting warmed up."

We run several strides.

"Your arms are good, but don't clench your fists."

We reach the halfway mark, and Tucker slows to a fast walk.

"Am I this bossy when I tutor you?" I wheeze.

"No. I'm just naturally bossy, and you're naturally nice. We're a good balance."

"Lucky for you," I grumble.

He laughs. "I totally got the better end of the deal."

We go around the track three more times, the last round, he has me run at quarter lengths. Tucker has watched my pace, slowing down to make sure I'm not too winded, then picking it up when I caught my breath. I'm tired, but I don't feel like I'm about to pass out on the side of the track. We slow to a walk that's not as brisk.

"This is your cool down. Some people skip it, but it's important to let your body slow down."

I nod, catching my breath.

We walk around once, then Tucker picks up our water bottles and hands me one. "Now we need to stretch."

We move to the side of the track and Tucker takes me through a series of leg stretches. I'm surprised how good they feel. We sit on the floor, just finishing butterfly stretches. Tucker grins at me. "Well?"

"Well what?" I tease.

"What did you think?"

"While I'm not a huge diehard fan of running at the moment, I can see the benefits. I feel more relaxed." Although if I'm truthful, I'm not sure if the run has relaxed me or if it's Tucker. "But I *do* know that you are an excellent tutor. Thank you."

"Do you want to do this again? I have to work out four or five days a week. It gets pretty boring, and I've been anything but bored tonight."

"I don't see how you got a workout if you're slowing down to my level."

He shakes his head. "It's the offseason, Scarlett. As long as I'm working out somehow, I'm good." Tucker gets to his feet then reaches down to help me up. His hand feels right in mine, which catches me by surprise. But he lets go and picks up his bag, and we head to the exit.

Tucker went out of his way to do something nice for me. The least I can do is help him. "You said you were nervous about your test on Thursday. If it makes you more comfortable, we can get together tomorrow or Thursday before your algebra class."

He opens the door to the lobby and looks down at me. "I don't want to inconvenience you, Scarlett."

"Tucker, if you need more tutoring sessions, we can set something up. I want you to feel comfortable when you go in to take your test."

We go over our schedules and determine that we're both free tomorrow from eleven until our noon classes.

"We'll need to meet on campus." He sounds anxious, which catches me by surprise. "But we can't meet in the library."

"Why not?"

He shakes his head. "I just can't."

I'd suspect he'd goofed around in the library and gotten banned, but he seems genuinely anxious. "Okay. No library. Where?"

"We could meet at the coffee shop."

I hesitate. Our first meeting was there, and that was disastrous. And I'm getting coffee with Daniel at the same place tomorrow. But why should that matter? It just means I'll already be there. "How about I meet you at the coffee shop, and if it's too noisy, we can go somewhere else."

"Thanks." He releases a heavy breath of relief.

"No, thank you. There might be something to this exercise thing."

He opens the outer doors, following me outside. "Where are you parked?"

I tell him, and we walk in silence, but it's not awkward. I'm amazed how comfortable I am with him.

We stop next to my car, and Tucker smiles. "Thanks for tonight."

I laugh. "You're the one who helped me. Why are you thanking me?"

"Because for the first time in a long time, I had fun working out." He hesitates, then opens my car door. "I'll see you tomorrow."

As I drive away, I shake my head in confusion. Just when I think I've figured Tucker out, he shows me another side, confusing me even more.

Chapter Ten

When I get home, Caroline wants to know where I've been, but I give her a vague answer. I know she won't understand why I met Tucker, especially after last Friday, and I can't say I blame her. If I were her, I wouldn't trust Tucker either. I can't explain what's going on with Tucker to myself, let alone Caroline.

But Caroline isn't easily fooled. She's sitting on the sofa with her laptop and she sets it to the side, narrowing her eyes. "Let me get this straight. You just decided—out of the blue—to start exercising. At eight o'clock at night?"

I shrug.

"Where were you? Really."

I hang my coat in the closet and wave to my clothes. "See? Workout clothes. I ran at the fitness center."

"And when, pray tell, was the last time you ever ran in your life? And running to class because you're late doesn't count."

I hate lying to her, and I suppose I'm not. Unless you call this a lie of omission. I sit on the arm of the sofa and gnaw on my bottom lip.

"You suck at secrets. Spill."

I take a deep breath. "I was running at the fitness center. I was with someone, but you have to promise not to freak out."

"Oh, God. You're freaking me out."

"I told you not to freak out, and I haven't even told you who it is yet."

"It was Tucker, wasn't it?"

"It's not what you think, Caroline."

She crosses her arms. "Fine, then tell me what it is."

I sigh and flop into the seat next to her. "He's not interested in me that way, if that's what you're worried about. He's been a *perfect gentleman*." I pat her leg.

"You and I both know that Tucker Price isn't a perfect gentleman. His reputation precedes him. He's up to something."

I turn to my side. "Why do you assume the worst in him?"

"It's totally unlike you to assume the best. Where's the girl who practically wears a chastity belt?"

Grunting, I smack her with a throw pillow. "I did assume the worst of him. And then I spent time with him. It's weird, Caroline. He's not like the person he is on campus or what we hear. He's nice. He's polite. He listens. He's thoughtful."

"What about the first time you were supposed to meet him at the coffee shop? He was none of those things then."

I sit back and bury myself in the pillow. "I know. But then he came to me and begged me to give him a second chance, and he was different."

"So what was tonight about?"

"He knows about my anxiety."

"You told him?"

"No, that's just it. I didn't. But he knows things about me."

"You mean he's spied on you?"

"No, I mean he's observant. He sees things about me that no one else does. He's been doing really well studying, and he said he wanted to teach me a way to de-stress."

She snorts. "I bet he did."

"He meant running, Caroline. He met me at the track, and he taught me proper form and how to warm up and stretch afterward."

Cocking her head, Caroline scrunches her nose in disbelief. "You're telling me he hasn't made any moves on you. At all?"

"No, I told you that it's not like that. We're just friends." And as I say the last sentence, I know it's true. I'm friends with Tucker Price. Why does that surprise me after the last couple of times we've been together?

"That's weird. It's like you're in one of those old *Twilight Zone* episodes."

"Tell me about it."

We sit in silence for several seconds before she says, "You're positive that he hasn't made a move. Maybe you're too naïve to pick up on it."

"*Caroline.*"

She shudders and picks up her laptop. "You can't blame me for asking. You haven't been on a date in a year." She turns to me again. "What's going on with you and that guy from the party?"

"Daniel and I are meeting tomorrow morning after my class."

"Why hasn't he asked you out yet?"

I make a face.

"Wait. What does"—she tries to duplicate my face—"that mean?"

"It means that he did ask me out, and I told him I wanted to take it slow."

"*Why*? I thought you liked him."

"I don't know, Caroline. I do but something doesn't feel right." I want to tell her about kissing him and feeling nothing but a slightly pleasant feeling, but I can't bring myself to do it.

"But you went out with Tucker?"

"I didn't go *out* with him. We went as friends. No pressure. I don't have to worry about what I say around Tucker because he likes that I tell him the truth. Daniel's a nice guy, but I'm still self-conscious around him."

"Just be careful, Scarlett. He's going to break your heart."

"Why do you think I'm going slow?"

"I'm not talking about Daniel."

I push myself up off the sofa, suddenly exhausted. "I'm going to take a shower and go to bed."

"I mean it, Scarlett. Be careful." I'm not sure I've ever heard Caroline sound so nervous and worried.

"I think you know me better than that. I'm not stupid."

"I'm sure many a smart girl has gotten her heart broken by Tucker Price."

"Maybe so, but I won't be one of them."

My legs have stiffened in the short time I've been on the sofa. I hobble to the bathroom, eager for the warm water to loosen my muscles.

When I go to bed, I sleep better than I can ever remember sleeping. Maybe there's something to this running thing after all.

~

The next morning, Daniel is waiting for me after my set and logic class. He's wearing a cheesy smile, and he looks cute, but my heart doesn't flutter and my stomach doesn't flip-flop. Isn't it supposed to? Aren't I supposed to get all atwitter when I see him? My stomach's a mess, but not in the right way. I feel slightly nauseated with nerves.

What if we run out of things to talk about?

My worry is needless. After Daniel asks a few questions and I give short, concise answers, he fills the silence by talking about himself. I easily glide through the conversation without having to add much to it. We walk to the coffee shop, and he opens the door like a perfect gentleman, but it feels automatic and not thoughtful.

Now I'm just looking for faults.

I nearly gasp as the truth hits me straight in the forehead. Is that what I'm doing? Looking for faults so I don't have to go out with him?

Before I have time to figure out why, I realize Daniel has asked me a question. I blink. "What?" We're standing in front of the pastry case.

"I asked you if you want something to eat."

"Oh." Since I'm meeting Tucker instead of eating lunch, I decide to get something. I pick a scone and order my coffee. The cashier tells me my total, and I realize Daniel has already paid for his drink.

He expects me to pay for my own.

I shouldn't be irritated. It's not like he's obligated, but he did invite me. Will our date be the same way? Or does he consider this pre-dating so he doesn't have to pay? I realize that a guy paying for the girl is outdated, but I'm kind of old-fashioned. Or maybe I'm looking for more excuses not to go out with him.

We sit by the window, and Daniel tells me about living in a frat house. He's not much of a partier, which I can totally relate to, but he says being in a fraternity will come in handy when he's in the business world.

Twenty minutes go by before he smiles and looks nervous. "I'd love to take you out on Friday night. Maybe we could catch a movie."

Panic brews inside my head. I don't want go out with him. Why? He's a really nice guy who has a life goal. Logically, he's perfect for me. So why do I want to turn him down "Uh..."

"Hey, Scarlett." Tucker walks up to me, then looks down at Daniel. The smile falls off Tucker's face. "Bailey."

Daniel stands. "Are you still stuck tutoring him?" The question is for me, but he glares at Tucker.

"I'm not *stuck* tutoring him. It's my job." I want to defend Tucker and add that he isn't a screw-up when I tutor him. That he pays attention and is learning and progressing, but I keep these things to myself. It's none of Daniel's business.

"Can't you get out of it?" Daniel asks dryly.

My mouth drops, but Daniel turns and leaves before I can respond.

"I'll see you Friday," he says without looking back.

I watch him go out the door and wonder if he means for coffee or for a date, because I most definitely didn't agree to a date.

Tucker drops into his vacant seat. "Did I interrupt something?" He tries to look apologetic but fails.

I grin and slightly shake my head. "You had perfect timing."

Tucker looks over his shoulder, out the window and watches Daniel walk to the business building. "Are you two dating?" He sounds strained.

Why does his question make me uneasy? "No, but we would be if Daniel had his way."

His eyes find mine. "You don't want to go out with him." It's a statement, not a question.

I shrug, and my back begins to prickle.

His face softens. "Scarlett, it's none of my business. Forget I asked."

But I can't forget. Why? Tucker's asking a harmless question, but it sets me on edge. I can't really come up with a good explanation why I don't want to go out with Daniel. It just doesn't feel right. Maybe this is the chemistry everyone's always talking about. But what if I'm broken, and I don't ever feel chemistry with someone? Or maybe I need to go out with him and give chemistry a chance to show up.

I decide it might be a good idea to get a guy's perspective. Tucker and I are supposed to be friends, right? "Caroline wants me to go. But something is holding me back."

His eyes darken. "What's holding you back?"

I purse my lips and look out the window with a sigh. "I wish I knew. There's little things that bug me"—I shoot him a glare and point my finger at him—"and if you tell him I said so, I'll kill you."

He laughs. "Don't worry. You won't catch me talking to Daniel Bailey."

I recognize the animosity between them, but I realize Tucker might have some information on Daniel that can help me sway my decision. "Why not?"

His eyebrows lift. "Let's just say we agree to disagree."

"Over a girl."

He smirks and leans back in his chair. "How'd you know?"

"When guys fight, isn't it usually over a girl?"

Shaking his head, he laughs and crosses his arms over his chest. "True enough."

"So you know him?"

He lifts one shoulder into a half-shrug and picks up his coffee. "Not that well."

"But you know him well enough to tell me whether I should go out with him or not."

Tucker is mid-sip. He chokes and begins to cough.

"Are you all right?"

When he catches his breath, he looks at me in disbelief. "Did you seriously just ask me to tell you whether you should go out with Daniel Bailey?"

"You said you know him. Maybe you know him better than I do."

When he stops coughing, his eyes find mine and lock for several seconds. "Scarlett, if you're asking a guy that you know doesn't play well with Daniel Bailey if you should go out with him, then you already know the answer to your question."

Maybe. Maybe not. I really need to get to the root of what's holding me back. Making me buy my own coffee and monopolizing the conversation can't be it.

"How are you feeling today?" he asks.

"Huh?" My mind is still stuck on trying to figure out why I don't want to go out with Daniel. "I'm good. Fine."

"No muscle cramps or aches?" His gaze is on my face, evaluating my response. He watches me more than anyone I've ever known, and I'm surprised it doesn't bother me more.

"Not too bad."

"Do you want to work out tomorrow night?"

"Not tonight?"

He chuckles. "You liked it that much?"

I shake my head. "No. That's not it. It's just that it takes twenty-one days to form a habit, which means it takes twenty-one days of consistency. I figured that I need consistency."

He leans his elbow on the table while a grin lights up his face. "While I appreciate your dedication, no. Give yourself a day off, let your muscles repair, and pick it up tomorrow. You need to ease into this, not rush it. So do you want to meet me tomorrow night?"

I nod. For some weird reason I do. I like hanging out with Tucker. But that's not why we're here, and we're wasting valuable time I could spend making sure Tucker is ready for his test. "Get your textbook out, and we'll go over a few things I know you struggled with."

His eyes stay on me for several more seconds before he pulls his books out and spreads them out on the table. We spend the next half hour going over problems. I have Tucker tell me why he performed the steps he chose. At eleven-forty, Tucker shuts his textbook. "I'm ready."

I smile. "I think you are."

"Thanks." His mouth tips up into the barest hint of a smile and his eyes are soft and warm.

There's a flutter in my chest that catches my breath.

"What class do you have after this?"

What was that feeling about? "Uh, ...Arabic."

"You really speak Arabic?"

"*Na'am. Lā atakallam 'arabi.*"

"And what did you say?"

"I don't speak Arabic very well."

He grins.

"Reading it is harder. Arabic doesn't have the phonetic alphabet the romance languages have. I'm an auditory learner so the visual is hard, and I can't connect the sounds to recognizable letters."

"But I'm sure you are good at it. I suspect there's not much you're not good at when you set out to do something."

I sink back in my chair, trying to figure Tucker out. Why does he pay so much attention to me? How is it he sees things no one else does?

Tucker packs his book in his bag. "I'll see you at Panera tomorrow."

"Good luck with your test."

But he stays in his seat, watching me.

A blush creeps to my cheeks, although I'm not sure why. I'm used to Tucker looking at me by now. But this seems different.

He shakes his head and stands. "I'll see you tomorrow."

I watch him go and wonder what just happened.

Chapter Eleven

On Thursday, Tucker is late to our Western civ class. This is a common occurrence, and the professor barely notices. As Tucker takes his seat, he looks back at me and gives me a half wave and a smile. Several of the girls in the class, who spend more time paying attention to Southern's star player instead of the lecture, turn to me with withering glares.

My face burns, and I ask myself why. Tucker and I are friends. There's nothing to be embarrassed about. It doesn't stop my blush, but my confidence builds a bit.

After class, I'm gathering my things when Tucker makes his way back to me, grinning.

Three girls have congregated at the door of the classroom, blatantly staring. I understand their curiosity and even their animosity. They are all much prettier and flashier than I am. They are obviously reading something into this that isn't here.

"Good luck on your test this afternoon. Oh, wait." I close my eyes, surprised I didn't think of this sooner. "You probably won't have a lesson today."

The corners of his lips fall a bit. "Yeah."

"Then there's nothing to go over." I'm surprised to feel disappointment washing over me in thick waves.

He watches me in silence. I can see he wants to say something, but he can't make himself say what he's thinking.

Why does it bother me so much that I won't tutor him today? "So I guess we'll get together after your class next Tuesday."

"But we're still on for tonight, right? At the fitness center?"

I smile. "Yeah, tonight. But if it takes twenty-one days to build a habit, will this be day two or day three?"

"Day two. Definitely day two." Relief fills his eyes, adding to my confusion. Last week he said he didn't have friends, which I considered a drunkard exaggeration at the time. But with someone like Tucker, maybe it's hard to have real friends. The gawking girls make me believe that even more.

"Do you still want to meet at eight?"

"I'll be there." He walks with me out of class and pauses in the hall, oblivious to the girls who openly stare at us. "Where are you headed to now?"

"The math lab, but I hope to study for linear algebra class first."

"There's more than one algebra?" he asks in horror.

I laugh. "Fortunately for me there is."

He shakes his head. We walk down the stairs to the exit and Tucker hesitates outside. "I'll see you tonight."

I grin. "See you tonight."

He heads the opposite way as I start toward the math building. I've packed my lunch so I can study during my break before tutoring.

"He'll just use you, too."

My head jerks to the side. A girl is walking next to me, a sneer on her face, but pain fills her eyes. Against my better judgment, I stop. "Excuse me?"

"He'll just fuck you and leave you. That's what Tucker Price does."

My chest squeezes, and I force out my response. "I'm not sure what you think—"

"It doesn't matter what I think. Just trust me. I know from personal experience that Tucker Price doesn't do relationships. He doesn't stick around to snuggle the next morning."

My pulse pounds in my head. "Why are you telling me this?"

She sighs and turns to watch Tucker walking away, then sweeps her long blonde hair over her shoulder. She's pretty, much prettier than I am. "You look like a nice girl, not his usual type. Trust me when I say he's way out of your league, sweetie. If you're smart, and you seem smart, you'll stay away from him."

She turns and walks away, but my feet are still rooted to the sidewalk.

Everyone keeps telling me the same thing. But I'm not looking for a relationship with Tucker. We're just friends, and I like it that way. I can be me around him and say what I want without blushing and feeling self-conscious. But I wonder if I'm deluding myself. Can there really be two sides to him?

I go to an empty classroom and can only partially concentrate on my work. I keep thinking about the girl and her warning. I feel nauseated and suddenly unsure if I want to meet Tucker tonight. It's one thing to hear about all his exploits from Caroline and Tina secondhand, and another to come face to face with one. The despair in her eyes haunts me.

The afternoon in math lab drags by, and Caroline is studying when I get home. She sees my face, and her eyes widen.

"What happened?"

I want to tell her about the girl, but the first thing she'll say is *I told you so*. I can't deal with that right now. "Tutoring was awful, and I've got a headache."

"So does that mean you're not going to meet Tucker?"

For the first time, I understand Caroline's fear and apprehension. I understand her worry for me. I could never be used like all those other girls and survive it. Caroline knows this.

"I don't know yet." I go to my room and shut the door, sitting on the bed. I need to put this in perspective. I'm not like those other girls.

I'm not Tucker's latest conquest. We're friends. Nothing more. Nothing less.

I change into my workout clothes and slip on Caroline's running shoes, which are tucked in my closet.

Caroline's face puckers with disapproval as I go into the kitchen and heat up some leftover pasta.

"So you're going?"

I nod and turn my back to her. I wish I could seek her advice, but I know what it will be. Shouldn't that set alarm bells off in my head? That should be my indication that I shouldn't do this.

Instead, I pick at my pasta and lift a forkful to my lips. "I like working out, Caroline. He's going to work with me a couple of more times, and then I'm on my own. Maybe you can run with me then."

She turns up her nose with disgust, at which suggestion I'm not sure. Probably both.

I leave the house even earlier than usual, needing time to prepare myself to meet him. But he's early too, even though I'm here at seven forty-five. He's looking the opposite direction when I enter the lobby of the fitness center. When he hears the door open, he turns to me and a smile lights up his face. I can't correlate this Tucker to the one everyone tells me about. I know they are the same. I just can't piece them together.

I know I should be leery. Tucker Price has broken many hearts, and not just here on Southern University's campus. I can't imagine how many he destroyed back in high school. But I think about all the things people said and believed about me back in Shelbyville. I wished someone had given me the benefit of the doubt. Stupid or not, I choose to have faith in the Tucker I see before me now until he gives me proof that I shouldn't.

"You're early," he says, then laughs. "Well, earlier than usual."

I shrug. "A nasty habit I can't seem to break. What's your excuse? I don't think you've *ever* been on time to Western civ."

"Maybe I just need a good excuse to be early."

A shy smile creeps onto my face.

"Are you ready?"

I nod and we go into the gym. Tucker has brought water again and hands me one after I take off my coat and toss it next to his bag. I take a drink and put down the bottle. "Okay. Let's do this."

We begin walking in silence, but it's a comfortable stillness. We make one full loop before he speaks. "One more lap and then we'll start to run again. I'm going to push you harder tonight."

I smile. "Okay."

"I was right, wasn't I?"

"Right about what?"

"That you like the challenge of controlling yourself and your body."

I snort. "You make me sound like a control freak."

He shakes his head. "I didn't mean it that way. Trust me. I understand the need to control a situation."

I turn to look at him. "Is that what you do with your out-of-control behavior? That seems the opposite."

His jaw drops.

I hold up my hands. "I'm sorry. I have no idea where that came from." I do, but I can't believe I actually verbalized it.

"No. You're right. What I do seems to be the opposite."

"Seems to be?"

He doesn't say anything for several seconds.

I grimace. "Tucker, I'm sorry. It's none of my business." What happened to giving him the benefit of the doubt? I think I still do, but there's no denying that he leads a wild life. I've seen proof of it myself.

"There's more than one way to control things, Scarlett."

I nod, sucking in my top lip.

"There's a lot most people don't know about me."

"Me, too." No one here knows about my past except for Caroline. Any of it. It's like I dropped out of the sky onto the Southern campus with no prior life whatsoever. But I don't have people watching me all the time either. "I'm sorry."

"No. Don't be sorry. Just be my friend." There's a sadness in his voice that breaks something inside me.

I reach for his hand and squeeze. "You already know I am."

His smile is tight and he squeezes back then drops it. "You ready to run?"

My answer is to break into a jog.

He laughs and moves in front of me, running backward and wearing a giant grin.

"Now you're just showing off."

Smirking, he holds his hands out to his sides. "It's what I do best."

I shake my head.

He corrects my posture, then turns around and runs beside me. "We'll do a couple of quarter-track stints, then pick it up to more half loops."

I nod, already feeling a burn in my legs.

Tucker is remarkably lighthearted after our brief delve into a serious conversation. Maybe he's relieved I'm still here. I know I like knowing he wants to be my friend.

On our second turn around the track, Tucker says, "Talk to me, Scarlett."

I shake my head and shoot him a *you've got to be kidding me* look. He was right about pushing me harder. Not only are we running longer stretches, but he's picked up the pace. He, on the other hand, is barely out of breath.

"How about we play a game?"

"You're kidding."

"Nope. You make it all the way around the track running, and I'll tell you anything you want to know."

His offer is tempting, but I'm not sure I really want the answers to some of my questions. I'm worried I won't like the answers.

"And if I don't?"

"I get to ask you anything I want, and you have to answer." His grin is mischievous. He knows what he's doing. He knows I like a challenge.

I'm out of breath and my calves are more sore than they were two nights ago, but I think I can do this. "Deal."

"But you still have to talk to me now."

"Screw you."

He laughs. "Why, Scarlett Goodwin. That was very unladylike of you."

"Who says I'm ladylike?"

"You, my darlin', are the epitome of ladylike behavior."

"Maybe you don't know me as well as you think."

"Maybe I'd like to change that."

He confuses me. One minute we're bantering with friendly chatter and the next he's flirting. Maybe he doesn't mean to do it. It could be as automatic as breathing for him. I know that Tina is a shameless flirt, and I don't think she realizes that she does it half the time. It's probably like that for Tucker, too.

I shoot him a teasing glare. "Too bad I'll win."

He winks. "Maybe we should pick up the pace."

"That's cheating!"

"Nope. I don't think so."

I'm struggling to talk, let alone sprint. "You go ahead and run faster if you like. I'm running at a good pace—a brisk jog, I might add —and I'll meet you at the finish line."

"I'm not going anywhere without you." He nudges his arm into mine.

We're halfway around the track, and I'm not sure I can maintain this pace and finish.

"Pick a spot just a short distance ahead." Tucker's voice lowers into a serious tone. "See that bench twenty feet ahead? Tell yourself you can make it to there. Count the steps if you have to."

I count my exhales as they leave my body. Inhale deep, exhale. *One.* Inhale, exhale. *Two. Just ten more feet.*

"Don't stop when you get to the bench. Keep going."

"Okay." My voice is barely audible, carried on exhale number eight.

"Good." Tucker says when we reach the bench. "Now see that bag next to the track? The red one. Aim for that. Don't slow down. Push yourself. You can do it."

Within ten seconds, we're there. A quarter of the track left and there's a pain in my side.

"Don't slow down, Scarlett. I'm going to ask you the most embarrassing question possible. You'll turn bright red and have to breathe into a paper bag to answer."

"Asshole."

Tucker laughs. "I'm kind of liking this unladylike side of you." He's winded but not nearly as much as I am. "Pick a new spot and tell me what it is."

"The pole," I gasp.

He watches my face. "Are you counting?"

I nod.

"Talk to me, Scarlett."

"Yes."

We reach the pole and the finish line is in sight, the white line painted across the track.

"I want you to run to that line," Tucker says. "I'll give you ten seconds and for every second you shave off, you get an extra question."

I turn to him in amazement. Why is he doing this?

His eyebrows lift. "Go."

I push off my back leg and concentrate on stretching my front leg out as far as possible, counting my steps.

I have no idea how many seconds it's taken me to make it to the line, but I know I haven't pushed myself this hard physically in years. My pace slows down.

"Don't stop." Tucker is beside me, his voice encouraging. "You can bring it to a slow jog, but don't stop."

I'm dying, but I try to keep going.

"How did that feel?"

"Exhausting."

"You're a natural, Scarlett."

"Are you *sure*?" I feel like anything but a natural. I also feel like I'm about to drop dead.

"You can slow down to a walk now."

My breath is coming in heavy gasps.

"You didn't ask me how many seconds it took you."

I'm afraid to find out. "How many?"

"Eight, which is quite impressive. I didn't think you'd get there in less than twelve."

"You didn't think I'd shave any seconds off your ten?"

"Nope."

I don't believe him. There's a hitch in his voice. He wants me to ask him questions. If I ask and he has to answer, he's off the hook for having to voluntarily share his past with me. He wanted me to win.

"So I get three questions?"

"Yep."

The problem is he's so secretive, I don't even know where to start. When we're halfway around, I've partially caught my breath. I decide to ask a simple question. "First question, tell me about your family."

His chin lifts. "Which one?"

"You have more than one? And this doesn't count as a second question.

He snorts. "Fine. It doesn't count and the indirect answer to your second question is"—he pauses, rolling his eyes to the ceiling—"seven families."

"Seven? How is that possible?" I stare into his face, searching for a sign that he's tricking me.

His mouth lifts into a grimace. "Foster care."

My mouth forms an *O*. That explains so much and yet so little.

"You get one family per question. Or you get one family and two more unrelated questions."

"Your first family."

He gives me a sad smile. He knew I'd ask this question. The realization is shocking. "My mother was a drug addict. Meth was her drug of choice, but she'd take anything she could get her hands on. When I was twelve, the state intervened and placed me in foster care. My mother wasn't the best of parents, but she was better than the multiple foster homes I made my way through."

He pauses, and I take in what he's said. I could have lived his life. I occasionally wondered if I should have had that life. My mother was neglectful when she was on a drinking binge, and she was on drinking binges more often than not.

"Next question."

I can't stop thinking about Tucker telling me that his parents want him to become a pro soccer player. "Tell me about your last family."

"My last foster family. I was placed with them when I was thirteen. It was toward the end of my eighth-grade year. They realized I had a talent for soccer and encouraged me to develop it. It didn't hurt that my foster brother played, too. I'm sure that's why I was with them until I graduated from high school. Because I was an all-state soccer player and received multiple scholarship offers. They liked the attention. They still do, although not all of it." His mouth lifts into a slight smirk.

He'd said that there's more than one way to control a situation. The door of understanding swings partially open.

"You think the only reason they wanted you was because you could play soccer?"

He's silent for a second. "I'm sure of it."

An ache fills my chest thinking about how unloved he felt. I wonder if he misses his biological mother or if he's tried to find her. "At least you felt wanted," I mumble before I realize I've said it aloud.

"What?"

I can pretend I didn't say it, but it hardly seems fair. He's shared deeply personal things. I need to reciprocate. I sigh and wipe the back of my hand against my forehead. "I said at least you felt wanted. I was a burden to my mother. The only time I ever felt wanted was when her boyfriends showed an interest in me."

His eyes widen in horror. "They didn't..." He can't bring himself to finish the sentence.

"No. But not because they didn't want to. Especially my junior and senior year."

"Scarlett. I'm sorry."

My face hardens. "I didn't tell you so you'd feel sorry for me. I thought it might help you understand me better. That's the point of this exercise, right? To understand each other better?"

"Yeah." He sighs. "You used up your last question asking me if I thought my foster parents only wanted me because I could play soccer. But I'll give you one more."

The question that springs to mind is one I'm not sure he expects but has plowed through my head since he told me about his last family. I plan to ask him if he's ever felt loved. I stop on the track and he comes to a halt next to me, looking into my face with nervousness and hope.

Why does he look at me with hope?

Once again, I wonder why he's telling me these things. I know for a fact he rigged this so he would be forced to share his past with me. A new question forms as I search his eyes. "How many people at Southern have you told about your past?"

The corners of his mouth lift into a sad smile. "Only you, Scarlett. Only you."

We stand on the track staring into each other's eyes as someone runs past, but neither of us moves.

Why me?

There's so much more to Tucker than he shows the world. A vulnerable, injured boy that created the man in front of me. Maybe he feels as trapped in his skin as I do.

That thought shocks me. Protected, cocooned, yes. I built the walls myself. I created the nest inside. But lately Tucker has made me question my decision to stay hidden, and never once have I felt trapped.

Until now.

Tucker walks to his bag and picks up our water bottles as I gather my wits and follow him. When I'm close, he hands me mine while keeping his gaze on the back wall. He takes several long gulps, then wipes his mouth with the back of his hand. "So how was your workout tonight?"

"Good," I say after drinking a quarter of the bottle.

We stretch in silence as I process what Tucker has told me and what it means. I feel like he's given me a precious gift, and I've given him nothing in return. But I'm not sure I can offer myself like he did, and then I realize Tucker has much more to lose by sharing himself with me than the other way around.

We're exiting the fitness building and walking across the parking lot as I search my brain for a comparable sliver of my past. "My mother was a drunk," I finally say.

He stops and turns to me. The lights illuminating the walkway make half his face visible while the other half remains in the shadows.

"It was just my mother, me, and my little sister. And the revolving door of guys she brought home. She was always looking for her meal ticket. Her way out of the trailer park she'd been born into and will probably die in." I look into his face and hope he can see how hard this is for me to share. "I swore I wouldn't end up like her and my sister and every other female in my family before me. I wouldn't end up pregnant at sixteen and living on welfare. That I'd make something of my life."

He watches me in silence.

"But I shut myself off from everyone and everything to survive. I'm hidden somewhere deep inside and sometimes I wonder if I'll stay buried forever. If I'll ever find my way out."

His hand reaches for my cheek, and he brushes away the stray hairs that have escaped my ponytail and whip around my face. "You will, Scarlett. You're closer than you think."

His hand drops, and we walk to my car in silence. He opens my car door and closes it once I've gotten inside, waiting and watching as I drive away.

I'm still stunned that I shared these things with Tucker. Shocked to realize the truth of the last part. I wonder if I'll ever climb out of this tunnel of isolation.

And I wonder if Tucker Price is the one to help me climb it.

Chapter Twelve

I'm achy when I wake up Friday morning. At first I think I'm tired and sore from pushing myself too hard the night before, but after I get up and moving, I realize I'm getting sick. My throat is burning, and I have a massive headache. I don't have time to get sick.

While I don't usually dress up to go to class, I definitely don't wear sweatpants like the ones I put on now. When I go into the kitchen to make a cup of coffee, Caroline takes one look at me and shakes her head.

"You look like shit."

I grab my travel mug from the cabinet. "I love you, too."

Her hand presses against my forehead. "You have a fever."

"Thanks. I figured that out by now." I press the large button on my single-serving coffee maker. It's days like today I truly appreciate its efficiency.

"See? I told you that running is bad for you."

I scoff, and it makes my throat hurt worse.

"You're not going to class, are you?"

I turn to face her, pressing my back into the counter. "I *cannot* miss set and logic. I might be able to get out of Arabic."

"*Scarlett.*"

I grab my coffee and find my coat. "This class is the most important class in my college career. I have a test next Friday. I *cannot* miss it."

"Then will you go to the clinic after your class? Please?"

I grin. I love this girl. "Yes, anything for you."

"That's not true, or you wouldn't be spending time with Tucker Price."

I walk out the door without answering. She's right. That's the one thing I stubbornly refuse to give in on.

Class is torture. My back begins to ache, and I end up slouching through the last half as I try to concentrate on the class discussion. When I gather my books and leave the room, I find Daniel waiting in the hall.

How could I forget that he'd probably be here?

His eyes widen as he moves toward me. "Scarlett. You look terrible."

"Why does everyone keep telling me that?" I grumble.

Daniel rubs his forehead. "That came out wrong."

"It's okay," I say, moving to the staircase. "I've looked in the mirror. I know it's true."

"What are you doing in class?"

"I couldn't miss the class discussion today." I cut him off as he opens his mouth. "And no, getting someone's notes isn't good enough. Not in this class."

"Are you going home now?"

"No, I'm going to the clinic. *Then* I'm going home."

"I'll walk with you."

I cast a skeptical glance at him. "I've got to warn you—I think I'm carrying the bubonic plague. Walk with me at your own risk."

He grins. "I'll take my chances."

We exit the building and dark gray clouds cover the sky. A blustery wind blasts my face and steals my breath. The chills from my fever intensify. All I want to do is go home and go to bed, but I suspect I have strep throat and need an antibiotic.

When we reach the building that houses the clinic, I turn to Daniel and smile. "Thanks for walking with me."

He opens the door. "What kind of guy would I be to leave you out here? I'll walk you to the clinic."

His offer is sweet and genuine, but all I want is to be left alone. Still, it's not like I can refuse. "Thanks."

When we enter the building, he presses the up arrow at the elevator. "I had hoped you'd agree to go out with me tonight, but I can see that's out of the question."

His statement is the one thing that makes me thankful I'm sick. I still haven't decided if I want to go out with him or not. Maybe the fact that I can't decide is my decision. "I suspect I'll be home all weekend."

The elevator opens and he presses his hand against the opening to keep the doors from closing. He's so nice and polite. How can I not want to go out with him? He has every quality I look for in a guy.

Maybe I'm just too broken to become attached to someone other than Caroline, who's more like a sister at this point than a friend.

The thought is upsetting, but I can't let myself ponder it as I exit the elevator and stop at the clinic door. "Thanks so much for walking with me, Daniel. It was really sweet."

"See you Monday after your class?"

I nod and give him a smile. I hope I have an answer for him, one way or the other.

The nurse practitioner confirms my strep throat diagnosis, and I send an e-mail to my Arabic instructor that I'm going to miss class. It kills me to miss a class. Any class. But not only do I feel like crap, I don't want to infect other people. The best place for me is home in bed.

When Caroline comes home, she pops her head in my door to check on me. "You still look like shit."

"I have good reason. Strep throat."

Her face scrunches with indecision. "You probably need someone to stay with you tonight."

I sit up. "Caroline, I'm twenty years old. You and I both know I've been taking care of myself since I was six. I'm not deathly ill. If you have somewhere to go, go."

"I was invited to a party with Tina."

I offer a smile. "Then go and have fun. I'm fine."

"Are you sure?"

"I have antibiotics, Netflix, and hot tea. I'm good."

She laughs. "You're so easy to please."

Not as much as she thinks. Not lately.

Caroline heads to her room to figure out what to wear. I check my e-mail to see if Anne in my Arabic class has responded to my e-mail requesting notes from today's missed class. Her response is in my inbox, but there's also an e-mail from Tucker.

I read Anne's first, although I'm dying with curiosity as to why Tucker e-mailed. Anne has attached her notes in a file, which I download to begin studying in a few minutes. Next I open Tucker's e-mail, which is titled *Just Checking On You*.

I stopped by the math lab to check on you this afternoon but they said you called in sick. I wanted to make sure you were okay, and that I didn't push you too hard.

Tucker

I smile and find myself happy, even though I'm sick. Tucker went to check on me. I click reply.

Tucker,

I survived the run but alas succumbed to streptococcus. No worries, I'll be back to normal by tomorrow night after penicillin has flowed through my veins for over twenty-four hours.

Scarlett

I send the email and open Anne's notes. We've been each other's fallback person since Arabic I. She's almost as thorough with her note-taking as I am. I'm reading the homework assignment when my e-mail dings.

I click over, surprised to see Tucker has responded. It's 8:10. Why is Tucker e-mailing on Friday night?

I was going to see if you wanted to run on Sunday afternoon. Do you think you'll feel up to it?

I find myself hoping I am.

Tucker was right. I like the challenge of pushing my body, but I have to admit that there's more to wanting to run than the physical activity itself. It's Tucker. But what exactly is going on in my head?

I like the freedom to be myself with him. No pretenses. No hiding. His wild partying and short flings with girls tells me he's not interested in me in anything other than a friend, which makes me feel safe. And while I love Caroline, it's nice to have someone else in my life. It's so easy with Tucker. The door to me, the me deep inside, has cracked open, and I'm emerging into the daylight for the first time in years. I like that he's part of that.

I e-mail him back and tell him to count on meeting me at four.

By Sunday I'm much better, and eager to get out of the apartment. I've been holed up since Friday.

Caroline doesn't approve, which comes as no surprise, but she's too busy getting ready to go out with a guy she met at the party on Friday night to put up much of a protest.

Tucker is waiting in his usual spot when I arrive at three-fifty. He's grinning as I walk up, a mischievous gleam in his eye.

His look makes me slightly nervous. He's up to something.

I lift an eyebrow. "I still don't understand how you can be *early* when you meet me to run and for tutoring, but you can never make it to Western civilization on time?"

He shrugs. "I told you. I just need the right incentive." I start to open the door to go to the track, but he puts his hand over it. "You probably shouldn't run, since you're still getting over strep."

Disappointment sinks like a weight in my chest. "I'm a little tired, Tucker. I'll just take it easy."

"We're still working out, just not running."

My eyes narrow. "What exactly are we doing?"

"I'm behind on my weight training. We're going to work out in the weight room instead."

"Oh." This is unfamiliar and unease blooms inside my chest.

"Scarlett." His face lowers to mine. "No one's going to pay any attention to you, okay? And I'll show you everything so you'll know exactly what to do."

"Okay." I'm still not used to him reading my subtle emotions.

He steps away from the door. "Come on." He heads up the stairs and enters a large room filled with weight machines, then tosses his bag on the floor. "Have you ever worked out on machines before?"

"No." Some of them are easy to figure out but others look completely foreign.

"We'll start slow. We won't overdo it." He moves to a piece of equipment with pads where someone's legs would go.

Tucker is focused on adjusting the weight and I watch him in confusion. I'm struggling to believe that he's here for such a simple reason as wanting to be with me. "Why are you doing this, Tucker?"

He turns around, surprise widening his eyes. "Doing what?"

"This." I point to the machine he's standing next to. "We were supposed to run. If you thought I couldn't run, then why are we up here instead? Why didn't you just cancel?"

Tucker takes a step toward me, worry wrinkling his forehead. "I told you. I'm behind in my weight training."

"You'd be much faster and more efficient without me."

His head tilts to the side, and his face hardens slightly. "Do you not want to do this?" The way he says it sounds like he means more than working with weights.

"No." I shake my head. "I mean yes." I exhale in frustration and brush a stray hair from my face. "I want to do this. I just don't get why *you* do."

He rests his butt against one of the machines and crosses his arms over his chest. "The truth?"

"Always. I only want the truth from you."

A soft smile tips his mouth up. "That's one reason. The fact you want the truth. No one else does. They want to hear what's going to make them happy, even if it's a lie. But you always want the truth, even if it's painful. Just like me."

I cringe.

"No, don't do that, Scarlett. Don't make a list of things in your head that you should have done differently."

I cock my head and lower my voice. "Why would you think I'd do that?"

"I've told you before. I know you better than you think."

This should scare me, the way he can peek at the inner me, but it's comforting. I believe he really does, that he wants to find the real me. I just can't figure out why.

"Look." He stands and moves in front of me. "You're the first real friend I've had in years. Everyone wants or expects something from me and while, yes, you do too in a way, you want me to succeed for my benefit, not yours."

We're so different. No one expects anything from me but me. Everyone expects something from Tucker. But we're similar, too. We're both very much alone.

"I like spending time with you," I finally say, looking down at the floor.

"Me, too."

I look up into his face and sadness crinkles his eyes. Then he grins his Tucker Price grin and cocks his head in his self-confident way. "So are we doing this or what?"

"We are." I'm surprised I don't feel more shy, more self-conscious, but Tucker has a way of making me comfortable so I not only say what I think, but I'm not embarrassed about it either.

"Come sit on this thing right here." He pats the seat back.

I have slight reservations about sitting on the machine, but I look up into Tucker's smiling face. He wants to help me.

The thought is strange and comforting at the same time. He values what we have, whatever it is.

I rest my back against the seat. "Is this some medieval torture device?"

"No, but remarkably close." He explains that it's to help strengthen my thighs as he sets the weights lower, explaining everything as he goes. "Now lift your legs slowly and slowly release. Don't drop it abruptly."

I do as he says, focusing on my thighs.

"Good. Now nice slow reps. Controlled movements. It's all about control." He's looking at my legs as he talks, and I'm thankful I'm wearing yoga pants.

Control. He's right. It's all about control. Control over my thoughts and feelings. Trying to control what the world thinks about me when it probably doesn't even give a flip. Even my anxiety is my mind's way of trying to control things I have no control over.

Maybe I need to give up more control and embrace moments of impetuousness.

Isn't that what I'm doing right now?

We spend the next hour with Tucker showing me how to use the machines. He gets in his own workout between his lessons for me.

I glance over at him while he's lifting at least quadruple the weight I used on my thighs. "I'm sure many a girl has swooned over your legs," I tease.

He cocks an eyebrow. "Are you making fun of my legs? They're my best attribute."

I laugh. "Your legs? That's a sad fact indeed. Your mind is much more useful."

"Perhaps, but my good looks get the girls."

"What are you going to do when your hair falls out and you get a potbelly gut?"

"Never." He winks. "And who says swoon anymore? What are you? From the nineteen-fifties?"

"I'm a bit old-fashioned sometimes." I shrug.

His face softens. "I know. It's cute."

After we finish in the weight room, Tucker asks if I want to walk around the track instead of run. I'm not ready to go home yet, and if I'm honest, I'm not ready to leave Tucker yet, either. I watch him, trying to name this foreign emotion floating in my head.

Lighthearted. I feel lighthearted.

We head down to the track and fall into a comfortable silence. We've made one full lap when Tucker looks down at me. "I told you about my past. I want to ask you questions this time."

Tucker asking questions about my past sends a sliver of worry poking my belly. "If I remember correctly, and I'm sure I do, I had to earn those questions."

He grins, reveling in the idea of a challenge. "So what do you want me to do?"

"That's a good question. I'm not sure it would be fair if you do something physical. Maybe I should make you recite the rules of distributive properties."

"Do you know how incredibly hard that would be for me?"

"Nothing easy is worth having."

He stops in the track.

I've walked several steps away and turn back to him. "Tucker?"

He looks in awe, as though he's had a revelation. "You're right."

"What do you mean?"

"Maybe that's why I'm so unhappy. Soccer and everything that comes with it is too easy."

I shake my head. "That's not what I meant."

"Maybe not, but it's true."

I stare up into his face, my heart aching. "Are you unhappy?"

A tiny smile lifts his mouth. "Not when I'm with you."

We stare at each other for several seconds until someone calls Tucker's name. His head jerks to the side, and he becomes a different person. His shoulders roll back and his chin lifts. A hardness fills his eyes. He's arrogant, cocky.

A dark-headed guy I don't recognize walks toward us, looking me up and down. He puts his hands on his hips. "What are you doing, Tucker?"

Tucker spreads his arms wide, tilting his head to the side with a grin. "Working out, dude. What's it look like?"

The other guy's face is expressionless, but one eyebrow twitches. "Looks like you're walking around and talking to me."

Anger puffs out Tucker's chest. "What, are you here to check up on me?"

"Somebody has to."

"Fuck you, Jason." Tucker sneers, then grabs my arm and pulls me away.

I turn to study Jason. He still stands in the middle of the track, his hands on hips, watching me. "Who was that?"

"No one." But Tucker's mood has darkened. He looks over his shoulder. "We should call it a day."

I nod, but I'm disappointed. "Yeah."

He grabs his bag and loops the strap on his shoulder, and picks up my coat. We walk out into the lobby and he helps me put on my jacket, but his movements are tight and controlled.

"How are you feeling?" he asks. "I didn't have you overdo it, did I?"

"No, I'm fine."

We walk outside, and Tucker's bare-armed, but he barely notices. He seems agitated.

"Are *you* okay?" I ask.

He stops. "I'm fine." But he doesn't elaborate. His demeanor has changed again. He no longer acts upset and instead has morphed into the caricature that greeted Jason. The guy who was twenty minutes late for our first tutoring session.

This arrogant Tucker is the shield he puts up to protect himself, and I suspect it's up most of the time. It has to be exhausting. His trust in me grants me the rare privilege of knowing the real him. I want to tell him that he should tell people like Jason to fuck off and really mean it, but we're not to that place in our friendship.

"Thanks for working out with me." I say, worried that he's put up his shield against me as well.

"Yeah," he mumbles before he walks away.

I walk to my car, hoping I haven't lost him.

Chapter Thirteen

Daniel is waiting for me after set and logic on Monday, and I suppress a cringe. What am I going to do about this situation?

"I don't have time to have coffee with you," he says, his eyes apologetic. "I've got to meet my advisor, but I didn't want to make you think I'd stood you up."

I smile. He really is a nice guy. He deserves better than me stringing him along.

"I realized I didn't have your number to text you."

"Oh." I pull out my phone, and he takes it from my hand to enter his number.

"If you want to get ahold of me"—he looks up and grins—"for any reason, feel free to call or text."

"Thanks," I say, looking at my phone in his hand.

He hands it back. "I'll see you Wednesday, unless you decide you want to see me sooner." His meaning is clear.

"Thanks." I still can't make myself look at him.

"You look like you're feeling better."

"Yeah," I shrug and finally look up. "I'm much better. Thanks."

He walks backward down the hall. "I'll talk to you later."

"Bye."

I didn't have my morning coffee at home in anticipation of meeting Daniel so I head to the coffee shop without him and wait in the line to place my order.

"I heard he's actually *seeing* someone." A girl in front of me says to her friend. "He was supposed to go to Scott's party on Saturday night, and he never showed."

The second girl lowers her chin and lifts her eyebrows. "Tucker Price skipped a party? What? Was he in jail?"

My ears perk up at the mention of Tucker's name, but I try not to look too interested.

"No, he stayed home. Jason said he was doing homework. On a Saturday night. How insane is that?"

"Was he with someone?"

"*He stayed home.* You know he never takes girls to his place. And Jason said he was at his place. All weekend."

Tucker's alleged activity this weekend goes against everything Caroline is always telling me as well. And who's Jason? I know he's the dark-headed guy who talked to Tucker at the gym, but is he Tucker's roommate?

I spend the rest of my time before Arabic trying to study, but I spend more time thinking about Tucker, and the gossip I overheard. What does it mean? Why should it matter to me? But Tucker and I are friends. He even admitted it. Doesn't that give me the right to care?

The rest of the afternoon flies by in math lab, and I'm exhausted when I leave ten minutes late. Tucker's standing in the shadows in the hall. He grins when he sees me.

"Tucker, what are you doing here?"

"We did it, Scarlett. We got a B-plus."

I stop in front of him, my heart bursting with pride. "No, you did it, Tucker. *You* got a B-plus."

He turns serious. "I couldn't have done it without you."

Shaking my head, I smile. "You could have easily had another tutor help you. This was all you. You just needed to have the steps explained slower."

"Well, thanks." He hands me a brown gift bag he had hidden behind him. His shoulders hunch as though he's worried I'll refuse.

My heart flutters, and I feel lightheaded. But not in the way I usually feel when I'm anxious. This is pleasant. "What's this?"

"A thank-you for helping me."

I look up at him and smile. Other than Caroline and Tina, I can't think of the last time someone has given me a gift. The bag is heavier than I expected. "What is it?"

"Open and see."

Gifts make me awkward. People watch while I open them, and although I'm used to Tucker staring at me, he's waiting for my reaction. That makes me more anxious than usual. I pull out the white tissue paper and start to transfer it to my other hand, but Tucker takes it from me, his mouth pressed into a tight line.

He's nervous. Confident Tucker is nervous. Why?

Tilting the bag, I look inside and pull out a rounded object. It's an alarm clock, but the face of the clock has equations in place of the numbers.

"I saw it and thought about you. It's kind of stupid…"

I glance up at him, smiling. "I love it."

"Really?"

"Really." I can't believe how *happy* I feel right now. It's such an unfamiliar emotion that I barely recognize it. "You didn't have to do this, Tucker. The university is paying me to tutor you. Besides, we're friends."

"I know. But I wanted you to know how much I appreciate you."

I'm nearly speechless. "Thank you." I finally get out.

"You're welcome."

We stare at each other for a couple of seconds. I have no idea what he's thinking, but I'm amazed this thoughtful guy is the same person who fuels the university's gossip. I'm so grateful he's part of my life.

"So what are you doing now?" he asks.

I take a deep breath. My nerves feel like they're about to jump out of my skin. "I'm meeting someone from my Arabic class at Panera to study for a test on Wednesday."

"Panera should give you some kind of frequent-customer discount."

"Yeah," I laugh. "Where are you off to?"

"Training. Then some quality time with Western civ."

"That's right. We have another test coming up next week."

"Maybe we could..." Tucker shakes his head, rubbing the back of his neck, then releases a long exhale. "When do you meet your friend?"

"At six-thirty." I shift the strap of my bag on my shoulder. "I need to get going." My clock is still in my hand, with the handle of my bag looped over my fingers. I should put the clock in the bag, but I can't make myself do it yet. I still can't believe he's given me a gift, let alone such a perfect one.

"I'll walk you out." He reaches for the strap of my messenger bag and slides it down my arm, then hooks it over his shoulder. It's a simple thing, but I can read so much into it. The gift. Taking my bag. What does this mean? Is that what friends do?

We head for the staircase.

"I've been thinking about Daniel Bailey," he says, his demeanor shifting again. He's quiet, thoughtful now, with a twinge of sorrow. "I...I hope I didn't sway you to not go out with him because of what I said."

"You didn't really say anything, Tucker."

"I know. Look, Bailey and I don't get along because I'm an asshole. He's entitled to his opinion of me. I earned it." He stops at the exterior door, his hand on the handle, keeping his gaze on my mouth. "I think he's probably a nice guy, Scarlett. If you want to go out with him, you probably should." His eyes shift to mine.

My breath freezes, and I'm not sure how to process everything that's just happened within the last few minutes. "You think I should go out with Daniel Bailey?"

A war of emotions flashes in his eyes and finally settles on acceptance. "You deserve a nice guy, Scarlett."

But what about you? stays tacked to the tip of my tongue. Where did that come from? How can I misinterpret our being friends to Tucker wanting to go out with me? And where did this sudden desire to go out with Tucker come from? I feel like I've been struck by a lightning bolt of want. *I want Tucker Price.* My knees start to buckle from the shock. It steals my breath, and I fight not to suck in a lungful of air. Instead, I smile, my chin quivering. "I'll think about it."

He pushes open the door and a gust of cold air blasts my face, springing tears into my eyes.

"I can walk you to your car." He looks down at me with sad resignation. Sorrow oozes from him, filling the air and choking me with it.

Or is it my own?

This revelation is shocking and strong, as though I've run headlong into a wall. I cannot confuse his thoughtfulness with romantic interest in me. This is why me trying to date is a terrible idea. I get caught in a quagmire of confusion and anxiety, unable to read simple social cues. Tucker is encouraging me to go out with Daniel. He's not interested in me other than as a friend. He's never hinted that we were more than friends.

Tucker waits for an answer. The wind blows his hair, making it stand on end. His cheeks are turning pink, and his hands are shoved in his pockets. He shifts his weight to one side.

How could this happen? *When* did this happen? This is terrible. Horrifying. The one person I want is the one person I can't have. Tucker Price flits from girl to girl, party to party, from one destructive situation to another. We live in different worlds that barely intersect, and that's only with algebra. Which I love and he hates.

"Scarlett?" His voice is gentle, and it sharpens my pain.

I shake my head. "No."

Confusion furrows his brow. "I can't walk you to your car?"

"I have to go." I turn and head toward the parking lot.

"Scarlett! Wait." Tucker runs in front of me and blocks my path. Worry pinches the bridge of his nose. "Did I do something?"

"No." I shake my head, desperate to get away from him. "I'm going to be late." I try to step around him, but he moves in front of me.

"Something's wrong. What did I do?"

You're too kind and thoughtful. You make me feel things I've never felt before. You see me, the me I keep carefully hidden behind facts and pretense. You see through the layers I've built up over the last twenty years. You give me hope when I have no right to feel it. That's what you've done. You've made me feel for the first time in longer than I can remember. But I say none of these things, and instead attempt to swallow the burning lump that clogs my throat. *I will not cry. I will not cry.*

"I'm tired. Maybe I overdid it yesterday." My smile is weak and is probably worse than no smile at all. "It's been a long day, and I still have hours of study time ahead of me." All these things are true. But only partially.

Tucker recognizes the half-truth, but doesn't respond. He steps toward me and wraps his arms around my back and holds me close. "I'm sorry," he whispers into my ear. Then he releases me, hands me my book bag, and he's gone.

I stand on the sidewalk, trying to stop shaking. The street lamp overhead casts long shadows around me. The shadows of the bench and the trash can and a nearby tree are dark and thick. But mine is gray and obscure, the hint of me is there, but only a ghost compared to the world around me.

How long have I existed in this nether world? Living in it but not part of it? Standing on the sidelines as a bystander? I'm like an alien, exiled to a foreign land in which I never fit, no matter how hard I try. For twenty years I've lived alone, keeping me safely tucked inside, but it's an illusion. A lie. I thought I could protect myself from the horror of my home life growing up, but all I've done is isolate and ostracize myself from the world. I'd always hoped someone would hold the key to open the door to my prison. Someone I felt safe letting in. Now I've found him.

And he doesn't want me.

I take several deep breaths, counting to ten before I find the energy to walk to my car. Studying with Anne is a blur, and I go through the motions, forcing myself to concentrate.

This is so unlike me that it shakes me to my core.

By the time I've left Panera, I've regained control and even decided that I'm overreacting. So I have some schoolgirl crush on Tucker Price. Who doesn't? This is a good sign, that I can actually have feelings about a guy, instead of the apathy I've had with every other guy I've gone out with.

When I get home, I close myself in my room and pull out my homework. My fingers curl around my mechanical pencil and the lead glides across the paper, the crisp, smooth sound filling the quiet of my room. My lamp pools light on my desk. I'm in my own little world. Numbers and variables fill the page and my head, easing back the prickly emotions that make me uneasy. This is my nirvana.

And for the first time, it's not enough.

Chapter Fourteen

I've seen movies and read books in which the girl secretly pined for a boy who didn't know she existed. I never understood why she didn't move on. Why she got so *stuck*. But now I get it.

I'm living it.

Only it might be better if Tucker didn't acknowledge me instead of showering me with niceness. We sit at Panera going over Tuesday's algebra lesson. I've convinced myself that being with him in some way, even as a friend, is better than not being with him at all. He's sweet and jokes with me, coaxing out my smiles. After thirty minutes, I'm more relaxed, and he seems relieved. He's not awkward with this moody me, just subdued until I open up more.

"Are we still on tonight?" he asks, but he doesn't look at me. He keeps his gaze on the notebook in front of him.

If I were smart, I'd say no. If I had any sense in my head, I'd convince the chancellor that Tucker needs another tutor. But my intelligence has fled along with my self-control and my common sense.

He glances into my face as I hesitate, probably because I hesitate, and I see the fear in his eyes.

He knows.

Of course he knows. Why else would he apologize yesterday? He'd done nothing to apologize for. He knows, and yet he pretends like he doesn't.

I take several deep breaths and count to ten. I'm never nervous around Tucker, at least not until now. Now I've ruined everything.

He's still waiting for an answer.

As much as I want to be with him, I can't. It hurts too much. "No."

His eyes widen and disappointment sweeps over his face. "Why not?"

I can't admit the real reason why, and I don't want to lie to him. I decide to tell him something that will make everyone happy. Everyone but me. "I already have plans tonight."

"Oh."

He doesn't ask any more questions, but he's quiet for the rest of our session. When our time is up, we pack up our things, and Tucker walks me to my car like he usually does. But this time feels different.

I twist the keys in my hand. "So I'll see you Thursday. You're doing great, Tucker. You may not need my help for much longer at this rate."

He doesn't respond for several seconds. "Then I guess I'll have to work on looking more inept. I like knowing I have you to explain the lessons. You're my safety net."

There's affection in the way he says it, and I can't help smiling. "I've never been called anyone's safety net before. But the arrangement is that I tutor you until your grades have improved, and you no longer need me. As long as you need me, I'm yours."

Horror rushes in my head as I realize what I've just said, but Tucker smiles his sad smile.

"You have no idea how much I need to hear that." Then he turns and walks to his car.

I watch him for a second then get in my car, processing the last hour in my head. I've made the right decision. For my own self-preservation, I need to create some distance between us.

Before I leave the parking lot, I text Daniel and apologize for the short notice and ask if he wants to go out tonight. He answers me back within thirty seconds, asking if I want to go see a movie.

This is good. I need to move on, and Daniel's a great guy. So why does my heart hurt so much?

I drive back to campus to finish my math lab hours. Between students, I text Caroline and tell her I have a date tonight. I'm glad it's a text when she sends an excited *Squeeeeeee!!!!!!*

Time drags, and I'm getting more and more nervous. Daniel texts and gives me the choice of a rom-com or an action movie. He seems surprised when I picked the action film and tells me it starts at seven forty-five, and he'll pick me up around seven-twenty since I work until seven. I'm thankful there are few students waiting for help, and I get to leave ten minutes early.

When I leave the campus, my stomach is a mess of nerves and fear. I reassure myself that people go on dates all the time. Daniel is not an ax murderer. We'll be in a public place. But when I walk in the door, Caroline tosses her afghan to the side and hops off the sofa.

"Where have you been?"

I squint my confusion. "Working. Like I always do on Tuesday afternoons."

"We have to get you ready." She drags me to my bedroom. Caroline seems more nervous than I am. I didn't think that was humanly possible.

"I've been on dates before, Caroline. Calm down." I really need her to calm down. She's freaking me out.

Her eyes widen. "Dates? You mean those encounters with that beady-eyed science guy last year?"

"He wasn't beady-eyed."

Her head shakes in short bursts. "Oh, he was beady-eyed all right. He doesn't count."

"He most certainly does count!"

"Not like this. Daniel is *normal*."

I could argue that I'd had three normal dates other than the physics major I'd gone out with last spring, but I don't see the point.

Caroline deems all my clothes "hopeless," and loans me a pink sweater that she says looks good with my complexion and dark hair. I draw the line at her putting on my makeup and fixing my hair.

"For God's sake, at least take out your ponytail."

Releasing an exaggerated sigh, I pull out the hair band and fluff my hair. "Better?"

"I wish you'd wear your hair like that all the time."

"One step at a time, Caroline."

Caroline hands me a plate of pizza rolls she heated up, since I haven't eaten since my partially eaten bagel at Panera. I'm brushing my teeth when the doorbell rings.

Caroline's eyes fly open. "He's here."

"I swear to God, Caroline, if you don't calm down, I'm going to slap you. One of us has to be calm, and it has to be you."

She takes a deep breath. "You're right. I'm calm." Barely. She opens the door and invites Daniel in. "So what do you crazy kids plan to do tonight?"

Daniel smirks. "We thought we'd go see a movie."

I grab my coat off the chair and try to settle my nerves. Why am I so nervous? "Don't mind her, Daniel. She's scheduled for her lobotomy next week."

"Very funny," she grumbles.

Daniel and I walk to the parking lot, and I stuff my shaking hands into my coat pockets. He stops next to a pickup truck and looks at me apologetically. Most of the guys back home drive trucks, but the guys here at Southern tend to drive cars.

"Sorry it's so tall. It comes in handy with construction." He shrugs and opens the passenger door.

I have to step on the running board to climb in. Caroline wanted me to wear a skirt, but I refused because of the cold. Now I feel justified with my decision.

On our way to the movie theater, Daniel tells me about his day and about working for his dad in Lebanon, Tennessee. He's doing all the talking, and I'm grateful. The pizza rolls aren't settling well in my stomach.

After we purchase the tickets, Daniel gets some popcorn and a drink, and we find a seat. Since it's Tuesday, the theater is only half full. We're early enough that we have a few minutes before the movie starts.

Daniel takes a handful of popcorn. "So are you still tutoring Tucker Price?"

My breath catches. I really don't want to get into this with Daniel. "Yeah."

"That must be a bitch."

My mouth parts and I gasp at his rudeness. "It's against the rules and unethical to discuss the people I tutor."

He scoffs. "Come on. Price lives his entire life seeking attention. You can't tell me that he doesn't expect you to talk about it. Hell, I'm surprised he hasn't begged you to."

Tucker may live an attention-seeking life, but that's not the Tucker I see. I refuse to share details of our time together. The Tucker I know seems vulnerable. I almost laugh at the thought, but I still feel protective of him. "It doesn't matter whether he wants me to talk about it or not. I'm not going to."

Daniel leans back and views me through narrowed eyes. "Don't tell me you have a thing for him. I thought you were different than every other girl at this school."

The blood in my veins catches fire, and I have trouble catching my breath. "I'm here with you, aren't I?"

He shakes his head. "That doesn't prove anything. It's not like he's going to ask you out. You're not his type."

His insult is clear. I'm not good enough to garner the attention of Tucker Price. I wonder what he'd say if he knew that Tucker had come over to my apartment the night I met Daniel and that Tucker spent the night in my bed. But the truth is he's right. Tucker will screw every other girl on campus, but he's not interested in me.

Daniel quickly realizes what he's said and panic spreads across his face. "That didn't come out right."

I clench my teeth to stop my chin from quivering. His statement has hit too close to home.

He leans closer and takes my hand in his. "Scarlett, I swear that came out wrong. I just meant that he usually goes out with girls who are loud, obnoxious, and flashy."

I agree with his assessment, but I'm still hurt and consider leaving.

"Scarlett, I'm sorry. Price and I have history, and I took it out on you. It wasn't fair."

The lights dim and the previews start before I can answer. I'm angry with myself when tears sting my eyes. The fact remains that Daniel's telling the truth. I'm not Tucker's type, and Tucker has made it painfully clear he isn't interested in me. Nevertheless, while I like Tucker, it's not for the reasons every other girl on campus does.

I like him for the person he lets me see and doesn't share with anyone else.

That thought is what keeps my butt glued to my seat, and my hand in Daniel's firm grip. That thought is more dangerous than anything Daniel might inadvertently say to me, because that thought encourages me to hope for things out of my reach.

I try to pay attention to the movie, but I can't focus when I'm concentrating on not hyperventilating. I start reciting prime numbers up to seven hundred and forty-three in my head, then move on to square roots with rational numbers. Old soothing habits I picked up in middle school. When one of Momma's boyfriends lived with us for two years of hell filled with drinking, smoking, loud arguments, and police visits every time he resorted to taking his frustration out on Momma with his fists.

When the movie's over, I'm exhausted in every way—physically, emotionally, and mentally. Daniel wants to stop and get something to eat, but I can't do it. I can't fulfill this social role a minute longer than I have to.

Daniel pulls into the parking lot of my apartment complex. I open the door before he has the engine turned off.

"Scarlett," he calls out, worry in his voice. "Hold up." He jumps out, running around the front of the truck. He intercepts me, grabbing my arm. "Wait."

I try to look into his face, but I can't make myself do it. I'm embarrassed both by my behavior and what he thinks of me.

"Scarlett, I think we got off to a rough start here, and it's entirely my fault. I'm sorry." He pauses, and I lift my chin to look at him. "Just because Price and I have had our differences doesn't give me the right to treat you the way I did. You're stuck tutoring him, and I should be understanding of that. I get it."

I want to tell him it's okay, but I can't make myself do that either.

"Will you give me another chance? Please?"

I want to tell him no, but when I look at the evening objectively I can't say he did anything terribly wrong. Everything he said was true, even if it came out wrong. No one is perfect. Lord knows I'm far from it. "Okay."

He wraps a hand around the small of my back and pulls me gently to his chest while his other hand cups my cheek and lifts my face. His lips brush mine, and when I don't pull back, he takes it as encouragement. His tongue runs along my bottom lip before seeking an opening to my mouth. I let him kiss me, and while I kiss him back, hoping that this time will be different, that this time I'll feel something.

His hand on my back slides to the front and finds the opening to my coat, then settles on my hip.

I wait for the feelings I'm supposed to feel and although it's pleasant, it's far from earth-shattering.

His hand slides upward, and I involuntarily stiffen. Daniel stops, lifting his head. "Can I see you on Thursday night?"

I shake my head. "I have a big test in set and logic on Friday. I need to study."

"Surely you can squeeze me in a couple of hours."

He knows how worried I am about this class. I've told him so multiple times. "No. It's Friday or nothing."

Irritation flashes briefly across his face. "Okay."

For the life of me, I can't help wondering why he wants to go out with me again. I can't figure out why I'm agreeing.

"I'll walk you to your door." He removes his hand from my waist and returns it to my back.

I lightly push his arm away. "That's okay. I'm fine. I'll talk to you later."

He doesn't look happy. Maybe he wanted another kiss at my door, but he says, "Okay," and returns to his truck. I walk across the parking lot as he drives away. I pause halfway up the stairs and turn around, sitting on the step and lean my head against the railing. I can't walk into our apartment and face Caroline. She's going to want details, and I can't bring myself to share them yet. There's no doubt that tonight was a disaster.

What the hell is wrong with me?

This isn't the first time I've asked myself this question, in a multitude of situations. But this time specifically I'm referring to my inability to feel anything when being kissed by a man. Maybe I'm just too broken.

That's the part that scares me the most. That I'm too broken to love anyone.

Chapter Fifteen

I sit on the steps for at least ten minutes, crying out my heartache and anguish. I've gotten control of myself when a dark figure turns from the street and jogs across the parking lot. He's wearing a gray sweatshirt, and the hood is over his head. His muscled calves stick out from under his long shorts, and I know who it is before he's at the bottom of the staircase, pulling back his hood.

Tucker.

He looks up and sees me.

I wipe my fingertips across my cheeks and keep my gaze on him.

He takes in my movement. I'm sitting in the shadows, and I'm grateful he can't see my face. I'm sure my nose is red, and my eyes are swollen.

He leans over his knees, out of breath, his eyes still on mine. After several seconds, he climbs the steps, one slow step at a time until he sits next to me and takes my hand in his, lacing our fingers and squeezing.

I close my eyes and lean my head into his shoulder.

We sit like this for several minutes, maybe longer. I lose track of time because all I know is that sitting like this with him feels so right, so perfect.

His thumb rubs the back of my hand, making slow circles, and I feel the tension leave my body.

Finally, he breaks the silence, his voice soft and soothing. "Want to talk about it?"

I shake my head, my temple still pressed against his shoulder. Tucker is the last person I want to tell about my night with Daniel.

He pulls his hand from mine, and I'm sure he's about to leave, but he wraps his arm around my back and pulls me against the side of his body. His free hand picks up my hand, curling over the top so his fingers now caress my palm.

"Do I need to kick the shit out of someone?" His arm tightens around my back. "Because if I find out who made you cry, I'm liable to do just that." His words are soft, but somehow I know he means every word.

I shake my head again, burying my cheek into his chest. I must be dreaming because this can't possibly be real. Tucker has not shown up outside of my apartment. He's not holding me in his arms. Why is he here?

I look up into his face and his gaze lowers to my mouth. His arm tightens around my back, and he closes his eyes, pressing his forehead against mine. For several seconds, our breaths mingle and we're breathing each other in. I'm amazed at how right this feels. Like I've been searching my entire life for this peace I feel in his embrace.

His head rises, and he gives me a sad smile. "I need to go." But he doesn't release me, instead looking into my eyes.

"Okay," I whisper.

"Thursday?"

I nod. "Thursday."

He sighs and climbs to his feet. His hand reaches for mine, and I put my palm in his. His fingers curl gently around my hand, and he pulls me to my feet. "Are you going in now?"

"Yeah." I feel calm enough to face Caroline, although I'm not sure what I'll say to her.

He releases my hand and smiles.

"Goodb—"

Tucker places his finger on my lips. "Don't say goodbye. I hate goodbyes." Sadness creeps into his eyes.

My lips tingle and butterflies fight to escape from my stomach.

His finger slides off my lip. "Thursday."

I smile. "Thursday."

He bolts down the steps and turns around at the bottom and grins.

I watch him jog across the parking lot and out into the street until he disappears behind a tree line on the side of the road.

Time to face Caroline.

She's waiting when I open the door, excitement on her face. "Well?"

"It was nice." I avoid looking at her.

"*Nice*? I need details."

Heaving a sigh, I take off my coat. "We went to the movie, and we talked."

Her perfectly tweezed eyebrow lifts. "And?"

"If you're asking if he kissed me, the answer is yes."

"And?"

"And what?" I know what she wants, but I'm sure she won't like my answer.

"Scarlett!"

I shrug. "It was nice."

She flops on the sofa, crossing her legs. "Again with the nice."

I sit on the arm of the chair. "What do you want me to say, Caroline? He's a nice guy. We had a nice time. It wasn't spectacular. It wasn't love at first sight. It was...nice."

She scowls. "I don't think you're giving him a chance."

My mouth drops open.

She leans forward, earnestness in her eyes. "He's a great guy, Scarlett! He's cute. He's funny."

"I don't know." I was confused before Tucker showed up. I'm even more confused now.

"Scar, this was one date. I know you. Give it a chance."

I cock my head. "What are you saying?"

"I know how you are. You get nervous, and you blush, and you don't talk. It's hard for you to open up to people. It's just going to take you some time to get used to him. He *did* ask you out again, right?"

Even though her advice is sound, I just don't see Daniel and me working out. Even if Tucker hadn't come over tonight. But I don't feel like arguing about it. "I'll think about it."

"Good." She reaches for my hand and pats it. "Things will smooth out. I promise. When are you going out again?"

"Friday."

She smiles. "Plenty of time to get yourself ready. Maybe you can practice some of your guided imagery stuff."

"Maybe." I want to cry, and I'm not even sure why.

"I love you, Scarlett. I just want you to be happy."

I give her a hug, then stand. "I'm tired. I'm going to bed."

"Night."

I get ready for bed, ignoring the sorrow that expands inside my chest, choking off my air. I lay down on the bed and tears burn my eyes until I can't hold them in any longer. They stream down my face, dripping on my pillow.

The pillow Tucker slept on.

Three different battles wage on three fronts. Daniel, Caroline, and Tucker.

I wonder if my expectations of Daniel are too great. That I've seen too many rom-coms that set unrealistic expectations that no relationship could ever live up to. Did I overreact to his comments, especially since he apologized multiple times?

Part of me wonders if Caroline is right and maybe I'm not giving Daniel a chance. I have to admit that I let him do most of the talking. And he does seem like a nice guy. A normal guy. Not like the guys Momma brought home every few months. That has to count for something.

129

Finally, Tucker.

He stirs emotions in me that I don't want to dredge up, yet when he touches me, all anxiety flees. When he looks at me, it's not with pity or disgust. It's with respect and something more. He really sees the real me, not the façade I wear to get through the day.

Why did he come over? Had he been jogging past my apartment building? There's no way he could have seen me from the road. He had to have come with the purpose of seeing me.

One thing's for certain. Caroline doesn't approve of anything with Tucker, simple friendship included.

Daniel is waiting for me after class the next day. I didn't get much sleep the night before, and I'm tired and cranky. I'm definitely not in the mood to tiptoe around him.

He's leaning against the wall again, and he moves toward me, looking unsure that I'll welcome him. "Hey, Scarlett." He gestures toward the door. "How was your class?"

I adjust the strap of my bag on my shoulder. "It was good."

"Do you have time to grab a coffee?"

We both know the question isn't *do I have the time*, but will I agree to it.

I'm tense enough with the test looming on Friday, I'm not sure I need this aggravation. I brush the back of my hand against my forehead. "I really need to study."

His mouth purses. "It's only twenty minutes. Then you'll have an hour before Arabic."

I'm irritated that he's trying to arrange my study time, but he's right. It's only twenty minutes out of the seven hours I estimate that I have left to study. "Okay."

He grins, looking so happy that I feel guilty for almost telling him no.

Daniel talks about the movie on the way to The Higher Ground.

Since I didn't notice most of it, I have little to contribute, not that he seems to notice. I could be offended by this but instead see it as a relief. I'm not required to carry much of the conversation.

He remembers how I take my coffee—medium roast, room for cream and sugar—and orders mine with his. *That's thoughtful, right?* Is it wrong that I have to ask myself?

He pays for both and we sit at a table by the window, and I see Tucker walking across the campus. He's with a group of people, and he's in the center. I recognize two of the guys from the party a couple of weeks ago. My heart seizes when I realize they are coming to The Higher Ground. What will he think about me sitting with Daniel? Then again, maybe he'll be happy. He was the one who encouraged me to date him.

My frustration mushrooms. This is why I need rules. I know he cares *something* about me, but I can't help thinking it's more than just friendship. He never told me why he came over last night, and his comforting seemed to be more than that of just a friend.

Life is so freaking complicated. People make it even more so. Why can't they just follow rules?

Daniel has stopped talking. His face is expressionless as he watches me, and I wonder what I've done or missed. A quick mental inventory reveals only one thing—my attention is at the door where Tucker came in, my gaze fixed on his group. My chest locks down, and I push against the panic that fills my head.

Why am I freaking out?

"You don't have a thing for Tucker Price, huh?" Daniel asks, his voice cold.

Tucker's face looks up from the pastry case at the sound of his name. His eyes widen when he sees me.

"Daniel," I say as calmly as possible, willing my racing heart to slow down. "You know I tutor him."

"Does that mean you have to check him out the minute he walks in the door?" he asks in a hateful tone. "I see the look on your face,

Scarlett. You have a thing for Tucker Price just like every other slut in this school."

Tucker's face contorts into an expression I've never seen him wear. Cold rage. He's next to our table in two seconds, looking at Daniel through narrowed eyes. "Is there a problem here, Bailey?"

Daniel stands and grabs his backpack. "I don't see how it's any of your fucking business."

"It became my business when you brought my name into it."

I'm in the middle of a nightmare. It has to be, because there's no way I could be caught in something like this in real life.

Daniel shakes his head with a sneer. "So what? You're an attention whore. You should love that I'm throwing your name around."

Tucker's jaw clenches. "I don't give a fuck if you talk about me. But I *do* give a fuck how you're talking to Scarlett."

Disbelief sweeps across Daniel's face. "You've got to be shitting me." His gaze moves to me and back to Tucker. "You don't think you fucked enough of the girls on campus? Now you're going after the academic type? Or are you *just* interested in the girls I want to fuck?"

I don't realize what's happened until Daniel falls to the ground. He clutches his face as blood gushes from beneath his fingers. Tucker has just punched him.

Tucker leans over him and points. "If I ever hear you talking about Scarlett like that again, I'll beat the living shit out of you. Got it?" His voice is cold and hard and scary.

Everyone stands around us in shock. Then their eyes turn to me.

I'm still in my seat, my mouth hanging open. My diaphragm is stuck, refusing to push up or pull in oxygen to fill my lungs.

Tucker's face softens as he squats in front of me. "Let's go." He grabs my arm and pulls me up, picking up my bag with his other hand. Since my feet have forgotten how to move, he drags me outside and around the side of the building where the gawkers can't see us. Pushing my back against the wall, he drops my bag to the ground and leans over into my face. "Scarlett, take a breath."

I look up at him wide-eyed. My head is getting fuzzy.

He cups my jaw, and his fingers softly stroke my cheek. "You're safe now. No one is watching you. Just relax."

His touch is magical because that's the only explanation I can come up with that explains why my body responds to his commands. My lungs inflate as I close my eyes.

"I'm sorry." His forehead leans against mine. "I'm so sorry you had to go through that."

My eyelids flutter open to see despair on his face.

He lifts his head. "Has anyone else given you shit about tutoring me?" His voice is quiet, but there's a hardness that tells me that he's about to hunt people down if I say yes.

I shake my head. "No. Just Daniel."

His eyes enlarge, and his words are tight. "Did you go on a date with him last night?"

"Tucker—"

"He's the one who made you cry?" He starts to pull away from me, but I grab his arm.

"Tucker, please. Don't."

His expression softens. "I'm sorry, Scarlett. I was the one who forced you into this situation. I encouraged you to go out with him."

"No. I decided to go out with him on my own."

"I just want you to be happy."

I gawk at him. He knows what will make me happy, yet he's not interested.

"I feel like I've screwed up your life, barging in and forcing you to tutor me. I'm sorry."

I shake my head. "I'm not sorry."

"How can you say that?"

How do I answer him? I want to say that he makes me feel like maybe everything can be okay, as long as he's with me. That he makes me realize things about myself I never considered before. That my short time with him makes me want to live my life, not just watch it pass by. But my tongue refuses to respond except for three little words. "I like you."

His eyebrows lift, then he laughs softly. "I like you, too." Then his laugh fades and his eyes darken. "I think I more than like you."

"I more than like you, too."

His hand returns to my cheek, tilting my face up to his. His eyes search mine. "I'm not good enough for you, Scarlett. You deserve a hell of a lot better than me and for sure a hell of a lot better than Daniel Bailey."

"That's for me to decide, not you."

"I'll hurt you, Scarlett. I hurt every single person who gets close to me. I *always* fuck it up."

I think about what he just did to Daniel and how he makes me feel. "I'll take my chances."

He draws a ragged breath and looks like he's in pain as he exhales. "If I kiss you now, I won't be able to let you go, and you'll end up hating me. Tell me to walk away right now before it's too late. Tell me to leave you alone so you can have the life you deserve, Scarlett Goodwin, and not get stuck with a fuckup like me." The agony on his face tells me he believes every word.

It makes me want him even more.

Chapter Sixteen

I reach my hand behind his head and pull his mouth to mine, but he stops millimeters away, his free hand moving up to cradle my other cheek.

"Tucker?"

He shakes his head. "I can't, Scarlett. I can't do this to you."

He drops his hands, and squats to pick up my bag and put it in my hands.

"Thursday?" he asks, his eyes pleading with me.

My eyes brim with tears. He's just turned me away, yet he expects me to still tutor him?

His hand caresses my cheek. "Scarlett, I don't want to lose you by fucking up our friendship. I want you in my life, and if we do this, I *will* lose you. If that means showing some self-restraint for once in my goddamn life, then I will." Both of his hands cup my cheeks. "You make me want to be a better person. This is me being a better person."

I want to argue with him, but I see that this is killing him. He's trying to protect me in his own mixed-up way.

I nod, a tear falling down my cheek.

His thumb brushes it away. "Thursday." His voice is choked.

"Thursday," I whisper.

He turns his back and walks away, toward the fitness center. I stand with my back against the wall for several minutes, trying to figure out what happened. And hoping he changes his mind and comes back, not that he does. He doesn't look back, not even when he enters the building.

Was this some kind of elaborate joke? But even as the thought crosses my mind, I don't believe it's true. There was too much pain in his eyes. He truly believes he will end up hurting me.

Common sense tells me to run away from him, as far and as fast as I can. But two things keep me here.

He makes me believe I can be more than the me I am now.

And I like the Tucker he keeps hidden from the world.

When my legs finally stop shaking so that I can move, I check my phone and see I have only thirty minutes until Arabic class. And I still have to get lunch. My already frazzled brain is having a hard time accepting the fact that I've lost over an hour of studying time. There's nothing I can do about that now.

At least I'm settled down enough to pay attention in Arabic, and I'm lucky when my instructor compliments my oral recitation. I'd planned to go over it one more time before class, and all the Daniel-Tucker nonsense made me completely forget.

Between my course load and my tutoring job, I have enough to fill most of the hours of the day. I should save dating for after college, once I've established my career. I've done just fine on my own. There are no surprises when there's just me. No pain and no heartache.

This may be true or not, but it's what gets me through the next two hours without breaking into tears.

Well into my shift in the tutoring center, I'm helping a freshman with problems from algebra 101. The image of Tucker walking in weeks ago asking for help rushes into my head. Frustration and hurt bundle together in the pit of my stomach. I have to find a way to let this go. It's not that he doesn't want me—that has to count for something—it's that he doesn't want to lose me. I don't want to lose him, either. I just need to find a way to keep these more-than-friendship feelings to myself.

I glance up surprised to see Jason, the guy who confronted Tucker at the gym, enter the math lab. I study him out of the corner of my eye. He's dark-haired, dark-eyed, and wears nicer clothes than most college students. He walks in with an arrogant swagger, making him stand out from everyone else. Most students have reached a place of humility by the time they come to our center, accepting that they can't do the work on their own and need help from someone else.

This guy looks like he wants to flip off the entire room.

His eyes are on me as he takes a seat against the wall. Tina walks over to him and sits in a chair next to him, but he keeps his attention on me, watching me with a calculating stare. Tina doesn't like what he says, getting up and mouthing *sorry* to me.

My heart skips a beat. Why is she sorry?

I keep the freshman for several problems longer than necessary, just to stall. It's now apparent the guy, who's attempting to kill me with hateful glares, is waiting to talk to me. Especially after one of the other tutors tries to help him, and Jason turns him away.

When the freshman finally packs up her books, Jason doesn't waste time approaching me, moving next to the vacated chair.

"Scarlett Goodwin?"

"Yes." I force air behind the word so I sound more confident than I feel.

"Is there someplace we can talk?" He looks around the room, wrinkling his nose. "Alone."

My first thought is that it definitely hasn't been my day to handle men. There's no way I'm going somewhere alone with him.

"It's a delicate topic. Regarding Tucker."

Tucker. I can't figure out why he wants to talk to me about Tucker. And I still don't trust him enough to be alone with him. "Can this wait? I still have two hours left."

"I've wasted enough of my time already. I'm fine discussing this here. I'm merely trying to shield you. Delicate topic, remember?"

My throat squeezes. I can't imagine what this could be about, but I've had my fill of embarrassment for the day. "And who are you?"

"Jason Wallace."

I wait for more explanation but none follows. There's only one student waiting to be tutored and hopefully this won't take long. I stand and take a deep breath, glancing over at Tina. "I'll be back in a few minutes."

Tina's jaw drops, but I ignore her as I follow Jason from the room into the hallway. He walks to the end, close to the stairwell and stops, putting his hands on his hips.

He doesn't waste any time getting to the point. "You're interfering with Tucker's progress."

The air sticks in my lungs. "What does this have to do with you?" I clip my words in annoyance.

"I'm his brother."

Tucker's last name is Price. Perhaps they are step- or half-brothers. Where does his brother Marcel fit in there? I blink. "I still don't see how this concerns you."

"When Tucker's not focused it becomes my problem. You're getting in the way."

It takes a moment for what he's said to sink in. "I'm tutoring him, and he's improved dramatically. How can that be interfering?"

He leans closer to my ear and half-whispers, "We both know that's not what I'm talking about."

I suck in my breath.

"I know Tucker was part of an altercation earlier today, and it was because of you."

I want to protest, but what he's said is true.

"And we both know that Tucker is under disciplinary probation."

I close my eyes. *Oh, God.*

"You're not Tucker's usual type. I confess. I'm confused by you."

I force myself to answer. "I'm not sure what you think is going on between us, but I can assure you that we're just friends." Not that I want to be, but here I am nonetheless.

He smiles, but it's cold and ugly. "You can pretend that's the case, but Tucker is infatuated with you, and it's distracting him."

"Then you're talking to the wrong person."

"No, I think you can fix this. As I said, it's easy to see you're not his usual type. He's not used to waiting, if you know what I mean."

His full meaning sinks in and the blood pools in my feet. "I'm done here." I turn around and start back down the hall, but he grabs my arm and pulls me to a halt.

"You may be done here, but I'm not. Tucker's worked hard to get where he is, and admittedly, he's hit a road bump here and there, but he'd gotten back on track. Until you."

I jerk my arm out of his grasp. "I'm not discussing this with you."

"Scarlett." His tone softens. "It's obvious you care about Tucker. So think of it this way. Do you really want to stand in his way? Don't you want to do what's best for Tucker?"

"I have no control over how Tucker feels or doesn't feel." I'm not fooled by his switch in tactics. I could tell him Tucker doesn't want a relationship with me, and I might have if he'd taken a less offensive approach. Let him stew. "If I don't fall in line, can I expect a visit from Marcel next?"

Confusion clouds Jason's eyes. "Who the hell is Marcel?"

I stare at him for several seconds. How can he not know Marcel? Did Tucker lie or was Jason lying about being Tucker's brother? I turn and leave him behind without a word.

"He won't stick around." Jason calls after me.

Against my better judgment, my feet stick to the floor, but I keep my back to him.

"Tucker's incapable of loving anyone. Why do you think he parties so much? He's terrified of getting close to anyone. The moment he starts to feel something real for you, he'll bolt. That's what Tucker does. He runs."

I close my eyes in horror. I believe him.

"Do yourself and Tucker a favor and end anything between you now."

My feet find their will to move, and they don't stop until I sit in my chair. I must look shell-shocked because Tina leaves the student she's tutoring and sits in the chair next to me. "What just happened?"

"I've been told to leave Tucker Price alone."

"By who? Who was that?"

"He claims he's Tucker's brother."

"Jason?"

My eyes sink closed. I'd hoped he lied, especially since he didn't know about Marcel. I'd hoped it was a sick joke by one of Tucker's friends. "Yeah."

"What are you going to do?"

I'm not used to standing up for myself except in rare occasions. It's always been a choose-your-battle thing, and most battles just weren't worth fighting for. Until now. "I'm going to keep tutoring Tucker. That's all there is between us."

Her eyes soften. "Are you sure that's all there is?"

My lips press together into a frown. "That's what he told me this morning."

"Ouch."

I shrug. "It's for the best." I lift my chin. "But I refuse to be bullied into not tutoring him. The math department needs that program, and he's done really well with our tutoring sessions. The only way I'll stop is if he tells me he's done."

"And maybe hope he changes his mind."

I can't deny it. Part of me hopes he does.

Chapter Seventeen

On Thursday, Tucker shows up for Western civ, but other than offering me a sad smile when he walks in, he doesn't pay any attention to me for the rest of the class. When the hour's over, he leaves before I can say anything to him. Not that I would. He made his choice. I won't beg him.

I don't want to arrive at Panera early, but it's like a sickness and I can't help myself. I'm not sure what I'll find. Will Tucker be early again? Will he even show at all?

But he's here. Waiting outside. The day is overcast, and his hands are stuffed under his armpits. He turns his head toward me, but there's no smile this time. Only sorrow and disappointment.

He opens the door for me, and we walk inside without saying a word. I head straight for our usual table, but Tucker goes up to the counter and returns with coffees and a bagel for me. I look up at him, and he stares back, his face expressionless, as though he's waiting for my reaction.

The events of yesterday come rushing back in to my head. My eyes well with tears. Tucker's eyes widen before he slides into the booth seat next to me, wrapping an arm around my back and pulling my head to his chest.

"Scarlett. I'm sorry."

I have no idea what he's sorry for—for my tears, for his unwillingness to take a chance on me—I only know that when he holds me close, the anxiety is gone even if the pain remains. For the last nine years, since my first panic attack, I've searched everywhere for a way to ease the panic. And here it is with Tucker.

Where is the justice in that?

We sit like this for a long time, like the night outside my apartment. Tucker presses his cheek to my temple.

"Are you better?"

I could tell him no, in hope that he'll hold me longer, but I refuse to lie to him. Especially him. Even if it gets me what I want most in the world. "Yes."

"Want to talk about it?"

What is there to say? He told me what he wanted yesterday. There's nothing to discuss. "I think we should get started with your lesson. We're already late getting started, thanks to me."

"Scarlett..."

I shake my head as he watches me. "Don't."

He nods and moves across the table, pulling his books out of his bag.

I reach for my coffee, and my hand shakes. *Damn it*. The stress of this week is destroying all the progress I've made in the last two years. All this time, I thought that if I worked hard enough at school I'd graduate and get the perfect job, and then I'd be totally self-sufficient and never need anyone to make me feel complete. My mother spent my entire life running after men, trying to find one who would take care of her. Admittedly, most were losers, but there were a few who were kind to me and stuck around long enough to fill in for the father I'd never known but always longed for. Yet every time I got attached one of them and relied on them to be part of my life, Momma soon moved onto *greener pastures,* and I was left with a giant hole in my heart. It didn't take long to see that I couldn't count on anyone or anything to stay with me. My life is a revolving door for people. I've accepted this, and despite my occasional dating attempts, I'm prepared to live my life alone.

What Tucker doesn't know is that I don't expect him to stay. I don't expect anyone to stay.

His hand covers mine, and I realize I'm looking out the window, crying. He wipes my tears from my cheeks and stares at me, his face unreadable.

He doesn't say anything, and my heart is breaking into pieces. How can I feel this way about someone I just met a few weeks ago? Perhaps it's because for the first time in my entire life, I'm not invisible.

Panic swims in his eyes when my tears still flow. "I think I get this part." He points to his notebook. "Do you want to work on something of your own?"

I pull out my own books, starting to freak out that I've spent so much time crying about my love life, or at least my pathetic attempts at it, that I've lost valuable study time for my math test on Friday. And when I have attempted to study, I've been unable to focus. I take several deep breaths. I need to calm down.

His hand reaches across the table and covers mine, and I close my eyes.

"I'm sorry," I push out. "I have a test tomorrow, and I'm not nearly ready."

"You'll do fine, Scarlett."

I open my eyes and search his face. His smile is full of confidence and pride.

"How can you possibly know that?"

He turns serious, his thumb stroking the back of my hand. "Because I believe you can do anything you set your mind to."

I bite my lip, uncertain how to respond. How can this boy I've known such a short time have more faith in me than my own family? More faith than anyone who's ever been part of my life?

How can he expect me to sit here with him when he admits he wants to be with me, yet refuses to do anything about it? I'd rather he take a chance and break my heart than tease me with something I can never have.

I close my books and pick up my bag. "I can't do this." I shake my head, and my fingers tremble as I try to open the clasp of my pack. "I thought I could, but I just can't. It hurts too much." Maybe I look like a fool telling him that, but I promised myself I'd be honest with him. If I'm telling him goodbye, he deserves to know why.

His face pales, and he reaches for my hand. I close my eyes as he cradles my palm, waiting for him to say something. Anything.

I wait for at least ten seconds.

Maybe we can be friends later, but for now, I need some distance. I pull my hand from his. My trembling fingers struggle to shove my books in my bag. Then I stand, hesitating. Giving him one last chance before I walk away.

He looks up at me in horror but remains silent.

My only thought is that I need to escape to the sanctuary of my room. I've held it together as long as I can. I walk as calmly as possible out to my car, but my fingers fumble with my keys. Frustration wells up in me, adding to my heaping pile of pain and fear, and a sob escapes. Why can't I open the damn door? It's such a simple thing. It's a fucking door, but I can't even do that right.

I can't ever do anything right. My own mother doesn't want me. Why would I think someone else would?

I've always known I'd be alone. How is it that for years I've accepted that fate without qualm, yet a few weeks with Tucker makes that feel like a death sentence?

More tears blur my eyes, and the keyhole is impossible to see. I need to calm down. I need to get myself together and get out of here before I make a fool of myself.

"Scarlett, wait." Tucker is behind me and wraps his arms around my stomach, pulling my back to his chest.

I lean my head against him and try to catch my breath. "You can't have it both ways, Tucker. It's not fair." Even as I say the words, I realize how ridiculous they are. Nothing in life is fair. I'm not naïve enough to believe in fairness, yet I'm insisting on it anyway. But this is something within my control, as limited as it is. And Tucker's right. I'm all about control.

"I know." His voice is heavy and choked. But he doesn't say anything else, and I know his answer. I've known it all along. He made it perfectly clear yesterday. Maybe Jason is right. Maybe Tucker is afraid to get close to me, and the only way he can handle it is to keep me at arm's length. I can't make him want me, and I'd rather be alone for the rest of my life than beg him. The choice is his. Unfortunately for me, he's already made it.

Taking a deep breath, some of my hysteria evaporates, leaving cold determination in its wake. I gently push Tucker's hands down and unlock my car. He doesn't stop me, and I have no idea what he's thinking or feeling because I refuse to look in his face. I start the car and grip the steering wheel. *You can do this.*

And I can. Even if it kills any hope of ever being loved in the process.

I back up and drive away, Tucker still standing where I left him. I watch him in my mirror until I turn the corner and he's gone.

With a shaky voice, I utter the word he begged me not to say, but I need to say it now because I need the closure. "Goodbye."

I call in sick to the math lab, and go home with the intention of studying. Instead, I lie on the bed and take a nap. When I wake up an hour later, I'm still depressed, but my head has cleared enough for me to study.

Caroline comes home and finds me in my room, huddled over my desk. "Why aren't you at work?"

I offer her a grim smile. "I have a big test tomorrow. I need to study so I called in sick."

Her eyes widen. "*You* called in sick when you're not?"

I offer her a teasing smile, but I'm sure she can see it's forced. "Maybe you don't know me as well as you think you do."

"Apparently not. I just found out from Tina that Tucker beat up Daniel in The Higher Ground yesterday." She's upset that I didn't tell her. It's thinly veiled, but there all the same.

"Tucker did not beat up Daniel. It was one punch."

She throws up her hands. "*Only one punch*? But it was over you, right?"

I sigh in exasperation. "What do you want me to say, Caroline? Daniel was making rude statements about me, and Tucker overheard."

"But Tuck—"

"Let's get this out in the open: No, I'm not going on another date with Daniel. No, Tucker and I aren't seeing each other. In fact, this afternoon, I quit being his tutor." I tilt my head to the side. "Now is there anything else you want to know?" I don't know why I'm taking my anger out on her. None of this is Caroline's fault.

She sags against the door frame, offering me a sad smile. "Is it true Tucker's brother came to see you yesterday?"

Tina and her big freaking mouth. "Yes, but it doesn't matter one way or the other. I quit, remember?"

"Yeah," she says softly. "How are you doing with all of this? That's a lot for you to deal with."

"I'm fine." I look down at my desk. "I just need to concentrate on this test tomorrow."

"Are you hungry? I can make you some mac and cheese."

I release a soft laugh. Comfort food. "Yeah. Thanks."

She hangs on the door jamb, kneading her lower lip with her teeth. "I'm sorry about Daniel."

I don't look up. "It's not your fault. Nothing for you to be sorry about."

"But I pushed you..." Her voice trails off.

I lift my eyes to hers. "You didn't know. And we both know how resistant I am to trying new situations. I need you to push me some-times. If Daniel had been great, I would have thanked you for it later."

After she leaves the room, I find a groove working the problems on my study guide. I stay up to three in the morning, studying. I hope it's enough. My concentration is off, and my mind keeps wandering to this afternoon. If I close my eyes I can feel Tucker's arms wrapped around me, not that it matters. Tucker let me go.

I suppose it's better to find out now. Before my heart is broken anymore.

Chapter Eighteen

On Friday night, it's Caroline's turn to be nervous. She has another date with the guy she went out with on Sunday. This is the first guy she's dated since she broke up with Justin in the fall. Honestly, I'm surprised it's taken her this long. Caroline is cute and outgoing. People love her, especially guys. But she cocooned within herself for a few months, emerging into this new, more self-reliant woman. A broken bone sets and becomes stronger than it was before. Perhaps this will happen to me. Perhaps I'll emerge from this situation, stronger and more confident. Seeing Caroline so happy makes me believe maybe I can be happy, too. Someday.

"You can come to the party, Scarlett. Tina says she'll swing by and pick you up."

I shake my head. "I'm exhausted, and I don't want to run into Daniel."

"He might not even be there."

"True, but I can't take any more drama right now. Maybe in a few weeks." I'm surprised to discover that I mean it.

"You should be celebrating passing your test today, not sitting home pouting."

"First of all, I'm not pouting. And second, I don't know that I did well, I only think that I did."

She waves her left hand while her right hand puts on a touch-up coat of mascara. "Please."

"Besides, I have an exciting evening planned with my abacus."

Her eyes widen as she stares at my reflection in the bathroom mirror.

I grin. "Or maybe I'll order a pizza and watch a movie on Netflix instead."

"Now you're getting wild and crazy."

Lifting an eyebrow, I laugh. "I know, right?"

Her date arrives, and Caroline leaves me instructions like I'm the babysitter staying with her kids. Even though my mood has lifted some, she's still worried about leaving me.

"Caroline," I groan. "Go already."

When her date gets her out the door, I actually consider going to bed. I'm exhausted but it's only nine-thirty. If I go to sleep now I'll be up around six on a Saturday morning. I'm not one to sleep in, but that's ridiculously early, even for me.

The apartment is too quiet without her, and the emotions of the week make the walls of the apartment close in. I grab my coat and head down the stairs, stopping midway to face the half-empty parking lot. I sit on a step, leaning over my knees and breathing in the fresh air.

Sitting outside, especially at night, has always helped clear my head. When I was growing up, and the fighting and the drinking got to be too much, I'd escape to the stairs out the back door of our trailer. Old habits die hard. The apartment is fairly quiet, but the outdoors has become ingrained as a partial cure for my unease. The cold from the concrete seeps through my jeans, but I ignore it as I take in deep, steady breaths.

I rest my head against the railing and close my eyes. The rational part of me assures the irrational part that life will go on without Tucker Price, and I know for a fact that it will. But that doesn't ease the pain of him being ripped from my life.

I hear a thud below me and open my eyes with a gasp.

Tucker is standing at the foot of the stairs.

He's been running again, wearing shorts and a sweatshirt. He's out of breath, and his shoulders rise and fall as he watches me.

Neither of us speak. The parking lot light washes half his face with a pale glow, but his expression is unreadable. He looks as though he's waiting for something. Is he waiting for me? He knows what I want. It's up to him.

He moves to the stairs, climbing them slowly until he's several steps down, squatting in front of me. "Do you know why I'm here?" he asks, his voice husky.

I shake my head, unable to find the words to answer.

"Everything just feels so right when I'm with you, Scarlett. I can be me. But it's more than that. You give me something I haven't had in a long time, if ever. You give me peace. It's like the jumbled mess in my head can settle down, and I can be still with you. Like none of the other stuff matters." His voice catches, and he swallows. "I had a bad day and usually I'd get shitfaced drunk, but the only thing I could think of was I had to see you."

"Me, too," I whisper, tears blurring my vision.

He takes a deep breath and closes his eyes. His tension washes away, then a grin tugs at the corners of his mouth. "You wanted to get shitfaced drunk?"

A soft laugh escapes. "No, you give me peace." I say the words, reinforcing how true they really are. When I'm with Tucker, my life makes sense.

He turns serious. "I don't want to hurt you, Scarlett. I tried to stay away from you, but I need you too much."

"Maybe I'll hurt you," I whisper as my eyes search his. "I'm broken, Tucker. I'm hopelessly broken inside, and I'm not sure there are enough pieces in me to put back together. But when I'm with you, I feel like maybe I can actually be whole."

I expect him to look at me with pity or disgust, but instead his eyes are full of desire. "That scares the hell out of me, Scarlett. I don't want to break you more," he murmurs, standing and pulling me to my feet. His left hand slides down my jaw to my neck.

"You'll break me more if you turn around and leave."

His lips find mine, tentative at first, as though he took my words to heart and he's afraid I'll shatter if he's not gentle. His tongue works slow magic on my lips before discovering the inside of my mouth. He's slow and tender, coaxing my tongue to join his.

My stomach tingles, and an ache deep inside my abdomen catches me by surprise.

I release a tiny gasp, and Tucker wraps an arm around my back, pressing me to his chest. His mouth is more insistent, and I'm light-headed as we stand on the steps.

His hand slips in the opening of my coat. I tense slightly as his fingers rest on my waist, but he wraps his arm around my back, his palm between my shoulder blades.

I reach behind his neck, one hand burying in his hair while the other pulls his mouth harder against mine. I'm breathless with anticipation and longing.

Encouraged, his lips are more demanding, and he presses so tightly against me that I can hardly move.

I have never wanted anything more.

I pull away from him and worry wrinkles his brow, but I offer him a gentle smile and take his hand, tugging him up the stairs to my apartment. When he shuts the door behind us, he watches me with fear in his eyes.

What is Tucker afraid of?

I'm about to ask him when he slides my coat off my shoulders and slides it down my arms, throwing it onto the sofa. Smiling softly, I take his hand again and lead him down the hall.

When he walks into my tiny room, he seems too big and out of place. He moves to the nightstand and turns on the lamp, filling the room with a soft glow. I close the door and press my back against it.

"Where's Caroline?" he asks, hesitant.

"Gone. To a party." My nerves make me breathless. For once I don't mind my nervous jitters.

I step toward him, and he pulls me to his chest, one hand behind my head and the other pressing on my back. I'm flush against him as he kisses me with pent-up longing . I wrap my arms around his neck. "I can't believe you're here."

"I shouldn't be here, Scarlett," he mumbles against my lips. "Send me home."

My response is to kiss him back. He makes me feel alive. His touch makes my body respond the way it's never responded before. Kissing him fills me with an ache for more.

I step back and grab the bottom of his sweatshirt, lifting up. I get it partway before he pulls it over his head and tosses it over the back of my desk chair. His t-shirt is next. I start to remove it, but he finishes, tossing it to the side as well.

He's bare from the waist up, and he's gorgeous. I knew his arms were muscular, but I had no idea the rest of him was so toned. I reach for his shoulder, wanting to trace the outline of his well-defined muscles. His eyes sink closed as my fingers travel across his shoulders, and down his arms, then back up to explore his chest. His arms hang to his side, but his fingers twitch.

His hands reach up for my shirt, unbuttoning the top button and working their way down until my shirt is hanging open. He pulls it off and throws it where his clothes went. His hands find my waist and skim my ribs as he stares into my eyes, searching for something.

He unhooks my bra and lets the straps slide over my shoulders and down my arms. Now we're both naked from the waist up.

One hand reaches behind my neck as his mouth lowers to mine. His other hand cups my breast and fondles it, sending a jolt to my core. I moan, and he becomes more insistent, with both his hand and his mouth.

I want to cry with happiness. Tucker is here with me, partially naked in my room, and he's making my body feel more alive than I ever thought possible.

"I'm trying to go slow for you, Scarlett," he groans, his lips moving down to my neck. "But if you keep making noises like that, I'm liable to rip the rest of your clothes off and finish this too soon." His teeth lightly graze my skin and his tongue follows.

If he's trying to stop my sounds, he's taking the wrong path. Another moan escapes and he reaches for the button on my jeans and zipper, quickly undoing both and pulling my jeans over my hips. I step out of my slippers as well as my pants, suddenly self-conscious that I'm standing in front of Tucker wearing only a pair of panties.

His eyes are on me as he kicks off his shoes and removes his shorts. He leaves on his underwear, as if he knows I need to take this in slow, manageable steps. But I don't find that surprising. He's always seen through me. Seen who I am and what I need.

It's one of many reasons I'm drawn to him. This man has the capability to help me heal.

I've only known him a few weeks, yet long enough to know it's true. Still, I keep the revelation to myself. Tucker may be willing to risk his heart coming to me tonight, but I have no doubt that a declaration of anything deep and meaningful will send him running.

I know he'll run at some point. I'm only trying to hold onto him as long as I can.

His hand gently lifts my chin as he gazes into my eyes, worry etching his brow. "Hey, where'd you go?"

I smile. "I'm here."

"No, you left me for a moment." He pulls me to his chest. "We don't have to do this, Scarlett. We don't have to have sex for me to stay."

I shake my head. "No, I want this." He makes my body feel everything I've hoped was possible, and I want it all before he walks out of my life. Ten years from now, I don't want to regret that I didn't share this with him.

"But—"

I reach for his neck and pull his mouth to mine, kissing him so that there's no question of what I want. It's the permission he needs, and he pushes me down on the bed, kissing me as he lies next to me.

His hand splays on my abdomen. My muscles tighten in anticipation. His breath is on my neck, and his mouth trails kisses on my neck and chest. When his mouth finds my breast, I gasp, and my hips rise off the bed. His hand on my stomach pushes me down, then slides lower over my panties.

I gasp for air as I'm bombarded by feelings I've only dreamed of. I'm not a virgin, although I'm far from experienced. Both guys I slept with before were inept and awkward. Tucker is neither. But it's more than that. For the first time in my life, I truly trust someone. I trust him enough to completely give myself to him. The irony that it's Tucker Price I've chosen to trust isn't lost on me.

His head raises, and he looks into my face. I pull his mouth to mine, needing more, needing him.

He pulls my panties down, then rises on his elbow and takes them off the rest of the way. I'm naked, exposed. But this is Tucker, and he stares at me with awe and longing, and it makes me want so much more. Sex, yes, but something more meaningful.

His hand slides between my legs as he kisses me again. I reach down and feel him through his underwear, and he moans. "Scarlett."

Then he gets up, and panic washes through me. Has he changed his mind? I push up on my elbows to see him sitting on the side of the bed, taking off his underwear. He reaches to the floor, digging in his shorts. When he turns around, holding a foil square, he sees my face and tenses. His free hand cups my face and lowers his mouth to mine, pushing me back down on the bed. "Relax. I'm not going anywhere."

I look up at him and smile.

His mouth finds my breast while his hand is between my legs again. An ache builds deep inside, begging to be filled. I lift my hips up as I gasp, "Tucker. I want you."

He's gone again, but this time he's putting on a condom, then positioning himself between my legs. He braces his arms on either side of my head and stares into my eyes. I close my eyes, wanting to feel every second of this. To make it last forever in my memory, if this is the only chance I get with him.

"Scarlett, open your eyes."

I do as he says, looking up at him with confusion.

His eyes burn bright with desire. "I want you to see me when I come into you. I want you to know I'm here. I want you to know I see you."

His words spin my world upside down. He knows. He knows me and my fear, even though I've never said it. My gaze is locked on his as he enters me, slow and gentle. When he's all the way in, his pace picks up and a knot of desperate need grows deep inside me. I need more of him. I tilt my pelvis up, and he sinks deeper, his eyes rolling back into his head. Then his gaze returns to mine. I'm climbing, and I'm spinning out of control.

His hand brushes my hair out of my face. I need more. So much more. "Tucker, please."

My words set something loose, and he kisses me and everything moves faster. His breath is hot on the side of my face. I cling to him, needing him deeper until finally, I'm falling off a cliff, and I call out his name in a strangled voice.

He's close behind me, grunting. Then he kisses me, his mouth demanding, claiming, as though what we just did wasn't enough to bind us together.

There's a crack in the armor encasing my heart. I've handed Tucker the opportunity to get closer to me than anyone has ever gotten.

Or I've given him the opportunity to destroy me.

Chapter Nineteen

When I wake, I'm lying on my side with Tucker pressed against my back. He's kissing my neck while his hand cups my breast. I suck in a breath and he chuckles, his chest vibrating my body.

"Good morning," he murmurs.

"We can say good morning but not goodbye?"

His mouth slows and his hand freezes. I've pushed him too far, although I don't know how. He rolls me to my back and looks into my face, concern drawing down his eyebrows. Then his eyes light up with understanding. "You need rules."

I tense. "What?"

"You need rules to help everything make sense. Especially with me. I keep you guessing and ungrounded."

I don't know how to respond.

"I've been watching you, Scarlett. Taking mental inventory of what makes you tick."

I laugh. "That sounds slightly creepy."

He looks taken aback, then shakes his head. "No, I've been trying to figure out why you're different. Why I can trust you when I don't trust anyone else."

There's that word again. Trust. How is it that we both feel the same way? "And what did you come up with?"

His fingertips slide gently down my cheek to my lips. His index finger glides across my bottom lip and his gaze fixates on it. Then his eyes rise to mine as his hand slides down to my neck. "It's your soul. You have an old soul. I can see it lurking deep inside your eyes. I wasn't joking when I told you I feel peace with you. My life is a fucked-up mess. It has been for years, but when I'm with you, I feel like I can breathe. Like I matter for something else besides what everyone wants from me."

I blink with understanding. That's exactly how I feel with him.

Tucker smiles. "But you need rules to make you feel safe and protected. So I'll give you rules, even though I've always hated them in the past. Then again, maybe that's my problem." He gives me an ornery grin. "First rule. No saying goodbye, never goodbye. Especially with you." He leans over and kisses me, long and slow. "Goodbye is too permanent. Goodbye has the risk of never seeing each other again. But *good morning* is full of possibilities."

"Who knew you were a romantic?"

His hand trails lower, between my breasts, stroking lighting over my breastbone and making me tense with anticipation. "I don't show this side of me to anyone. I can be me with you."

"Me, too," I whisper.

He smiles, his eyes full of happiness and possibilities. "We were made for each other, Scarlett." His hand cups my breast as his thumb finds a task of its own and I gasp. He studies my face. "You need rules for your life to make sense. But I've ignored most rules so I could find a way to survive."

I'm trying to concentrate on his words despite the onslaught to my senses.

"The thing about rules is that they can keep you safe, but box you in so you can't truly live life. We'll have to find a way to meet in the middle."

I stare into his face, stunned that he's willing to become this serious about us so fast.

His eyes darken. "Just remember that the goodbye rule always applies. Always."

He makes it sound like what we have between us could be permanent. Like we have the chance of a future together. I can't let my heart count on that. Even before Jason told me Tucker was incapable of staying with someone, I knew it was true. But now, I can't help wondering if that's the other Tucker. The Tucker he shows to the world. Maybe the real him *is* capable of staying with me.

"I don't want you to think I'm weird," I say, looking over his shoulder at the window. "I don't mean to be a control freak."

He kisses me gently. "Scarlett, that's not what I meant."

I look up at him. "I know." Can I trust him with my past? If I want a chance of something real with him, I have to share all of me, my pain included. "My mom was a terrible parent, and I never knew my dad. He ran off when I was two. I grew up in a trailer park in Shelbyville with my mom and my little sister. My mom was a drunk. She lived off of welfare and was always looking for a man to save her. Momma saw my sister and me as a burden, except for the extra welfare she got because we were dependents. Most of my clothes came from the Goodwill, and we had subsidized lunches. I didn't care about any of that, not really. It was just stuff. I just wanted my mother to love me."

I pause and take a breath. "I've taken care of myself since before I can remember, and my sister, too. Momma never cared about my grades or what I wanted. There were no extracurricular activities, except for the few years my elementary school teacher gave me free piano lessons after school. Momma told me I was full of myself wanting to go off to college because I thought I was somebody." I turn to him. "I started having anxiety issues when I was in middle school, after one of Momma's boyfriends lived with us and beat her."

Tucker's hand tenses on my stomach. "Did he ever hit you or your sister?"

I hesitate for several seconds. "Once. He hit me once, but my teacher noticed my bruises the next day and called the police. Momma kicked him out soon after that, not because she wanted to keep my sister and me safe, but because she was worried we'd get sent to foster care and she'd lose our welfare."

"That can't be true."

I knew what he was saying. What parent could be so callous? I look into his eyes, my shoulders tensing. "She told me herself, Tucker. She was furious with me for my teacher turning her boyfriend in."

"She had to love you, Scarlett, even if it was in her own way."

"My mother is incapable of loving anyone or anything."

He's quiet for a moment, and his voice lowers into a soothing whisper. "You're not her. You're not your mother."

I gasp as I look into his eyes, shocked that he can see my secret fear. That I'm so broken I'm incapable of loving someone. The fact I never felt anything with men before had always confirmed it. Before Tucker. Tucker makes me think anything is possible.

"I went to therapy after I came to Southern, and my therapist said my life before was so out of control that I created my own boundaries to feel safe." I suck in my lower lip. "That's why I'm the way I am."

He leans down and kisses me with possessiveness, as though he's about to lose me, and he wants to make every second count. I kiss him back, his urgency pushing at my own fear. If he sticks around, will I always feel this way? Will I worry that each time together could be our last?

We make love in a frenzy of fear and desire.

Afterward, when I lie in his arms, I realize that every intimate moment I spend with him chips away my protective shield. I'm handing myself to him and he eagerly takes, but he's holding part of himself back. He's still hiding himself from me.

Tucker sits up and leans forward. My fingers explore his back and I find small, circular dimpled scars on his lower back and bottom.

He jerks when I touch one and swings his head around to me, his eyes hardened. "Don't."

Pain pierces my heart, not because Tucker has hurt my feelings, but because I know what caused his scars. I climb to my knees and put my hand on his cheek, staring into his eyes. I place a gentle kiss on his lips.

I have no idea about the circumstances of his scars, but the fact that his lower back and butt cheeks are scattered with cigarette burns explains so much. Tucker is as broken as I am. Maybe more.

He realizes that I know and panic fills his eyes, but I gently hold his face in my hands. I kiss him with tenderness and love.

"Don't feel sorry for me, Scarlett." His voice chokes.

I lean back and search his eyes, hoping he sees deep into mine and knows I'm telling the truth. "I don't feel sorry for you, Tucker. I feel sorry for the little boy who had to endure that." I slide one hand over his shoulder and down his back.

"But you *do* feel sorry for me?" His entire body tenses, and I realize I run the risk of sending him away from me. But I also realize that I have the chance to help him heal, to escape the horrors of his childhood, just as I hope he can help me escape mine.

"Only that you feel unworthy of being loved."

He inhales sharply. "Don't psychoanalyze me."

So much makes sense now. "Yet you can psychoanalyze me?" I say it softly and full of love so there's no way he can misinterpret my meaning.

I straddle his lap, resting my hands on his shoulders. We're both naked except for the sheet over his lower half. His hands encircle my waist, and it feels automatic instead of intentional. Like he needs to hold onto me to ground himself.

"I have no idea what you've been through, Tucker, and I won't push you. Not now, but I've shared some of my past. You know I won't judge you."

His eyes widen and flash with anger, then tears, which seem to catch him by surprise.

The burning lump in my throat makes it nearly impossible to speak. "I've tried to put my past behind me, but it's always there.

Always taunting me. It's holding me back. I can see that now. And I think yours is holding you back, too."

He shakes his head, closing his eyes. "I can't think about it."

"At some point, I think you need to. Just like I do." I wrap my arms around his back and hold him. He leans his head on my shoulder, and we sit like this so long that I'm sure his legs must have gone to sleep from my weight, but when I try to move, his arms tighten and keep me in place.

I'm still shaken by the pain and abuse in Tucker's past. How it contradicts the person he pretends to be with everyone else.

"You don't know what I've been through, Scarlett. What I've done."

I lean back and look into his eyes. "Tell me. I want to know."

He shakes his head. "No. Never. I don't want to risk losing you."

"I'm not going anywhere."

His head lifts, and his hand grabs the back of my hair and pulls my head back so I'm looking into his eyes. They are full of dark fury, and I inhale with a moment of fear. His mouth is rough as he kisses me. He's punishing me for pushing boundaries I didn't know existed, but even so, I know he'll never hurt me. I know this deep in my soul.

He yanks the sheet and flips me over, pinning me to the bed. He's hard against my belly and I'm not surprised when he lifts my hips and enters me in one big push.

I cry out his name before his mouth covers mine, hard and demanding. He's exorcising his demons and I offer myself to him, feeling myself climb with him. He's already helped me with my own fears. I'm grateful for the chance to help him face his.

It doesn't take long for either of us, despite the fact it hasn't been long since we had sex earlier. He collapses next to me, his arms tightening around me and holding me tight to his chest.

"Oh, God, Scarlett." Panic is in his voice and he pulls me back to look into his eyes. "Did I hurt you?"

"No." I stroke his cheek with my fingers.

"If I hurt you—"

I kiss his chin. "I'm fine."

He pulls me to him again. "I'll hurt you. I hurt everyone I touch."

My hand rubs his arm. I hesitate, worried my response will send him into another panic. I don't think Tucker is willing to accept good things in his life, which makes it all the more surprising that he caved and came to me last night. "No, Tucker. You help make me whole."

His arm around my back tightens. "I have to go." Regret is heavy in his voice. "I have mandatory team training today."

"It's okay." I kiss him to prove that it is.

"I don't want to leave you. Once I walk out that door, the real world takes over." Disgust drenches his words.

"Don't let it. You're stronger than that."

He shakes his head. "I wish I were, but I'm not."

"Yes, you are. You're stronger than you realize."

He places a gentle kiss on my mouth. "I don't deserve you."

I want to tell him that he does, that he deserves so much more, but he's already running from me. To tell him that will send him farther away. Instead, I say, "Thank you."

He looks down at me, confusion knitting his brow. "For what?"

I want to tell him that his tenderness is my undoing, that his concern for my emotional well-being over everything else is the most precious gift anyone has ever given me. I want to tell him that for the first time ever I think maybe I can love someone, really love someone and maybe, just maybe they might love me, too. But I'm not sure he's ready to hear it, and I know I'm not ready to say it, so I smile and kiss him tenderly. "You give me hope."

He kisses me back, and it tastes of promise and optimism. Tenderness and devotion. He sighs and pushes off the bed, reaching for his clothes. He's stepping into his shorts when he looks back at me. "I can skip this practice. I don't feel right leaving."

I remember Jason reminding me of Tucker's precarious situation and how he saw me as the blame. "No, Tucker. I'm fine. Go." I get up and put on my robe.

After he puts on his sweatshirt and ties his shoes he stands and pulls me to his chest, smoothing my hair from my face, gentleness in his eyes. "I'll call you later, okay?"

I nod and stand on my tiptoes to press a kiss against his lips.

His face twists in agony and he groans, dropping his hold on my arms and opening the bedroom door.

I follow him down the hall and into the living room. "Tucker, since you ran here last night, do you want me to drive you home?"

He shakes his head. "The run will do me good. Help me psych myself up for training." He leans over and kisses me one more time, then leaves. I stand in the open doorway, watching him go. Unease squirms in my stomach as he fades from sight. I'm pragmatic enough to know my future with him is murky.

Caroline groans behind me. "Oh, dear God. Please tell me I didn't just see what I thought I saw."

I close the door and turn around to face her. How do I explain this to her? How do I explain it to anyone else when I can barely explain it to myself? "Caroline."

Pain and anger contort her face, then disappointment, disappointment in me. Tears fill her eyes along with fear. She's terrified for me. "He'll hurt you, Scarlett. And not just hurt you. He'll destroy you."

I don't answer. I already know he will.

Chapter Twenty

Later in the afternoon, Tucker calls and tells me that he has a mandatory team meeting Saturday night. "I'm sorry, Scarlett." But I'm sure I hear relief in his voice.

"I never told you that you had to see me, Tucker. It's okay." I know I sound a little defensive, and I hate it.

He's silent. "I'll call you tomorrow."

"Okay." I try to be as nice as possible and not let my disappointment show. I'm not disappointed that I won't see him. I'm disappointed that he's running away from me already, because I'm sure that's what this is.

Thankfully, Caroline doesn't bring up Tucker again. I think she hopes he was just a bad dream instigated by her hangover.

After my phone call, Caroline is eager to get out of the apartment. I'm sure she's figured out what it was about. "Let's do something tonight."

"Like what?" My defenses are up. I can already tell it will probably be something out of my comfort zone.

"Let's go dancing."

"I don't dance."

"What happened to your trying new things?"

"Look how well that's worked out for me," I say dryly.

Caroline scowls. "Just because you had one bad experience doesn't mean you should give up." I'm not sure if she's referring to Daniel, Tucker, or both.

Before I know it, Tina is involved and the two of them nag me mercilessly until I agree. This is a terrible idea. First of all, the crowd will be too much for me to handle. I'll have to drink to be able to stay. Second, I know I'm attractive enough when I put some effort into my hair, makeup, and clothing. I'll attract attention, and I really don't feel like dancing with other guys and fending off their advances. Tucker and I have made no commitment. We haven't discussed being exclusive, but I can't go from what we experienced during the last twenty-four hours to seeking the attention of other guys.

We decide to splurge and actually go out to dinner before we go dancing, but I'm distracted while we eat, and Tina orders us drinks from a bartender she knows working in the bar. She hands one to me. "Here. You're making *me* jumpy."

I take the tall glass full of brown liquid. "What is it?"

"Does it matter? It's alcohol. Drink."

I take a sip, surprised I can't taste much alcohol. "You could have left me at home."

"Nope." Caroline shakes her head, sipping her drink. "No staying home and pouting for you. I left you home pouting last night and found Tucker Price in your bed. Again."

Tina spurts her drink over the table. "*What?*"

My stomach knots, and I shoot Caroline a glare. What happened with Tucker isn't what she thinks, but then I understand her reasoning. Tucker sleeps around. Why would she assume my experience was anything different?

Then again, why would *I* assume our experience was anything different?

Several hours have elapsed since this morning, and I can't help but wonder if I'm fooling myself into believing there was more there than a hookup. While I know I have to be prepared for it, I can't face that possibility tonight. Maybe tomorrow, but not tonight.

I sigh as Tina waits for an explanation. "The first time was that night I took him home from the party a couple of weeks ago, he passed out in my bed after I brought him to my apartment to clean up his hands. Nothing happened."

Her eyebrows rise as a grin spreads across her face. "And last night?"

I blush.

Her eyes widen with excitement, and she leans forward. "Was he good?"

I don't feel like discussing Tucker's sexual proficiency, or whether it was a one-night fling or something more.

Caroline grimaces. "From what I heard in my room this morning, it was pretty damn hot."

My mouth drops open in horror. "*You heard us?*"

She rolls her eyes in disgust. "Our walls are paper-thin. Of course I heard you."

Tina picks up my glass and hands it to me. "Drink this."

I grab the glass with shaky fingers and drink several generous gulps.

Tina turns to Caroline. "Now what did you hear?"

I gasp. "Are you *insane*? Why would you ask that?"

"Because Tucker's not the least bit interested in me so I'll have to live vicariously through you." I start to put my glass down, but she makes me lift it back up. "Drink some more. You'll be less mortified."

Against my better judgment, I obey her order. I'm already nervous, and we haven't even gotten to the club yet. I'm seriously regretting this decision.

Tina waves her hand to the bartender and points to me, waggling her eyebrows, then turns to Caroline. "Details."

Caroline scowls and shakes her head. "No freaking way. I'm trying my best to purge it from my mind."

The waitress brings another drink and sets it in front of me.

Tina turns her attention on me. "You're nervous, right? I want you to have fun tonight. You're too worked up most of the time. Now the fact that you fucked Tucker Price—"

"Tina!" I hiss.

"—is a step in the right direction to getting your freak on. But you skipped a bunch of steps you need to go back and hit tonight."

Caroline leans over the table and takes my hand. "I agree with Tina, except for the fucking-Tucker part." She shoots Tina a glare. "Don't encourage her." She turns back to me. "You need to relax and have fun. If you need a little alcohol to help you do it, so be it." She points to my glass.

I feel like they're trying to force cough syrup down my throat, except my drink tastes nothing like cough syrup. In fact, it hardly tastes like alcohol at all, yet I'm feeling pretty buzzed. "What is this?" I ask taking another sip.

Guilt washes over Tina's face. "Long Island Iced Tea."

"What?" I set the glass on the table knowing I'm going to be drunk very, very soon. But then again, what's the harm in that? I'll pay for it tomorrow, but tonight I want to forget everything. Forget Tucker and all my past. I want to forget about my carefully plotted life, and I just want to have fun like everyone else. I shake my head. "You know what? Who cares? My goal tonight is to get drunk." I bring the glass to my lips and take several swallows.

Tina's eyes light up. "Well, look at you. You go, girl."

Caroline doesn't look as ecstatic about my announcement, but I realize Tina and I are on opposite ends of extremes—Tina's the wild child, and I'm the boring one. Caroline straddles the center line. For me to skip right over Caroline into Tina's territory is shocking. Ordinarily, I would ask myself if this was a good idea, but I have enough alcohol floating around in my bloodstream to shove aside any concerns.

For once in my sorry life, I'm going to have fun.

I finish my drink, and Tina drives us to the club. I've never been here before, but Caroline used to go here with her ex-boyfriend, and I know Tina frequents the place. She's tried to get me to come with her half a dozen times. She's had a fake ID ready for me for months.

We're not wearing coats, and although I'm wearing Caroline's sequined sleeveless shirt and a skirt, I'm not as cold as I would be without the alcohol. We walk across the parking lot, and when a couple enters the building, loud music blares from the doorway. I wobble across the asphalt on Caroline's borrowed heels, already feeling the rhythm soak into my bones.

Caroline shoots me a weird look. "Tina, we have to take turns watching her tonight."

Tina scrunches her nose. "Whatever for? She's a big girl. You have to let our baby bird fly."

"She's so drunk she can hardly walk, and we're not even in the club yet."

I groan. "Sure, I'm pretty tipsy, but I'm having trouble walking because I'm wearing your three-inch stilettos." I point to my feet.

Caroline remains unconvinced. "You don't drink that often, and Tina filled you with enough alcohol to fuel an ethanol-powered car for fifty miles."

Tina shakes her head. "And you're telling me that you've never been drunk? Come on, Caroline."

"You know that's different," Caroline protests.

"Scarlett's smarter than you give her credit for. She's not that drunk, and we're in a public place. She'll be fine." Tina sighs. "But if you think she needs watching, you take the first shift."

After we pay to enter, Tina heads straight for the bar, and she and Caroline order drinks. I'm tipsy but not drunk. Contrary to what Caroline thinks, I'm no stranger to alcohol. You don't grow up in the home of an alcoholic and her friends and not become acquainted with it. I had my share of drinking binges in high school with the handful of people I hung out with. I just left it all behind in Shelbyville when I came to college.

Leaning against a tall table, I look around the room. We're on a raised level that surrounds a sunken square floor, which is half full of dancers. A DJ is set up on the opposite side of the room.

Tina comes back and hands me a drink. "There's a good selection to choose from tonight."

I turn to her in confusion.

"Guys. We're here to look for guys." She says it slowly as though I'm deaf, which I partially am from the roar of the music and the crowd.

"I thought we were here to dance."

Tina grins and sips her drink.

I taste mine and realize she's gotten me another Long Island Iced Tea. She doesn't just want me drunk. She wants me wasted.

Caroline stands next to me, swaying to the music. She leans toward my ear. "I trust you, you know. I just worry about you."

I give her a smile. "I know."

We stand at the table and finish our drinks, then Caroline grabs my wrist and tugs me toward the dance floor. We descend the stairs and stop close to the edge. Since I'm not used to wearing heels, and I'm on my way to being drunk, it takes me a second to regain my balance. Caroline begins to dance, watching me. I close my eyes, and let my body move to the music. The anxiety-ridden me, currently drowning in alcohol, claws to get out of this loud, crowded place. But I stuff her deeper while the newly liberated me basks in her freedom.

Someone stumbles into me, and I totter on my heels, but a hand grabs my elbow and helps me find my balance. My eyes fly open, and I see it's a guy I don't know, but he smiles and shouts. "Sorry."

In my fuzzy head, I recognize that I should be horrified and mortified, but this new me smiles.

I like the new me.

The guy stays next to me and dances, keeping his gaze on my body and my face.

An undercurrent of anxiousness prickles my nerves, but I decide to ignore him and dance. When the song ends, he leans close to my ear. "Want to get a drink?"

I'm still sober enough to question if this is good idea, but the liberated part of me shouts that he's asked me to get a drink, not sleep with him. I need to loosen up. "Sure."

We make our way to the bar, and I lean my elbow on the counter to steady myself. The loud noise is starting to make me restless, adding to the unease over the situation I find myself in now. My shoulders tense, and I tell myself this is not a big deal. Men buy women drinks all the time.

"I'm Ben," he says as he waves to the bartender halfway down the counter.

I force a small smile. "Scarlett."

The bartender stands in front of us, and Ben glances at me with a raised eyebrow.

I realize I need to slow down and be in control of the situation, contrary to Tina's plan, so I ask for a Diet Coke.

Ben orders a drink and speaks into my ear. "You come here often?"

It's a ridiculous pickup line, and I start to giggle. Some of my tension slides down my back, unknotting my shoulders in the process.

He gives me an odd look, but thankfully doesn't look offended.

I shake my head. "Nope. First time. What about you?"

"Every week."

I may be slightly drunk, but that tells me all I need to know. Not that I'm interested in him anyway. I'm here to appease Caroline and Tina. I have no idea what's going on with Tucker and me, but even if it's over before it's begun, I'm not ready to go out with someone else. My eyes scan the room looking for the girls. Caroline is still dancing, but Tina is at our table talking to a guy.

I look up at Ben, and he's handing me a glass with an expectant look. I realize he's asked me something. When I start to answer, I see Tucker behind Ben.

Tucker?

He's at the bar in the midst of a rowdy group of guys. I guess his mandatory team meeting included hanging out with his friends at a dance club. It's further confirmation that he's run away from me. From us. I'm not totally surprised, yet it still hurts, a dull ache that spreads throughout my body. He turns in my direction, and his eyes widen when he realizes I'm here, and he's been caught.

I give a little shake of my head to clear it. Tucker can do whatever the fuck he wants, even if that means giving up on us. I ignore the well of dismay bubbling deep in my gut and look up at Ben. "I'm sorry. What did you say?"

"I asked what you do."

"I'm a student at Southern. You?"

Before Ben can answer, Tucker is next to us, his face expressionless. "Scarlett. I'm surprised to see you here."

I suppose me being here looks just as bad as him showing up. He told me he was spending the evening with his team, and look where I headed. But he has to know while it's part of his normal lifestyle, this isn't usual for me. He of all people knows me well enough to know Caroline has probably dragged me here. "I'm sure you are." I give him a tight smile and take a sip of my drink. "I'm here with Caroline and Tina. What about you?"

"I'm out with the team. I told you that." He frowns. "So where are your friends?"

"Around."

I take another drink so I don't fidget in front of him. Ben looks uncomfortable. I'm not really sure how to handle this. I'm not going to beg Tucker to be with me, but I'm also not going to sit around and wait for him to decide he wants me. Still, I'm not good at games. With the help of alcohol-induced courage, I decide to be honest. "Did you come over for a reason, Tucker?"

His eyes widen in surprise. "No, I just came over to say hi." He looks unsure of his answer as he turns his attention to Ben. "Is he a friend of yours?"

"We just met. Ben, meet Tucker. Tucker, Ben." I wave from Ben to Tucker and back.

A battle of emotions sweeps over Tucker's face until he finally settles on acceptance. He looks Ben up and down while Ben shifts his weight. Tucker's jaw works as though he wants to say something but holds back. Finally, he turns back to me. "Are you having fun?" His question sounds genuine.

I'm not but don't want to admit that to either guy. I'd rather be home in my pajamas, huddled over my math problems.

Tucker leans close, his mouth next to my ear. His breath tickles my neck and my body involuntarily reacts to his nearness. "I only want you to be happy, Scarlett."

Again, I'm not sure how to respond. Tucker's made it obvious he doesn't want to be with me tonight and he has to know that hurts. Perhaps this is similar to him encouraging me to go out with Daniel. This is his way of making sure I end up with someone he thinks I deserve. Part of me wants to tell him he deserves happiness and love, too. He deserves *us*, but my pride stops me.

He glances over at his group. The guys seem interested in our conversation, even if they can't hear.

After several uncomfortable seconds, when I realize he's not going to change his mind, I say, "You better get back to your friends."

"Yeah." He swallows and leans into my ear again, his voice tight. "Can I see you later?"

My heart races. I can't believe what he's asking. Am I just a booty call after all? My voice hardens. "I don't think that's a good idea."

He leans back and his brow lowers with concern. "That's not what I meant, Scarlett."

I steel my back. "If you want to talk to me, just call me tomorrow."

He nods sharply, his mouth pinched into a tight line. He glances at Ben again, then goes back to his friends.

"What was that all about?" Ben asks, watching Tucker walk away.

"Good question." I'm exhausted. I'd psyched myself up to come out tonight and the drinks have helped, but I wasn't prepared to deal with Tucker. I'm not sure how to handle my emotions regarding him. My heart begs for him to come see me tonight, but my pride balks. He either wants me or he doesn't. No waffling. It still doesn't make the rejection any easier.

I'm on the verge of tears when I see Caroline weaving her way through the crowd toward me. Judging by the look on her face, she saw Tucker.

I take a long drink before I set the bottle on the counter. "Thanks for the drink," I say to Ben and make my way to Caroline, meeting her halfway.

She looks into my eyes. "Are you all right?"

This is stupid. I will not cry. "I'm fine." At least he's hanging out with his friends. I could have found him draped over some hot, gorgeous girl. This could have been so much worse. I need to stop overreacting.

She shakes her head, looking past me in Tucker's direction. "No, you're not. Do you want to go home?"

Caroline's having fun, and I don't want to ruin it for her.

This is life. It's messy and unpredictable, full of wonderful surprises and mind-numbing disappointment. The uncertainty of it all is why I hide, trying to avoid all the pain and the heartache. But now that my cage door is open and I've had a peek outside of it, I realize I've missed out on so many good things, too. If I run home now, it might take me a long time to emerge again. Just like when Tucker pushed me to keep running, even when my body begged to stop, I push myself to stay. "No. I want to stay."

She looks uncertain. "Are you sure?"

"Yeah." I flash her a smile and lead the way to the dance floor. Ben is at the bar watching us with a dazed look, but I decide to let that go. I never promised to hang out with him, just like Tucker never promised me anything. Ben only made assumptions, just like I did with Tucker.

I push deeper into the crowd so I'm not visible to Tucker. Or maybe so he's not visible to me. I can pretend that he's not here. But I can't, not really. The best I can hope for is to make it through another half an hour or so, then figure out a way to get home. My new resolve to experience life is in its infancy and is still finding its strength. No sense pushing it too far.

Caroline dances through several songs, and I'm happy that other guys don't approach us. I can't really deal with that right now. A fine sheen of sweat covers my brow and the back of my neck. When a slow song comes on, I'm relieved. I may have run with Tucker in the gym a few times, but I'm miserably out of shape.

We begin to weave through the crowd toward our table when I see Tucker making his way toward me. My heart skips a beat, and I continue to follow Caroline until Tucker reaches us and blocks my path. His mouth is pursed, but his eyes plead with mine.

"Scarlett, I want to dance with you."

I like that he doesn't ask and make me wonder his motivation. Instead, he makes it clear this is what he wants. How can he be so clear yet so obtuse at the same time?

I want to tell him no, but I can't, so I nod.

A soft smile lifts his scowl, and he takes my hand and pulls me out onto the floor, stopping in the middle of the crowd.

I've abandoned Caroline. I turn back to find her and see her staring, her mouth hanging open in disbelief. I know she doesn't understand. I don't totally understand, and I'm the one in this relationship, if that's what I can call it.

Tucker drops his hold on my hand and wraps his arms around my waist, pulling me close to his chest. I reach my hands around his neck and look into his face, trying to figure out what's going through his head.

He doesn't speak, just looks into my eyes, his arms tight around my back, as though he's afraid I'll walk away. My body responds being this near to him, tensing and relaxing at the same time, a weird tug of war over self-preservation and need. The heat of his body flows into mine, and my breath comes in shallow pants as I stare at his lips, only inches from mine. I think about what he did with those lips last night and this morning. My body betrays my resolve, and I release a soft moan.

There's no way he could have heard my sound with this noise and the crowd, but he does, his eyes sinking closed. His neck tenses, and when he opens his eyes, they are full of lust and desire. "I want to take you home."

My reaction to his request is confusing. I want us to be together, but I don't want him with me because he's worried someone else is going to pick me up. "Let's go somewhere and talk first."

He nods and takes my hand, pulling me to the back of the club, toward the restrooms. We go down a long hall toward a storage room. Tucker knows where he's going, and it's obvious he's been here before. I try not to think about what that means.

When we've entered the backroom, Tucker's mouth finds mine. His hands are on my waist and slipping under my shirt.

My body, already at a slow simmer, instantly responds, igniting into a blaze. I want him even more than I did last night and this morning. But I need to think, and I need some answers. I don't expect the answers to everything, but I at least need a few. He owes me that.

I put my hands on his chest and push him away. "Tucker, we need to *talk*."

Chapter Twenty-One

He nods, but his hands are still on my waist, partially under my shirt.

I find it difficult to concentrate when he's touching me, but I've wanted this for so long, this connection to someone else, that I can't make myself break away from it. "You told me you love that I tell you the truth. I want the same from you. Even if you think it will hurt me."

"Okay." His face is solemn, and I know he's taking my request seriously.

"Are you running away from me?"

His hands drop and he backs up, running his hand over his head. "*Shit*. You don't waste time, do you?"

"I don't see the point."

A grin flickers briefly on his face before his seriousness replaces it. "Yes."

I knew it. I expected it, and I hoped he'd admit it, but now that he has, my breath catches in my throat.

"But it's not what you think, Scarlett."

"Okay," I say without criticism. "Then tell me what it is."

"I wasn't leaving you forever. Just for tonight. It got so intense, so quickly. I just needed to give it some space."

"By coming here tonight?"

He closes his eyes. "I know how it looks."

I press my back against some storage shelves. "I don't expect anything from you, Tucker. I just want you to be honest with me."

His head jerks up, his face splotchy. "Don't do that, Scarlett. Don't let me treat you like shit. I *need* you to expect more from me. You're the one person who does."

Is his self-destructive behavior a test to the people around him, to see if they think he's worth fighting for?

I step toward him and touch his cheek. "It's like you set yourself up to fail on purpose."

He closes his eyes and tries to turn his face away, but I cradle the other side of his face, holding him in place.

"You told me that I make you want to be a better person, and I know you can be, Tucker. But you need to want to be a better person on your own. Not because of me."

He looks into my eyes. "Maybe I need something worth fighting for."

I stand on my tiptoes and press a soft kiss on his mouth.

His arms wrap around my back and pull me to him as he kisses me with desperation. "I need you, Scarlett."

My heart soars, dragging the weight of Tucker's pain with it. "I'm here."

His hands are everywhere. He's tugging my shirt up, then stops. "Not here. Will you come home with me?"

I nod. "Yes."

He kisses me again then grabs my hand and opens the door, pulling me into the hallway. He heads for the back door and into the parking lot. A soft rain falls, hitting my bare arms and sending a shiver up my back. Tucker wraps his arm around me. "Did you have a coat?"

"No." But I realize I'm leaving without telling Caroline or Tina that I left.

Tucker stops next to his car and opens the door. I look at him before I get in. *Be smart, Scarlett* a little voice says in my head. But how is this wrong? How can it be wrong to feel this close to someone?

He's in the car before I have time to muddle through my thoughts. Tucker reaches for me, his lips on mine, his tongue exploring my mouth with impatience. His hand slides up my leg and under my skirt, resting on my upper thigh. With a groan, he pulls back and starts the car, driving out of the parking lot.

"I need to tell Caroline I left."

Tucker turns to me.

"I don't have my phone."

He shifts in his seat, pulls his phone out of his pocket and hands it to me.

I look at the screen, trying to decide whether to text her or call. Texting is the chicken-shit way out, and she won't recognize the number, but if I call her, she's liable to give me a lecture, if she even hears her phone. I need to suck it up and call her. I sigh with resignation and tap in her number.

She doesn't answer and the call goes to voice mail. Talk about luck. "Caroline. I left the club, but I'm fine. I got a ride. Stay and have fun. I'll see you later." When I hang up I feel a mixture of guilt for not being honest and relief I didn't have to argue with her.

Tucker shoots me a look. "You didn't tell her that you left with me."

"She doesn't understand."

He nods, and I wonder what he's thinking. "She's a good friend."

"Yes."

I look out the window and realize we're not going to my apartment. "Where are we going?"

"Home."

"But my—"

"*My* home."

The significance of what he says sinks in. "Oh."

"I don't want this to be a one-time thing, Scarlett. I want to try to make this work."

Hope flutters in my chest.

He stops at a red light and reaches for my neck, pulling my mouth to his. "You're worth fighting for."

Tucker kisses me, and I lose track of where we are until a car honks. He drops his hand from my face and grins before driving through the intersection. His apartment is close, and he parks in the half-empty parking lot. He's out of the car in seconds, moving to my side and opening the door. His mouth is on mine for a brief moment, the promise of more to come, then he wraps an arm around my back and leads me to the entrance.

Tucker's apartment complex is nicer than mine. A door leads to a hallway with indoor entrances to the apartments. We go up two flights of stairs to the top floor, and he stops partway down the hall, unlocking the door and ushering me inside.

His hands tug at my shirt before the door is closed. He pulls the shirt over my head and presses my back against the door, his pain-filled eyes searching mine. "I've never wanted anyone as much as I want you, Scarlett. That scares the shit out of me. Everyone I love always leaves." His voice breaks. "I'm scared I'm going to lose you."

I reach for his face. "I'm here, Tucker. I'm where I want to be. With you."

He kisses me again then leads me down the hall to a closed door. When he opens it, I'm surprised to see a tidy, organized bedroom. His bed is made. His books are stacked on a dresser.

I don't have time to give it much thought because he's pulling off the rest of our clothes while kissing me. The only thing I'm aware of is Tucker. His hands and his mouth make my body feel things I never thought were possible.

He lowers me to the bed, and I'm exactly where I'm supposed to be. With him.

"Scarlett, you're so beautiful. Inside and out." His lips trail along my jaw and down my neck.

My hands reach for his chest, and they slide across his muscles to his shoulders.

"I love it when you touch me," he says. His dark, passion-filled eyes look up to mine. "Every time you touch me, I know you're not a dream. You're really here."

"I'm here," I whisper with a soft smile.

He props on an elbow. The fingertips of his other hand glide across my breast.

I gasp.

His eyes search my face while a smile lifts his mouth. His fingers continue their dance, driving me crazy with want. I close my eyes and moan.

His voice is low and husky. "I love your little sounds. I love that I can do this to you."

I open my eyes and heave a breath. "Only you, Tucker. You're the only one who's ever made me feel this way."

His mouth is on mine, hot and hungry. I wrap my arm around his back, pulling him closer. The need for him outweighs everything else. There's only Tucker and me, everything else fades away. His head lifts, and he stares into my face with such love and adoration that tears spring to my eyes.

He shifts and leans over to his nightstand, grabbing a condom from the drawer. After he puts it on, he moves between my legs, hooking a hand under one of my thighs and pulling it up to his waist. He enters me slowly, and I arch my back with a low guttural sound. I've never wanted anything in my life as much as I want Tucker right now. He finds a slow rhythm, and I'm climbing, needing more.

I reach for his waist, my hands sliding up his sides, to his back and he quickens his pace. I open my eyes and find him watching me, the same look of adoration and longing. Our eyes are locked as my body ascends to heights it's never reached before, never knew existed. "*Tucker.*"

"There's only you, Scarlett. Only you."

My eyes sink closed as the onslaught of sensations bombards every nerve ending in my body until I'm only aware of Tucker above me, pushing me higher and higher, and this desperate craving for more. When I'm so high I don't think I'll ever find my way back, I shatter into a million pieces, plummeting to earth. But Tucker's here, catching every sliver and putting me back together, but not into the person I was.

I'm someone new.

Afterward, I lay in his arms, the steady rise and fall of his chest against my cheek, and I'm amazed. I never thought I could feel so content. So happy.

We fall asleep in our cocoon of peace. I'm dreaming about Tucker and the way his eyes twinkle when he smiles, when a ringing jars me from my sleep. I rouse enough to realize the sound is Tucker's phone.

We're a tangle of limbs and sheets, so he has trouble rolling to the side of the bed and reaching his jeans. When he pulls the phone out of his pocket, he checks the screen and fear fills his eyes. He sits upright, swinging his feet to touch the floor as he answers.

"Yeah." He listens, then hunches over his knees. "*No.*" Pain fills his voice.

I sit upright, worried.

"What the hell are you thinking?" He breaks into a sob. "For God's sake, don't do it." After few seconds he hangs up and tosses his phone on his table.

I reach for his shoulder. "Tucker?"

Tears streak down his face, and he struggles to catch his breath. "Someone I know is in trouble."

Climbing to my knees, I pull him into a hug and stroke the back of his head. "I'm sorry."

"It's all my fault."

"How could it be your fault?" I ask in confusion. "You've been with me."

He leans back and stares into my face. He looks so shattered that my heart breaks for him. "You don't understand."

I caress his cheek. "Then help me understand."

He shakes his head, determination replacing some of his agony. "No. I can't."

"Tucker, you don't have to do this alone. Let me help you. Let me in."

He pulls away from me and stands. "I can't."

I watch his shoulders shake with the tears he tries to suppress, and I wonder how much progress we've made after all. He's with me, but he won't share what's bothering him, and he's pushing me away in the process. I know I can't expect him to change overnight, but I also know we'll never really be close if he's hiding things from me. "Do you need to do anything? Do you need to go anywhere?"

He closes his eyes, and shakes his head, pressing his palm into his forehead.

"Is it Marcel?"

He turns to face me, rage in his eyes. "How do you know about Marcel?"

I resist the urge to shrink away from his anger and instead hold my ground. "*You* told me, Tucker. The night I found you punching the Dumpster. You told me that Marcel was your brother, and whatever he was doing was your fault."

Horror washes over his face, and he sits on the edge of the bed. "Did you tell anyone?"

I scrunch my forehead in confusion. "Who would I tell?"

"I don't know. Caroline? Your friend in the math lab? You didn't answer my question, Scarlett. Did you tell anyone?"

I don't understand why his brother is a big secret, but he's obviously agitated. "No. I didn't tell anyone." Then I remember my conversation with Jason. "Wait."

His panic-filled eyes shoot to my face.

"I mentioned him to Jason, but he didn't know who he was."

Tucker bounces off the bed to his feet and paces, rubbing the back of his head. "You told *Jason*?" He turns to me. "*When did you talk to Jason?*"

His swinging pendulum of emotions scares me, but not for my

physical safety. "He came to see me in the math lab earlier this week. He told me to end things with you. That I was distracting you."

Rage covers his face. "And you didn't tell me this?"

I shake my head, my breath sticking in my chest. "You and I weren't exactly speaking then. You'd made it clear you weren't interested in me. I didn't see the point. There was nothing to end."

"How did Marcel come up in the conversation?" His voice is cold.

I pull the sheet up to my chest, suddenly feeling vulnerable. "Jason told me he was your brother so I asked him if I could expect a visit from Marcel next."

"And?"

"And what?"

"What did he say?"

"He asked me who Marcel was."

"Did you tell him?"

Anger burns in my chest. I feel sorry for Tucker and the pain he's in, but he doesn't have the right to treat me like this. "No. I didn't answer him."

He nods.

"So is Jason your brother?"

Tucker glares.

Resentment and disappointment threaten to swallow me whole. I slide my feet to the edge of the bed.

"Where are you going?"

I grab my panties on the floor and step into them, keeping my back to Tucker. I'm exposed enough without having him see me naked right now.

He grabs my shoulders from behind, his fingers digging into my flesh with his tight grip. "Where are you going, Scarlett?"

Jerking from his grasp, I reach for my bra and slip it over my arms, fastening the back before I turn to face him. "Home."

"*Why*?" Pain fills his voice again. "You're leaving me?"

"Tucker." Tears clog my throat. "I want to be with you more than I've ever wanted anything in my life, but you can't even share something as simple as who your *brother* is. If you don't trust me enough to tell me about your family, then this isn't going to work."

His eyes narrow with anger. "So you're running away from me."

I step into my skirt, tears blinding my vision. "No, Tucker. You're the one running away from me."

"You're the only person I see leaving."

I can't find my shirt and then I remember Tucker took it off when we came home to his apartment last night. How did everything change so quickly? My chest shakes with a sob. I look up into his face. "I don't want to go. I want to stay with you, but you have to open up to me. Give me one thing. Just one thing, and I'll stay."

He turns to the side.

"Who's Marcel? Why do you think it's your fault?"

His eyes close, and his chest rises and falls.

"Who is Jason? Why do you have different last names? Is he your foster brother?"

His hands fist at his sides.

"Tucker. *Please.*" I wonder how fair this is. He's clearly upset, and I'm pushing him to do something that he's uncomfortable doing. But he needs me, and the only way I can help him is if he lets me in.

"Yes. Jason is my foster brother from my last family." He sits on the side of the bed, defeated. "We have different last names because my foster family didn't adopt me. Jason lives with me here."

I sit next to him and wrap my arms around his shoulder. "Thank you," I whisper.

"Don't leave me, Scarlett." He chokes on the words.

Tears stream down my face, and I brush the tears off his. "I'm here."

He turns and kisses me, his hands grabbing my cheeks. "But for how long?"

I stare into his guarded eyes. I can't answer. I'm surprised he doesn't realize he's the one who has the answer to his question.

Chapter Twenty-Two

J ason is gone for the weekend, so I spend most of Sunday with Tucker, but he's reserved, which is understandable given the fact someone close to him is in trouble. But he seems raw and wounded, and I wonder if he needs to spend some time alone. He takes me home by mid-afternoon, only because I insist I need to study.

Caroline is frantic with worry when I walk in the door. "*Where have you been?*"

"I told you..." My voice trails off as I realize I only told her someone was bringing me home. I close my eyes. "Caroline, I'm sorry."

"Where were you?" Anger replaces her worry.

I'm silent. She has every right to be upset with me. How could I be so thoughtless and careless?

Her eyes narrow. "You were with Tucker." Her words are clipped.

"Caroline..."

"Don't." She shakes her head. "Just don't."

I spend the rest of the afternoon in my room, studying and feeling miserable. Isn't falling in love supposed to be wonderful and magical? Am I doing it wrong? Leave it to me to screw this up, too.

Caroline's chilly attitude thaws by early evening, but we don't talk about it, pretending that the incident never happened. We snuggle under an afghan and watch several episodes of *Gossip Girl*, my apology gift to her. For the first time, I realize the show isn't just about a bunch of rich kids, but the pain and turmoil they experience as they fumble their way through figuring out who they are and what they want. Their lifestyle is only expensive window dressing. Turns out rich kids struggle with the same things the rest of us do.

We're between episodes, and she gets up to get the ice cream container and two spoons. When she sits, she hands me a spoon then digs into the container of rocky road.

"I worry about you, you know," she says, focusing her attention on her spoon. "You're the closest thing I have to a sister. I just want you to be happy."

"Thanks, Caroline." I lay my head on her shoulder.

"I won't say anything else about Tucker. If you want to see him, I won't stand in your way, and if it all crashes and burns, I won't say I told you so. But ask yourself this: does Tucker make you happy or does he make you more miserable than you were before?"

Her question meanders through my head the rest of the evening. When I'm with Tucker, it feels so right, but when we're apart, the doubts begin to creep in.

I'm in my room studying when the doorbell rings.

"Are you expecting someone?" Caroline shouts from the bathroom.

"No."

I get up and go to the front door, looking through the peephole. Tucker stands outside the door, his hands shoved into his hoodie pockets.

I open the door, and we stare at each other.

He's been running, but it's drizzling outside and his clothes are wet. His mouth is turned down, and he looks miserable. His lips open, and he hesitates before he finally speaks. "I lived in six foster homes. I was at my last one four and a half years. I don't like libraries because one of my families would make me sit in a room full of books for hours on end, insisting I read. They give me claustrophobia now."

Tears spring to my eyes. He's trying to open up. "Thank you."

He's still standing outside the door, his hands still buried. "I'm not the only one with secrets, Scarlett. You have plenty of your own."

"You're right. I'm sorry." My chin trembles. What can I tell him? My past is tucked inside a vault. I sort through my neatly filed baggage. "My sister is three years younger than me. She dropped out of high school when she got pregnant at fifteen. She lives in a trailer in the same trailer park I spent the first eighteen years of my life."

He reaches for me, and I take a step toward him, my bare toes curling on the cold concrete outside the door. His face lowers and his mouth hovers over mine. "I miss you, Scarlett," he whispers.

"I miss you, too," I whisper back.

His lips are soft and gentle, and his hand softly caresses my cheek.

I sigh as the now-familiar sensation of peace fills me with his touch. Taking his hand, I pull him inside.

Caroline pads down the hall in her robe and stops when she realizes that Tucker is standing in our living room.

"Hey, Caroline," Tucker says with a hesitant smile.

Her mouth parts, and she takes a step back.

His weight shifts, and he looks uncomfortable. "I know you're worried that I'll hurt Scarlett. I know you don't trust me, and I don't blame you."

Her eyes widen, and she turns to me.

"Scarlett didn't say anything." Tucker adds. "But I know you're friends, so of course you'd be worried about her."

Caroline tries to look indignant, but she's having a hard time since Tucker is being so blunt. "You have to admit you have a reputation of leaving girls strewn in your wake."

"I know, but Scarlett is different. I won't hurt her if I can help it."

She lifts an eyebrow. "*If you can help it*?"

"I can't promise I won't hurt her, Caroline. Nobody can. But I promise to do my best not to."

She's not sure how to respond.

"I plan to be around a lot. I hope you and I can get along."

Caroline lifts her chin. "I guess that depends on you. If you hurt her, I'll cut your balls off and shove them up your ass."

I gasp, but Tucker bursts out laughing. "Fair enough."

"Then we might just get along." Caroline spins around and stomps off to her room.

Tucker grins at me. "I like her."

I've never loved her more. "Me, too."

"What were you doing when I showed up?"

I smirk. "You have to ask?"

"We have a history test this week. We could study together."

I can't help smiling. "I'd like that."

I get my textbook and notes and we sit next to each other on the sofa, going over my notes. Lifting my eyebrows, I give him a playful glare. "I think I see the reason you're with me now. You just want my notes."

He kisses me long and slow, then grins against my lips. "Damn. You saw through my devious plan."

I kiss him back. "I like it."

After we've studied for thirty minutes, it's obvious that history comes more easily to Tucker than math. When I mention it, he shrugs. "Why do you think I'm majoring in it?"

I tilt my head to study him. "You're serious?"

He sighs. "Look, I have to get good grades to keep my scholarship and stay on the soccer team. So my parents insisted that I majored in something that I'm good at. The fact is, I might not even come back for my senior year. There's an agent who wants to sign me and work on getting me signed pro a year early."

"An agent?"

He chuckles. "I told you I was good."

"You'd really quit school to go pro? What about your education?"

"If I can make enough money playing professional soccer, then I don't need an education."

"But is that what you really want to do? You don't even love soccer that much."

He turns serious. "I lived most of my life with *nothing*. I have a chance at *something*."

He's shared more of himself. Granted, it's not much, but it's something. I understand having nothing, but I can't help wondering if Tucker is selling his soul just for the *chance* of having more. "I still don't understand why you can't major in what you want, in case your professional soccer plans fall through. You want to major in education. You'd be fantastic at it."

He pushes me backward on the sofa and leans over me, kissing my neck. "I told you already, Scarlett."

I laugh. "I almost forgot *Mr. Beckham*."

He pins my hands to my sides. "Oh. Insulting my soccer skills, huh?" A wicked look fills his eyes. "Have you even seen me play?"

My voice lowers, and I grin. "Oh, I've seen you *play*."

His mouth gapes, then he laughs. "You're full of surprises, aren't you?"

No one is more surprised than I am that I have a playful side. I stretch up to kiss him.

He releases my arms and his hand slides down my neck to the exposed area on my chest above my oversize t-shirt. "I want to study something else."

"I thought you loved history."

He turns serious. "Maybe I love something else more."

My smile falls as I wonder what he means by that, but he kisses me until I'm breathless and forget everything but Tucker.

On Monday morning, Tucker is the one meeting me after my set and logic class. He's waiting outside The Higher Ground and kisses me as though he hasn't seen me for days instead of only a few hours.

"I missed you," he says.

"I missed you, too." I'm surprised I mean it. I'm so used to being alone, it scares me how attached to him I've already become.

We go inside and sit after we order coffee. "Tucker, I'm going to cancel our official tutoring sessions."

His eyes widen. "Why?"

"It's not right, for one thing. The university is paying me to tutor you, and it seems a conflict of interest since we're..." The blood rushes to my cheeks. "Together."

He grins. "You're cute when you blush like that."

I glance down at the table. "I'm glad somebody thinks so."

He lifts my chin and looks into my eyes. "You're perfect, Scarlett. Don't be embarrassed about who you are."

How does he do that? How can I go from feeling embarrassed and nervous to relaxed and at peace in a few seconds? No drug, no therapy for my anxiety, has ever been able to accomplish what Tucker can do with a smile and a touch.

"I'll still work with you, but we both know that you really don't need me except to explain a few things. You have me anytime you want me now."

"I like the sound of that." He leans over the table and kisses me. "But I hope I can come up with a better use for my time with you other than studying algebra."

"I happen to like studying algebra."

"Then you study algebra and I'll *do other things*." His voice lowers on the last words and I feel flushed for a reason other than embarrassment.

"Do you want to work out with me tonight?" he asks.

I waggle my eyebrows. "And here I thought we *were* working out."

He laughs. "God, I love you."

I suck a breath and lean away, pressing my back into the chair.

His smile falls, and he takes my hand. "I love you, Scarlett."

How can he know that? We've only known each other a few weeks.

"I know it seems fast. But sometimes you *just know*."

I gnaw on my lip, unsure how to respond.

"I don't expect you to say it back. Not yet. But I don't want to pretend I don't."

I feel like I should be scared. This is so huge, but it feels right. Like we're supposed to be together. I'm not sure if what I feel is love or not. I know it's strong, and I want to be with him, but is this love? I can't say the words until I'm sure.

"You didn't answer my question. Do you want to work out?"

I nod. "Yeah. I do."

"I'll pick you up at your apartment at seven-thirty. Okay?"

Why does the idea of working out fill me with such happiness? It's because of the person I'm working out with. "Sounds perfect."

Tina is in the math lab when I show up for my shift in the afternoon. "*Well*?"

"Well, what?"

"What happened with Tucker?"

How she knew I was with Tucker when Caroline didn't is beyond me. But Tina seems to know everything that happens around Southern University's campus.

"I'm on my way to resign from tutoring Tucker. What does that tell you?" I ask.

Her mouth drops open, and I laugh. Let her get the wrong idea.

Dr. Carlisle is in his office, and he's thrilled when I tell him that Tucker has learned the subject well enough that he no longer needs me. "I heard he made a B-plus on his exam. Great job, Scarlett."

"Thanks."

The afternoon is busy so I'm caught off guard when I glance up and discover Jason sitting in a chair against the wall. I have no idea how long he's been there, but the scowl on his face tells me he's not happy. His gaze is locked on me, and pure hatred flows from him. The muscles in my back tighten and blood rushes to my head. The student

I'm working with looks up when he realizes he's lost my attention. I clench my hands in my lap and try to concentrate on the student's problem.

When we finish and the student gathers his things to leave, I stand. "Tina, I'll be back in a few minutes."

She nods and casts a worried glance toward Jason.

I walk into the hall, all the way to the end, and cross my arms to hide my shaking hands, staring out the window onto the university campus. My panic is about to explode, but I push it down. *I can do this.* I sense him approach, and he stands next to me, too close.

"I told you to stay away from him."

My pulse pounds in my head, and I force my breaths to come in slow, even waves. "What I do or don't do is none of your business."

"It is where my brother is concerned."

"Your foster brother."

He pauses. "I know what's best for Tucker. You don't know him. For some reason you think you do, but you don't."

I turn toward him. "I'm not going to discuss this with you."

"He's skipping team training sessions. He's only half-playing in the practice games. He's losing his edge, and it's because of you."

Could that be true? I know Tucker can't work out as hard with me as he would on his own.

"Scarlett, do the both of you a favor and leave this now before someone gets hurt."

It's too late for that. If either of us leaves, we'll be devastated. "You keep making vague threats. What exactly do you think is going to happen?"

Jason leans his hand on the window in front of me and lowers into my face. "Tucker was born to play soccer. He's got a gift most players dream about. A gift I would *kill* for. But when he's complacent he loses his edge. He has a good shot of being picked up by a pro team within the next few weeks. A few scouts are supposed to be coming to check him out and we're expecting a couple of offers, but they won't make an offer if he's lost his edge. And trust me, their scouts *will* come to watch him."

Complacent? Does he mean happy? But I can see how Tucker might be missing things because of me. Other than the mandatory practice last Saturday, I've never heard him mention working out with his team. "Don't you think Tucker should finish college before going pro?"

He scoffs. "Tucker won't need a degree. He'll be a professional player."

I can't believe what he's saying, "That's pretty shortsighted."

His eyes widen. "Shortsighted? It's more shortsighted to hope he doesn't get some career-ending injury. Tucker has the opportunity to make a lot of money if he can make it to the European circuit."

"But what about whether he's happy or not?"

Shaking his head, he laughs. "Happy? Money and fame will make Tucker happy."

Tucker's attention-seeking, destructive behavior fits with that kind of life. Jason's insistence that Tucker not alter his behavior makes me wonder if his foster family encouraged this public persona. "Do you even know what Tucker really wants?" I ask.

"Do *you*?"

No, but I intend to find out.

Chapter Twenty-Three

When I get home, Caroline is sitting on the sofa, eating macaroni and cheese from the pot.

"Bad day?" I ask, tossing my coat on a chair.

She shoves a wooden spoonful of noodles in her mouth.

"Want to talk about it?"

"Who gives a shit what the difference is between nylon and polyester?" she grumbles.

"I take it your test in textiles didn't go well."

She shoves another bite into her mouth.

"I'm sorry."

Caroline shrugs, then looks up at me. "You've made the gossip at Southern."

I sit on the arm of the sofa. "*What*?"

"People are talking about you and Tucker."

"Me?"

"Of course they are. You had to know this would happen. Tucker Price is acting completely out of character, and everyone is saying it's because of you. Which means a lot of girls hate you."

I stand. "Great." I go into the kitchen and make a peanut butter sandwich and take it to my room. "I'm going to work out. Tucker's going to pick me up in about fifteen minutes."

"Working out, huh? Is that what you crazy kids call it?" she calls down the hall.

"Very funny."

I know I shouldn't care what people say about me, but I do. The thought of other people talking about me, and it being completely out of my control makes the hair on my arms stand on end. I'm close to hyperventilating when Tucker shows up.

I answer within seconds of his knock. He takes one look at me and his forehead creases with worry.

"What's wrong?"

I shake my head. "It's stupid. Let's go." I head for the staircase, but Tucker grabs my arm and pulls me back.

"If something has upset you, then it's not stupid."

"Jason came to see me today."

His eyes widen, then darken with rage. "He did what?"

No matter what Jason's motives really are, he does seem concerned about Tucker's future. "He's worried about you."

"I told him that my life is none of his fucking business."

"He told me that you were skipping team training and practices. Because of me. Is that true?"

He inhales deeply and exhales my name. "Scarlett."

"It is, isn't it?" I move to the stairs and sit down.

He sits next to me, our hips touching. "It's not that simple."

"But you *have* missed practices and training because of me."

"Yeah." He threads his fingers with mine.

Guilt floods my head even though I tell myself I didn't ask him to. "Why?"

"I'd rather be with you."

I tilt my head to look into his face. "I know you don't love soccer, but do you hate it?"

He leans his forehead into mine. "It's not that simple."

"I'm pretty smart." I say, making sure it doesn't come across as snotty. "I understand plenty of complex things."

He kisses me and I lean into his chest, content to be with him. But Tucker is anything but content, even if he claims to be happy with me.

"Tucker, do you like playing soccer at all?"

He sighs and pulls my body flush with his. "I used to. Back when I was in middle school and high school. I loved it. But once I came to college, set on becoming pro, it wasn't fun anymore." He kisses my forehead. "But I'm good at it. I may fuck up everything else in my life, but soccer is the one thing I get right."

"You and I are good together."

He shakes his head slowly. "I'll fuck that up, too. Eventually."

"We're going to fight. We're going to disagree. But that's not fucking us up, Tucker."

He doesn't respond, and instead looks lost and forlorn.

"Now that you can see me anytime you want, you can go to the all the practices and trainings, right?"

"Yeah." But he doesn't sound happy.

"When's your next practice that you actually *play* soccer?"

"We have a scrimmage on Saturday afternoon."

"I want to come see you play and judge for myself whether you're awesome or not."

He smiles. "Promise you'll come?"

"I promise." I press my lips against his. "Are you missing something to be with me tonight?"

A small smile turns up his lips. "No."

"Then let's go work out."

We head to the fitness center, and I realize I haven't told him about my anxiety over being the center of gossip, but the attention we garner once we get to the gym takes care of the issue for me.

Tucker's so used to being the center of attention that he doesn't realize people are watching us. Not until he realizes I'm anxious during our second lap walking around the track.

Concern darkens his eyes. "What's wrong?"

"Dating you comes with drawbacks." When I see the panic on his face, I realize I've worded my answer badly. "Not you, Tucker. It's the attention that comes with you."

His shoulders relax and understanding dawns on him. "I'm sorry. We can go somewhere else."

I want to run far and fast and out of the sight of curious eyes. But Tucker's belief in me gives me strength I didn't have before. "No. I need to deal with it. Once people get used to us together, we'll get less attention."

He doesn't seem entirely satisfied with my answer, but we fall into silence as we finish our run.

We spend every night together at my apartment and part of me worries this is all happening too quickly. When I broach the subject with Tucker, he shakes his head in disbelief. "How can something so good be too much?"

"Haven't you ever heard of everything in moderation?"

He pulls me flush to his chest and kisses me. "The person who said that obviously never loved you."

Tucker has gotten several secretive phone calls while we're together. He refuses to share any details, but he's always subdued for hours afterward. He knows his secrets upset me so each time he compromises by telling me something else from his past. He hates chocolate. His birth father is serving time for second-degree murder after killing a convenience store clerk in a robbery. His mother died of a drug overdose when he was twelve. He lived on his own for a month and half before anyone realized he was unsupervised and put him in foster care. He never mentions a brother, and I know better than to inquire.

Every time he shares something, I share something, too. I was on the academic team in high school. (Although he told me this information is too obvious to count.) My first boyfriend was in my freshman year of college and only lasted a couple of months, mostly due to my lack of interest. I was friends with a girl in the fifth grade and I spent every minute I could at her house, wishing I was part of her family. She moved away before the beginning of sixth grade and I was depressed for a month.

On Thursday night, we're in bed after making love for the second time. I'm lying in Tucker's arms, and his fingers lightly stroke my arm. I've never felt so at peace. I never knew this happiness was possible.

"I've been thinking," Tucker says softly. "Maybe we should get an apartment together."

I prop up on one elbow, feeling slightly panicked. This is a big step. "What about Caroline?"

"She can keep this one."

"What about Jason?"

Tucker shrugs. "He won't care."

I rub my forehead, staring at Tucker's clock, which is perched on the nightstand. "He's your roommate so he can keep an eye on you. He'll never agree."

"So what? Fuck him."

"Jason hates me. He thinks I'm destroying your career. He's not some random stranger or friend. It's your brother. This will make him hate me even more."

"So what? You of all people should know that family doesn't necessarily mean jack shit." Irritation pinches his mouth. "What difference does it make? We spend all our time here anyway."

"You don't—"

Tucker's phone rings and guilt washes over his face as he glances at it.

I'm sure it's one of his secretive phone calls. I climb out of bed, reaching for my robe. "It's okay. Answer it."

His demeanor changes within seconds of answering. He stands and begins to pace. "Slow down, Marcel. Slow down."

My head jerks up.

Tucker notices my attention and sits on the edge of the bed, stepping into his jeans. "Don't do that, man." He pauses. "I'm coming. For God's sake, just wait until I get there, okay?"

I know I'm eavesdropping, but this seems important enough for me to know about.

Closing his eyes, Tuckers pleads, "Promise me you'll wait. *Promise*."

He hangs up and continues dressing.

"Where are you going?"

"Out."

"I can see that, Tucker. *Where*?"

"Nashville." He refuses to look at me.

"*Nashville*? Why are you going somewhere two hours away at this time of night?"

He stares into my face, his own etched with worry. "I'll be back tomorrow." He gives me a peck on the lips and opens the door.

"Who the hell is Marcel, Tucker?"

He shakes his head.

"You owe me an answer."

His eyes harden. "Do I, Scarlett? There's a fucking hell of a lot I don't know about you."

"You don't see me running to Nashville at midnight either, do you? You seriously think you'd let me run off without demanding an explanation?"

He sighs, and his face softens as he reaches for me, but I back out of his reach. As soon as I'm in his arms or his lips touch my skin, I'll give in and I don't want to. "You have to trust me, Scarlett."

I sit on the bed, tears burning my eyes. It's not that I don't trust him. It's that he doesn't trust me.

He squats in front of me and takes my hands in his. "I'll be back tomorrow night. I promise."

I don't answer. I'm not sure what to say. Finally, I square my shoulders. "Go."

"I'm sorry."

I shake my head. "Go. But when you come back, I think you should spend the night at your place tomorrow."

Disbelief lifts his eyebrows. "You're breaking up with me?"

"No. But I think this is moving too fast, and you aren't ready to commit to me yet. Not if you don't trust me enough to tell me what's going on. So I think we need a break. At least for a day or two."

He stands but doesn't protest my announcement. "You'll still come to my practice to watch me play Saturday?"

"I promised that I would."

Tears fill his eyes as he steps backward and grabs the doorknob. "I love you, Scarlett."

"But it's not enough, is it?"

He turns and leaves, and I wonder how my life can turn so quickly from happiness to despair.

Chapter Twenty-Four

Turns out I'm miserable without Tucker, which is beyond ridiculous. We've only known each other a few weeks, only been together for one, yet I feel like my heart has been torn out, ripped to pieces, and stuffed back inside my chest.

I tell Caroline about our fight in the morning and seek her opinion. "Am I wrong?" I secretly hope she tells me that I am.

Tears fill her eyes. "No, Scar. You're not wrong. This is huge if he's running to a city two hours away and won't tell you why. For all you know, Marcel is a girl."

That thought steals my breath before I make myself calm down. "No, he called Marcel his brother."

"What are you going to do?"

"I don't know." I rub my aching temple. Crying half the night has given me a massive headache. "But I promised I'd go to his practice tomorrow and watch him play."

"Do you want me to come? I'm supposed to work in the fashion department workroom for extra credit, but I can get out of it."

I shake my head. "You need the extra credit after your test. I'll be fine."

"How about we order pizza tonight? We can watch *Twilight* and make fun of it."

I grin. "I thought you had a date tonight."

She shakes her head with a sad smile. "Not anymore."

I give her a hug. "Then it's you and me tonight."

"And what if Tucker shows up?"

A scowl purses my lips. "He won't. I told him things were moving too fast and we needed to take a day or two off. Besides, who knows if he'll even be home tonight? He might still be in Nashville."

I spend the rest of the day trying not to think about what Tucker is doing in Nashville or who Marcel actually is. When I'm worried about something, my mind usually comes up with half a dozen outrageous scenarios to fuel my anxiety, but in this instance, I come up with nothing.

When Jason shows up in math lab around five, I groan. He doesn't even waste time for me to come into the hall.

"Where's Tucker?"

I ignore him as I brush past. When I leave the room, and I'm out of earshot of anyone in the math lab I cross my arms and face him. "Tucker told me he was going to Nashville, and he'd be back today."

"He's not back yet, and he's not answering his cell phone."

My heart seizes, and I force back my panic.

"Why did he go to Nashville?"

"I honestly don't know. He took a call from someone and then told me he had to go."

"And when was this?"

"Last night. Around midnight."

Jason's eyes fill with anger. "Are you lying to me?"

My mouth drops open. "Why would I lie to you? I'm not happy about him running off, either."

Jason begins to pace and rubs the back of his neck. "He has to be back tomorrow. I've heard from someone in the know that a scout from the Chicago Fire will be at practice to evaluate Tucker."

"What does that mean?"

Jason glares. "It means this is Tucker's big shot, and he might miss it."

I inhale sharply. "He'll be there. He made me promise I'd be there tomorrow to watch him play."

With a grunt, Jason shakes his head. "Let's hope for his sake you're right."

When I get home, I tell Caroline about Jason's visit and the possibility of the scout showing up.

"What are you going to do if they recruit him?"

A lump fills my throat. "I can't even think that far ahead. I just hope he shows up." But my hope is even simpler than that. I just hope he's okay.

The practice is at two on Saturday, close to the university. Metal stands line both sides of the practice field, and I've brought some blankets and a travel mug of coffee to keep me warm on the dreary February afternoon. Dark gray clouds hang heavy in the sky, and my umbrella is next to me in case the clouds decide to open.

My stomach is a bundled mass of nerves. I haven't heard anything from Tucker, and from the anxious look on Jason's face as he paces the edge of the field, he hasn't either.

I tell myself it's only one fifty-five. Tucker is notoriously late to everything. Everything that's not related to me.

But he knows I'll be here, so wouldn't he be here early?

I've sworn that I wouldn't call him, but I'm beginning to panic. I pull out my phone just as I see his car pull up in the parking lot on the other side of the field. Releasing a long exhale, I push my pent-up fear with it. Tucker jumps out of the car and runs past his teammates and across the field toward me.

I stand and walk the few steps down to the field, relief making my knees weak.

When he stops in front of me, he's hesitant, his face tight with apprehension. "You came."

I swallow the lump in my throat. "I told you I would. I was worried *you* weren't coming."

He leans down and gives me a gentle kiss. "I couldn't pass up the opportunity to show off for you." His words are teasing, but he's holding back. "So is our break over? After this practice I can be with you?"

My chin quivers. Have we solved anything other than proving I'm a miserable mess without him?

"I've missed you so much, Scarlett."

I nod as tears stream down my face. "I missed you, too."

He wraps an arm around my back and pulls me to his chest. A whistle sounds, and Tucker reluctantly drops his hold on me and gives me his cocky Tucker smile. But it's tempered by his eyes as they search my own. "Wish me luck."

I grin. "I didn't think you needed it, superstar."

He laughs and runs across the field to warm up with his teammates. When I look out of the corner of my eye at Jason, he's scowling. I'm irritated that Jason seems more relieved that Tucker is here to impress a scout instead of being relieved he's safe. But then again, maybe Jason is used to Tucker running off for days at a time. My happiness sobers. Just another reminder of how much I don't know about him.

I know very little about soccer, but once they begin to scrimmage, it's obvious that Tucker has talent. He outshines everyone on the field. My heart bursts with pride for him, and sorrow when I see a man walk up to the stands halfway through the match. He sits at the top row and takes notes on an electronic tablet. At one point, he pulls out his phone and holds a serious conversation, his eyes on Tucker the entire time before he leaves.

Tucker's side easily wins, and when the match is over, Tucker heads straight for me, wearing his trademark grin. Some of his teammates watch him with curious expressions.

Jason has moved during the match so that he's sitting two rows behind me, which I suspect was to move to get closer to the scout. I stand, keeping my eyes on Tucker, but ask loud enough for Jason to hear. "How'd he do?"

He hesitates, but then I hear pride in his voice. "He was excellent. Beyond excellent. They're bound to offer him a contract after that. I've never seen him play that well."

A soft smile warms my heart as I move toward the stairs. I can't help thinking my presence played a part in it, proving that I'm not a bad influence after all.

Tucker reaches the edge of the field, and Jason stomps down the metal stairs, intercepting Tucker before he reaches me. I'm close on Jason's heels.

Anger reddens Jason's face, and he glares at Tucker. "Where the hell have you been?"

"None of your fucking business."

"It becomes my business when you almost missed a scout from the Fire."

Tucker's eyes widen. "You're shitting me."

"Dude, he was here, and *you* were on fire."

Tucker runs a hand through his hair. "Why didn't you leave me a message with one of your fifty phone calls and texts?"

Jason grins. "I didn't want you to know and possibly freeze up." He gestures toward me. "Besides, I figured you showing off for Scarlett was motivation enough."

Tucker reaches for me and swings me around, letting out a whoop of excitement. "This could be it, Scarlett!"

I'm happy for him, but I'm scared about what this means for us. There's no denying that Tucker truly does have a gift. But will this make him happy? I'm not so sure. "You were amazing, Tucker. Truly amazing."

He kisses me then swings me around again. When he sets my feet on the ground, Tucker keeps his arm around me and looks up at Jason. "How long until we know for sure?"

"I called my friend after the scout left. He thinks he'll hear something within the week."

"And then what?"

"It depends. There's a chance they'll bring you in right before the regular season starts."

Tucker's eyebrows rise. "That soon? That's only a couple of weeks."

Jason's grin spreads across his face, and it occurs to me this is the first time I've really seen him smile. "That soon. This could move really fast."

"But what about this semester?" I ask. "Will Tucker just drop out of school?"

Jason smirks and looks at me like I'm an idiot. "Scarlett, I told you Tucker doesn't need a degree if he's a pro."

Tucker's arm tightens around my waist. "Nothing's a sure thing, Scarlett. We'll see what happens."

I nod, then head back up into the stands to get my blankets. My fingers shake as I fold the blankets into neat squares. Tucker seems genuinely happy about this, and that's what I want, for Tucker to be happy. He beams with pride, standing on the sidelines, deep in conversation with Jason. He's gorgeous, with the soft breeze blowing his short blond hair, and his cheeks rosy from physical exertion and the cold breeze.

My breath catches as I realize I'm losing him.

I knew this would happen. From the moment I met him, I knew he would leave and break my heart, yet I can't fault him for it. He's following his dream, and what more could I hope for him? If only I was certain it really *is* his dream. His excitement convinces me that perhaps it is. Maybe these last three years of college soccer *are* merely a stepping stone to becoming pro. I hope he finds the joy he had when he played in high school. If the way he played this afternoon is any indication, it's there. Maybe he just doesn't recognize it anymore.

He looks up and our eyes lock, his smile fading slightly. He says something to Jason, and Jason waves and walks away.

It's Tucker and me, and we're on his turf, literally. It only seems fair after I've had the advantage of most of our time together. I wonder how much time we have left before he's gone.

I'm stuck in the stands, my feet unwilling to move as my tears fall. He bounds the few steps to me and pulls me into a tight embrace, pressing my cheek to his chest. He doesn't say anything. He doesn't need to. We both know we're on borrowed time. If I barely made it through a day and a half without him, how will I last a lifetime?

"Don't cry, Scarlett. Please, don't cry. We can make this work."

But we can't. Not really. He'll go away and be on the road most of the year while I'm here going to school and hoping to move to Washington D.C. when I graduate.

I stand on my tiptoes and pull his mouth to mine, kissing him with an urgency that fills every cell of my body. I may be losing him, but I'm not going to waste a moment of what I have left. My heart is going to break whether he leaves now or in a few weeks. Trying to protect myself is pointless.

His arms press me tighter against his chest, and he kisses me until we're both breathless. "I want to take you home."

I nod with a weak smile.

He picks up my blankets and takes my hand before we descend the steps. A soft rain begins to fall as we walk to where my car is parked on this side of the field. Tucker opens my door and tosses the blankets onto the passenger seat.

"I have to get my things. How about you go home, and I'll be there soon?" There's a sadness in his voice, and it occurs to me that most of our relationship has been filled with sorrow since the beginning. Perhaps this is a sign that we're not meant to be.

I nod again and get into the car, not trusting myself to speak. Tucker takes off running across the field. He stops midfield, his head back, and his eyes uplifted to the sky as the rain coats his face. I wonder what he's thinking, or if he's even thinking about me.

Caroline is still at school when I get home, and I'm unsure what to do with myself as I wait. My nervousness makes me jumpy. Should

I do something before Tucker shows up? Brush my teeth? Put on lingerie? That's a laugh, since I don't own any. I decide to do nothing. Tucker loves me for me.

Tucker loves me.

I've known this, but the reality of the situation sinks in. I can name only a handful of people who really loved me, and with the exception of Caroline, every single one of them has walked away. I'm not sure which is better—the chance to experience love and lose it, or to live my life without it.

Too late to determine that now.

Tucker knocks on the door, and I open it before the second rap. He's wearing a half smile, but his eyes are glassy. "Jason's friend at the Fire called. He says they want me. They're going to make me an offer."

I take in a deep breath, unable to say anything except for one word. "When?"

"Jason's right. They'll want me for the first of the season. If it all gets worked out, I might leave next week."

I nearly stumble with the news. My head bobs in acknowledgement even though I'm dying inside.

He grabs me and kisses me with all the grief and pain I feel. I'm barely aware of him closing the door as his hands slide up the back of my shirt, his cold hands erupting goose bumps on my arms.

We go into my bedroom and I cling to him, hating myself for it. I've become the very thing I hate. My mother. She always picked men who were either derelicts or destined to leave.

I'm no different than her.

Instead of analyzing it, I surrender to my feelings, surrender to this man, even though I know it's emotional suicide. But he already owns half my heart anyway. I'm merely handing him the rest.

We're both silent as he strips off my clothes, then takes off his own. No words are necessary. We both know this is goodbye.

We stand together naked, our bodies pressed against one another, and I catalog every feeling, every sensation. When he's gone, at least I'll have the memories of him.

He's looking into my eyes, his hand sliding from my cheek to my neck. "I love you, Scarlett."

The words are on the tip of my tongue, but I can't say them. My heart burns with grief and love. Those three words are the last piece of my soul, and even though I've given him everything else, I'm not sure I'll survive if I hand over this final piece.

I close my eyes, and his lips press against mine. He lowers me to the bed, and we make love with tenderness and regret. How can something so beautiful be so devastatingly sad?

Tucker holds me close, brushing my hair from my face. "Marcel was my foster brother." His voice breaks on the last word.

I turn to look up at him in surprise. Tucker's eyes are closed.

"He was a foster kid, too. We were in the same foster home together. I was a year older than him and he looked up to me." He sighs and a tear falls from the corner of his eye and slides into his hair. "His mom died too, like mine, but unlike me, he had a good mom. Her boyfriend got drunk one night and accused her of sleeping around. He shot her right in front of Marcel. The guy tried to shoot Marcel, but his gun jammed, and Marcel got out the back door." Tucker takes a deep breath. "The Browns were his first home, but they were my third, so I knew the drill by then. He'd cry himself to sleep every night, missing his mom, wishing he'd died, too. The other kids made fun of him, but I tried to look after him. I got a few black eyes for it." He smiles but it's wobbly, and his chin quivers.

I put my hand on the center of Tucker's chest and he places his hand over mine.

"Marcel had an aunt who lived in Texas, but she couldn't afford to come to Nashville to get him. The Browns were mean sons-of-bitches, but most foster homes for kids our ages were rough, and Marcel was soft. He had no business being in foster care. So I decided we needed to find a way for Marcel to get the money to take a bus to Texas." His laugh is hard. "God, I was stupid.

"The problem was that thirteen-year-olds can't get jobs and in the neighborhood the Browns lived in, the neighbors didn't exactly hire boys for yard work. Marcel was ready to give up, but things were getting worse at the Brown's house. I could have turned them in, but we'd most likely be split up and sent to different foster homes."

He pauses, and his chest rises and falls. His heart races beneath my palm.

"We passed a convenience store every day walking home from school. One day, I remembered that my dad got two hundred dollars once, robbing a store. Two hundred dollars would be more than enough to buy two bus tickets to Midland, Texas, because we'd both decided we were sticking together, no matter what. I was going with him. We even did a stupid secret blood-brother ceremony." He shakes his head with a derisive laugh.

"Marcel didn't know what I planned to do before I went inside the store. I told him to stay outside and keep watch. I didn't have a gun, but I figured the clerk didn't know. I put my hand in my jacket pocket and pointed it at him, telling him to hand me all his money. Marcel came in a minute later to see what was taking me so long—just moments before the police showed up."

My heart aches for the thirteen-year-old boy who only wanted to help his friend.

"We were both arrested for attempted robbery, but plea-bargained down to a misdemeanor. We were lucky enough to only spend a few days in juvie, but we were split up after that. We tried to stay in touch, but we both moved to several homes and had no way to keep track of each other until I graduated from high school. I found Marcel, but he'd changed. He'd run away from his last foster home and joined a gang." His eyes open and he looks into my face. "A couple of weeks ago, that night at the party when you took me home, Marcel called to tell me that he was being promoted, but he would have to kill a guy. After I talked to him, he told me he'd think about it."

I squeeze his hand. No wonder he was beating the Dumpster.

"He called me later and told me he didn't do it. He couldn't. But then last Saturday night, he told me he didn't have a choice. The only life he knew was gang life."

"Tucker, I'm so sorry."

"He didn't do it. He'd changed from the boy I knew, but he couldn't kill someone in cold blood. When he called Thursday night, he told me it was either he follow through with the murder or the gang would kill him. So instead, he decided to kill himself. I told him I'd come there and to wait for me." His voice breaks. "I found him and bought him a plane ticket to Midland, like I'd tried to do years ago."

"Tucker, why didn't you tell me?"

Pain fills his bloodshot eyes. "I was ashamed, Scarlett."

"*Why?*"

"It was my fault. Marcel's awful foster homes. His joining a gang. It was all my fault."

"No, Tucker. You were a kid."

"I knew better." His eyes plead with mine to understand. To condemn him. "I wasn't stupid. My father went to prison for the very thing I did. I knew it was stupid, but I did it anyway."

"Maybe so, but Marcel didn't have to make the choices he made after you were split apart."

Tucker sits up, his face contorting with his inner turmoil. "Don't you see? It's not fair. I ended up with Jason's family. They found me on Jason's middle-school soccer team and took me in for the sole purpose of honing my soccer skills. While Marcel lived in filthy, low-class foster homes, I lived with the Wallaces and their upper-middle-class lifestyle. The whole fucking debacle was my fault, and I got rewarded for it while Marcel paid the price. For what *I* did. "

It all makes sense now. His self-destructive behavior. He thinks he doesn't deserve everything he's been given. Marcel received the punishment Tucker should have been given. "Tucker, you may have lived in a nice house, but did they love you? You said they took you in because you could play soccer and they wanted to make you into a star. You may not have lived in the terrible places that Marcel did, but you never felt loved. You weren't happy. You aren't happy now."

He shakes his head with disgust. "Are you sure about that? Look where I'm at now. I'm about to go pro."

"You're about to leave everything behind to pursue a dream I'm not sure belongs to you." My voice shakes. "I think you're leaving me to follow someone else's dream."

He sits up and leans over his legs, sucking in deep breaths as though he's about to hyperventilate.

Oh, God. He thinks that's his punishment, too. That he deserves to lose me.

I sit up and take both of his hands. "Maybe you think you owe the Wallaces for taking you in. Or maybe you think you owe Jason for—"

"Scarlett, stop." His face hardens. "I want this."

"Do you, Tucker?"

"You saw me play. I'm good."

"You're more than good. You're fantastic. But does it make you happy?"

His eyes narrow with anger. "I thought you made me happy but look how well that's working out."

I gasp.

He takes several deep breaths. "I love you, Scarlett." His shoulders shake as he climbs out of bed. "But you know it's not enough."

I struggle to keep my wits together and remember that he's doing this on purpose. He's trying to hurt me so I'll be the one to leave this relationship. "You're doing it again. You're trying to destroy what you think you don't deserve."

"Stop trying to psychoanalyze me, Scarlett." He pulls his pants on. "You don't know anything about me."

"But I do. I *know* you."

"You spend a couple of weeks with me and you think you know me? You don't know shit about me, Scarlett." Hatred fills his eyes as they pierce mine, but I know the hate isn't directed at me. It's directed at himself. "I've fucked every girl I could get into bed, and quite a few anywhere I could screw them. I've been arrested more times than I can count and the Wallaces get me out of it. Every fucking time. You think I can just walk away from this soccer contract? Well, guess again, Scarlett. I'm the Wallace's whore. They've paid to get me out of all of those things with the sole intent on making bank with me. Guess what? I let them." He inhales deeply and stares at the ceiling. "I fucking let them."

"Tucker, you didn't know."

His gaze lowers to mine, his anger simmering. "See? You don't know shit about me. I knew exactly what they were doing."

We stare at each other in silence while I struggle with what I can possibly say to make him realize he has a choice in this. Whether he stays with me or not, he doesn't have to play professional soccer.

But he knows me, too. "Keep your arguments to yourself. It's wasted breath. There's nothing you can say that will change my mind."

"So what does this mean for us?"

He shakes his head. "You already know what this means. You knew the second you opened your door this afternoon."

I know I should be upset, but I'm numb from disbelief. How can this be happening? "So this is it? Right now? You're just going to walk away from me? From us? Because you feel like you owe a rich couple who bought you to be their source of pride?"

"Everyone's always telling me to be more responsible. Maybe that's what I'm finally doing."

"Walking away from me is being responsible?"

He shakes his head, self-disgust covering his face. "I never deserved you. I'm getting exactly what I deserve." He pauses in the doorway. "Goodbye, Scarlett.'

And then he's gone.

Chapter Twenty-Five

It's a Saturday in spring in Tennessee, and the campus at Southern University is full of youth and excitement. The Chicago Fire is about to play Sporting KC and students at Southern have become professional soccer fans since Tucker's addition to Fire. The student body has taken over the student union to watch the match on a big-screen TV every Saturday for over a month.

"This is a terrible idea," Caroline grumbles as we walk across the campus. "Why are you doing this to yourself?"

I wish I knew. Tucker's been gone for over two months and just the mention of his name shreds my soul, but I feel like I owe him my support. No matter how much it hurts.

"She just needs to move on." Tina loops her arm through mine. "Let's attend this thing, look for a new guy for you, and call it closure."

I shake my head with a condescending smile. I'm nowhere near ready to think about another guy. I'm not even close to having recovered from the last one.

"Have you heard about your internship with the FBI yet?" Caroline asks in an attempt to change the topic.

"No, but since the math department got that new computer program, it makes me much more likely to get accepted." I'm counting on that. Most internships I'm interested in are in Washington D.C. or New York, which means additional living expenses I can't afford. This internship is at the local FBI office and would be great on my application for a job at the CIA. My heart may have been broken, but I refuse to give up on my own dreams.

The student union is crowded when we arrive. This is the fifth party they've had to watch Tucker play, but it's the first time I've attended. I was still too raw before, and I'm not entirely sure why I'm coming this time. Perhaps Tina is on to something. Not about hooking up with another guy. Maybe I need more closure than watching Tucker walk out of my life. Maybe I just need to see him playing and prove to myself that he's happy.

As stupid as it sounds, I just want him to be happy.

People give me curious glances when we get drinks and hang out in the back. They know I dated Tucker briefly, but it was longer than he'd dated anyone else. They are curious about our current status. Most think I'm just one more in a long line of women caught in Tucker Price's aftermath.

Perhaps they're right.

When the game starts, the crowd hushes. The announcers introduce the players on both sides and seem confused that Tucker isn't on the field. They begin to speculate where he might be.

"Price has been the model player, despite the fact that he had quite the reputation for partying at Southern University—"

The students shout and cheer at the mention of the university's name, drowning out part of the announcer's statement.

"—hasn't been any official word from the Fire's camp, leaving us to wonder where he might be. But word has been leaked that he's battling a flu bug and won't play in today's game."

Everyone groans, and I'm suddenly feeling claustrophobic. I needed to see him play, but I can see that's not going to happen.

Caroline has found a friend from one of her classes and Tina has disappeared with a guy. I lean over to Caroline. "I'm going to go to the bathroom. I'll be right back."

She nods, but worry wrinkles her forehead.

I offer her a smile to reassure her that I'm not about to freak out. I'm not. I just need a moment alone.

I practically bolt up the stairs and out the doors, needing the fresh air to sooth my nerves. I find a nearby courtyard and sit on a concrete bench, focusing on the daffodils blooming around the patio edge.

Tears burn my eyes, stoking the anger that lies smoldering in my chest. I needed this. I needed to see him. For some stupid reason, I can't move on until I know he's okay.

"Scarlett?"

I shake my head as I wipe away a tear from my cheek. I'm hallucinating now. I'm sure I hear his voice in the distance.

"Scarlett."

His voice is closer now, and I whip my head around to see Tucker standing ten feet away.

"What..." I shake my head, trying to make sense of what I'm seeing. "What are you doing here?"

"I had to see you."

I'm lightheaded from shock and I blink to make sure I'm not imagining him. "But you're supposed to be in Kansas City. You're supposed to be playing in the game."

He grins, his cocky Tucker Price grin, but there's fear in his eyes. "I know. Since when did I follow the rules?"

"What are you doing here?"

"Seeing you."

I twist my hands in my lap. I can't let myself dare to hope that he's here for the reason I hope for.

He sits down on the bench, but leaves several feet between us. "I said some ugly things to you, Scarlett. I can't live with myself, knowing that I hurt you like that. I need you to know I'm sorry."

Tucker needs the same thing I do. Closure.

His voice breaks. "I didn't mean the things I said."

I look up into his face, searching for some sign of his intentions, but his face is carefully guarded. "I know. You were trying to push me away."

"You have no idea how sorry I am. How many nights I've laid awake wishing I could take it back."

I smile, frustrated that tears fill my eyes again. "I think I do."

He sighs and his mouth twists. "I'm here to tell you I'm sorry for what I said, and I am, but there's more. So much more." He takes my hand. "Do you know what I'm most sorry for?"

My chest tingles when he touches me. I've spent more time away from him than we ever spent together and I still have the same reaction to him. I shake my head. "No, what?"

"I'm sorry I left you. You were the best thing that ever happened to me, and I not only left you but hurt you in the process." He pauses. "You were right. About everything. I thought you were too good to be true. I wanted you more than I've ever wanted anything, even playing professional soccer, but I didn't think I deserved you. I tried to hurt you when I left so there'd be no chance of you taking me back."

"Tucker."

He closes his eyes and scrunches them shut, then exhales as he opens them to stare into my face. "I know I don't deserve you now, and I have no right to hope you'll let me back in your life, but I want you to know leaving you will always be my biggest regret, and we both know I've made a shit-ton of mistakes."

I swallow a sob building in my chest. I can't believe he's here. I can't believe he's telling me this.

"I've quit the team, and I'm coming back to Southern. I'll take some classes this summer to make up for missing this semester, but I'm changing my major to secondary education, so I'll need to go at least another year to take the classes I need."

"You're changing your major?"

"You were right. You're right about everything. I want to teach high school history and coach soccer. Maybe work with some foster teens and help them make better choices than Marcel and I made. I've already talked to the counseling department here, and they'll let me back in."

"What about your soccer scholarship?"

"I lost it, but I'm glad, even if it means I'm going to be stuck with a ton of student loans. I'm thinking about joining a rec league so I'm playing just to have fun and there's no pressure. Maybe I'll love it again."

He's so good at soccer, I want him to love it again. "I suspect the teams will be fighting over you."

"Maybe, but I need to get my grades back up first." He gives me a sheepish grin. "I dropped algebra so I need to take another math class. I'll have to take a statistics class, and I hoped maybe you'd tutor me."

I'm trying to get the words out to tell him that I've missed him, and I want him back, but they're stuck in my throat, tangled in my building tears.

"Scarlett, I have no right to ask you this, not after the way I've treated you, but I'm going to ask anyway." He takes a deep breath and squeezes my hand as though he's worried I'm about to bolt. "I'm miserable without you. I need you. I understand if you don't trust me and you need me to earn back your trust. I understand if you need to go slow—"

"Tucker."

He sounds desperate now. "Nothing makes sense without you. I love you, Scarlett. Please give me another chance."

"I love you, too."

His eyes widen. "What?"

"I love you, too. I need you, too."

"You... don't you..."

"No. I don't need time. I need you."

He leans forward and wraps his arms around my back, kissing me and showing me how much he's missed me. "I'll spend the rest of my life making you happy, Scarlett."

I smile, still not believing this is happening. "You're off to a great start."

Epilogue

Butterflies fill my stomach. "I think I'm going to throw up."

"You are not going to throw up." Tucker says in my ear, pressing his chest to my back and wrapping his arms around my stomach. "Take several deep breaths, close your eyes, and picture yourself walking into that FBI office for your internship, feeling confident and in control."

His belief in me fills me with confidence. "I love you."

He kisses my neck. "I love you, too. You're going to blow them away. Now let's get you some coffee before you go."

We head to the kitchen, weaving through towers of boxes stacked everywhere.

Tucker pours coffee from his coffee maker into my travel mug. He looks up with a grin. "I know it's not the one-touch coffee maker you and Caroline shared, but I'm not shirking on my coffee-making duties yet."

Grinning, I shake my head. "You've only been at this two days."

"And I haven't failed you yet." He hands the mug to me. "Does Tina need help moving her things into Caroline's apartment?"

Caroline's apartment sounds strange. Home with Caroline these past three years has been more of a home to me than my mother's ever was. "No, I think she's good, although she may fake needing help, hoping some of your soccer buddies will show up and help."

Tucker laughs. "We might be able to arrange something."

"What about you? Are you nervous about your summer session at school? It's your first day, too."

"Nervous? Nah. Not with these classes. But I suspect I will be nervous when I start working with actual students next fall."

"You'll be great." I wrap my hands around his neck and pull his mouth to mine. "I'll miss you today."

"I'll miss you, too. But later I'll show you how much I missed you."

I grin and realize Tucker has helped ease my anxiety. "Something to look forward to tonight."

He smiles, love in his eyes. "We've only just started a lifetime of *something to look forward to*s."

I like the sound of that.

Redesigned (Off the Subject #2)
Caroline's story
Available now

Join the Denise Grover Swank newsletter to for news about my latest releases, sales, and bonus content!

You can also join the romance newsletter I share with Angela Casella.

Redesigned Preview

CHAPTER ONE

I push damp hair off my forehead, irritated with the heat. It's too hot for late September, even in Tennessee. Still, if I'm honest, my irritation is partially due to the man drinking a beer six feet away from me.

He's exceptionally good-looking—blond hair, blue eyes, a tan that doesn't end at his biceps. I've seen him without a shirt, and it's easy to see why many of the girls on campus have nicknamed him Adonis. But more importantly, Dylan Humphrey is pre-law, and he comes from a family of lawyers. Not ambulance chasers, but a prestigious firm in Memphis. I should be happy I've finally gotten this close to him, but right now he's not paying the least bit of attention to me. His attention is focused on my roommate Tina.

"Caroline." My best friend Scarlett calls my name and pulls me into a hug. I'm a good three inches taller than her in my brown suede stiletto boots. I heard Dylan would be here, and I came dressed to impress with my boots and a jersey dress even though it's an outdoor party. Scarlett squeezes my arm. "I miss you."

A lump burns in my throat, but I swallow and force my lips into a smile. "I find that hard to believe with Tucker Price in your bed."

She swats my arm. "You've been hanging around Tina too much."

"Whose fault is that? I needed a roommate after you moved out."

I try to keep the bite from my words, but a hint of it is there none-theless.

Tina is the world's biggest flirt and some would call her a slut, which is probably why Dylan is paying more attention to her right now instead of me. But everyone knows that good southern boys don't bring bad girls home to their mommas. They bring home well-behaved ladies. I may not have been born a cultured Southern girl, but I play the part well now. I just need to bide my time.

Scarlett rolls her top lip between her teeth and studies me. I recognize this look after living with her for three years—our freshman and sophomore years in a dorm room and our junior year in an apartment. But Scarlett moved out the end of May and into an apartment with her boyfriend, Tucker.

Who would have ever thought that math major/introvert Scarlett Goodwin would end up with a perfect devoted boyfriend—an ex-man-whore before settling down with her—while I'd been single for eleven months? A year ago, I'd felt sorry for her. Funny how things change.

Scarlett finally breaks her silence, her face expressionless. "I'm sorry to hear about the dress store closing. Are you going to be okay?"

I'm trying not to freak out that I'm currently without a part-time job. "I'm fine. I saved a bunch of money working overtime there this summer." I force a smile. "But I've had to talk to Tina about being more prompt with her share of the rent and utilities."

"I'm sorry I deserted you."

I shrug. "At least my night life is livelier with Tina."

Scarlett rolls her eyes. She's been out with Tina a few times. She knows how wild Tina is. "Well, I'm glad you came to our party, even if you didn't find a date. Although why you think you need one is beyond me."

Of course, it's beyond her. Scarlett wasn't looking for love when she found Tucker. The boy practically fell in her lap. "Time is short, Scarlett. I'm a senior and have less than a year to find the future Mr. Caroline Hunter."

"You don't need a man to make your life fulfilling." Scarlett sighs. This has to be Round Twenty-Eight of some variation of this discussion. "You need to make yourself happy first."

"Says the woman with the sexy soccer player for a boyfriend."

"You forget he left me for two months before he came back. I found my own happiness without him. He only makes my life so much better."

As if hearing his name, Tucker sneaks up behind Scarlett, wrapping his arms around her stomach and pulling her back to his chest. She looks up at him and smiles. Her face is so full of joy, I nearly gag with envy. I'm not jealous of my friend. I'm happy Tucker came into her life. Scarlett deserves every bit of happiness he brings her and much, much more. I'm jealous of what she has, of what remains so elusive for me. I've never had what she has, not even with my two-year relationship with my ex-boyfriend.

"Great turnout, Tucker," I finally say with a smile. "I'm glad you gave Scarlett a party for her near-perfect GRE score. She'd never celebrate it on her own."

She turns around to face me, lowering her voice. "You know I hate parties."

I shake my head. "Talk about an understatement. But you deserve a celebration. Besides, Tucker's invited mostly people you know, with only a few soccer players sprinkled here and there for my and Tina's amusement."

Tucker laughs. "You have to admit I'm a great host."

I lift my eyebrows in a smirk and take a sip of the wine in my red plastic cup. "That you are. Now if you can just get Dylan Humphrey to pay more attention to me than Tina, I'd be a happy girl. Getting him to go out with me would be icing on the cake."

An ornery look spreads across Tucker's face. "Done."

I groan, but I'm secretly happy. Tucker's not one to back down from a challenge, and I'm positive he'll follow through without embarrassing me.

For a guy who was narcissistically self-centered less than a year ago, he's remarkably attentive to Scarlett and her needs, always mindful that social situations tend to make her anxious. And concern for her friends, specifically me, seems to fall under Tucker's attentiveness. He hardly seems like the guy he was before Scarlett. The guy I'd repeatedly warned her to stay away from. I'm glad he proved me wrong.

"Congratulations, Scarlett." A male voice interrupts my thoughts.

Scarlett turns around and her face lights up. "Reed! I'm glad you came."

A guy at least a half-head taller than me stops next to Scarlett. An awkward grin tugs at the corner of his mouth as he hands her a small wrapped box. "I wasn't sure what type of gift one was supposed to give for passing your GRE with such a remarkable score." The wrapping is crisp white and the bow is gauzy and perfectly tied. It's obvious he didn't wrap it unless he's gay. I look him over. Even though he's impeccably dressed in pants, shirt and tie, his shoes are scuffed. Not gay.

A rosy color spreads across Scarlett's cheeks. She hates getting gifts. "I'm sure it's perfect. Thank you." Scarlett turns to me in an attempt to take attention from herself. "Caroline, this is Reed. He's just moved here from Boston and started his first year as a grad student in the mathematics department."

A math man. That explains the professorly attire. He's cute in a geeky kind of way. His dark, brown hair is a bit shaggy and in need of a trim. His dark chocolate-colored eyes are framed by long lashes. His face is pale, which tells me he spends a lot of time inside. He's wearing a long-sleeve light blue shirt and a navy tie, but he doesn't seem to break a sweat even though it has to be at least eighty-five outside.

One of Scarlett's math department friends wanders into the courtyard, and she goes over to greet him.

"Mathematics graduate student?" I know most of the people in the math department are conservative, but Reed has run past conservative headlong into the middle of the last century. "Do you plan to go into analytics like Scarlett?"

He studies me for a moment. "No, my focus is the analysis of algorithms."

"And what will you do with that? Something with the CIA or Department of Defense?"

His eyebrow rises in surprise and a hint of appreciation. "No, I hope to find a university position and teach."

I strike him off as potential date material. For one, he's in the math department so we would have nothing in common, but most importantly, I can't imagine a college professor makes much money. I've seen the cars parked in the faculty parking lot. "Boston? Where did you go to school before coming to Southern?"

He looks wary of my question. "Out east."

Totally vague answer, but I decide it's not worth pursuing. "So how do you like Tennessee?"

"It's hot." He tugs at his sleeve. "Are you from Tennessee?"

It's a simple question, common conversation, but it always makes me edgy. "Yes, born and raised."

"I thought so. You have a southern drawl."

I can't tell if it's a compliment or an insult. "Most everyone around here does."

"Not everyone," he murmurs, and I realize he's really looking at me now.

My skin flushes from his examination, and to my surprise, it's not from embarrassment.

"As Scarlett mentioned, I'm new here this semester and my courses and teaching schedule keep me busy. I don't know many people." He clears his throat. "Would you be free to go to dinner next weekend?"

I stare up into his dark brown eyes, and I'm so very tempted. They're pulling me closer to him. Literally. There's something about him I can't pinpoint, like a physical awareness arcing between us. But a relationship needs more than physical attraction, and I've wasted the past six months going out with good-looking guys. It's my senior year, and it's time to think of my future. Even if some inexplicable part of me wants to kiss him right here and now.

All the more reason to say no.

The question is, what should I tell him? He's a bit abrasive, but I tack that up to his left-brain tendencies. Scarlett does the same thing and needs to be reminded from time to time that the rest of us aren't robots. Still, I don't want to be rude and flat-out decline. I decide to pick up on his busy theme. That's believable. "Thanks for the invitation, Reed, but I'm a fashion design major, and I have a fashion show coming up that could possibly determine my future." My excuse sounds lame, even to me. "I'm hoping to make it on the committee so I have to give every spare moment proving I'm capable."

I expect him to get irritated, but he smiles with approval. "I respect hard work. Maybe I can get a rain check for next semester."

I certainly hope I'm not still single next semester, so I nod. "Sure."

Tucker drags Dylan toward us, his arm around Dylan's shoulder, and I resist the urge to cringe. Talk about terrible timing.

"Caroline, there you are. I was telling Dylan all about you."

I smile, but it's not natural as I cast a worried glance to Reed. "I hope you didn't spill *all* my secrets," I joke.

"Don't worry. I saved a few for you to share." Tucker winks, then notices Reed. "Reed, have you met Dylan Humphrey?"

Reed extends his hand, but his face hardens as Dylan shakes it. "I haven't, but I've heard a lot about you." He doesn't look happy about what he's heard.

Tucker misses Reed's glower. "Say, Caroline, I was telling Dylan about my friend's band playing at the Voodoo Lounge next Friday night. Dylan's interested in coming to check them out, you still in?"

I finally get the full meaning of being caught between a rock and a hard place. It would be rude of me to accept after I just told Reed no, but this might be my only opportunity to go out with Dylan. I've had my eye on him since the beginning of the semester. The reality is that I really don't have a choice. "Sure," I say, but I purposely avoid looking at Reed. "I'd love to."

Dylan's eyes move down over my body, hesitating on my breasts. "It was nice meeting you." His gaze rises to my face.

I'm suddenly unsure this is a good idea.

Reed releases a hard cough.

Tucker whacks Reed on the arm. "You all right, dude?"

"Surprisingly, great" is his terse reply.

Tucker remains clueless as he winks at me again, then follows Dylan to a huddle of his old soccer teammates. Tucker came through for me, so why do I feel so miserable?

"Is it my major that throws you off or the fact you can't do your laundry on my abs?" Reed's voice is unyielding.

The truth is that I feel much more drawn to Reed than Dylan, apparent lack of abs and all. I feel a connection to Reed I've never felt before and the tension between us only feeds my libido. "Reed, let me explain."

"Caroline, that really isn't necessary. Perhaps I'm just not your *type*."

I want to lie to him and say he's right, I'm not attracted to him at all, but that would be a flat-out lie. For some reason I can't make myself say it. Maybe because it's so far from the truth. "What type would that be?" I finally say. Because for some inexplicable reason, I can't walk away from him.

"Rich, good-looking, *powerful*." Ugliness drips from his words, snapping me out of my lustful stupor.

I lift my chin. "There's nothing wrong with any of those attributes."

He shakes his head in disgust. "I've seen *your* type before, and I can usually spot them a mile away. Somehow you slipped past my radar."

Anger boils the blood in my veins. "My type? And what exactly would that be?"

"Isn't it obvious? You're a fortune hunter. An opportunist. A gold-digger."

My mouth drops open in shock, partially that he's pegged me, even if he makes it sound so vile. What's so wrong with wanting to be assured that I'll never be poor again? But even so, what gives him the right to speak to me like this? Ugly words slip over my tongue before I can stop them.

"There's no way you'll make much money as a professor. Nothing that could compete with a respected attorney. Besides, Dylan looks like a Greek god and his family has money. Why wouldn't I want to go out with him?"

The moment I finish, I want to take back every word.

His face reddens, and I'm about to apologize when a perky blonde literally bounces up to him. She wraps her arm around his and pulls him to her in such a familiar way that it's apparent they aren't casual friends.

Reed Pendergraft just asked me out with his girlfriend on the other side of the courtyard. And he has the nerve to condemn *me*? Nausea rolls in my stomach. And here I was about to convince myself I should blow off Dylan and accept Reed's date instead. I'm grateful his girlfriend has saved me from myself.

"Reed, are you going to introduce me to your friend?" She looks up at Reed's face, her big blue eyes shining with happiness. I wonder if I should tell her what just happened, but I won't be the one to destroy her. I'm sure Reed will take care that himself.

Reed pauses, long enough for me to jump in. "I'm no one." Then I turn and walk away.

∾

Read Redesigned now!

About the Author

DENISE GROVER SWANK was born in Kansas City, Missouri and lived in the area until she was nineteen. Then she became a nomad, living in five cities, four states and ten houses over the course of ten years before she moved back to her roots. She speaks English and smattering of Spanish and Chinese, which she learned through an intensive Nick Jr. immersion period. Her hobbies include witty Facebook comments (in own her mind) and dancing in her kitchen with her children (quite badly if you believe her offspring). Hidden talents include the gift of justification and the ability to drink massive amounts of caffeine and still fall asleep within two minutes. Her lack of the sense of smell allows her to perform many unspeakable tasks. She has six children and hasn't lost her sanity. Or so she leads you to believe.

For mystery and romance: denisegroverswank.com
For urban fantasy: dgswank.com